AWESOMELY
ALLY'S WORLD

Sadie ROCKS!

Happiness, and All That Stuff

Deep Joy, or Something Like It

It's All Good (In Your Dreams)

Smile! It's Meant to be Fun

Collect all 16 fabulous titles!

7 sunshiney, seasidey, unmissable books

And her novels

Marshmallow Magic and the Wild Rose Rouge

An Urgent Message of Wowness

The Seventeen Secrets of the Karma Club

The Raspberry Rules

Karen McCombie

AWESOMELY
ALLY'S WORLD

SCHOLASTIC

Scholastic Children's Books
An imprint of Scholastic Ltd
Euston House, 24 Eversholt Street
London, NW1 1DB, UK
Registered office: Westfield Road, Southam, Warwickshire, CV47 0RA
SCHOLASTIC and associated logos are trademarks and/or registered
trademarks of Scholastic Inc.

First published in two volumes as *The Past, the Present and the Loud,
Loud Girl* and *Dates, Double Dates and Big, Big Trouble* by Scholastic
Children's Books, 2001.
This edition published in the UK by Scholastic Children's Books, 2010.

ISBN 978 1407 11608 2

A CIP catalogue record for this book is available from the British
Library.

Printed in the UK by CPI Bookmarque, Croydon, Surrey.
Papers used by Scholastic Children's Books are made from wood grown
in sustainable forests.

3 5 7 9 10 8 6 4 2

www.scholastic.co.uk/zone

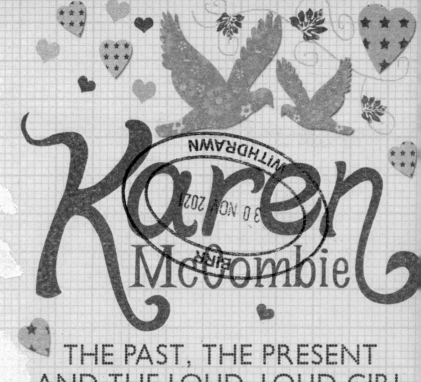

Karen McCombie

THE PAST, THE PRESENT AND THE LOUD, LOUD GIRL

Welcome to the weird and wonderful world of Ally Love, age 13…

ALLY'S WORLD

Contents

PROLOGUE

Dear Mum,
I've decided to do something.

Don't panic: it's not like I'm about to pierce my lip, or enrol for the next Mars mission, or run away with the circus and juggle clowns or something. (Although you'd probably think all that was cool.)

It's just that, you know how I've been keeping a box with all our photos and school reports and stuff for you to see? Well, no you don't – which is the problem – but trust me, that's what I'm doing.

Well, anyway, apart from those bits and pieces, I've decided that I'm going to start writing down some of the things that happen to all of us; the things that matter, anyway. It's not going to be like a diary or anything – I don't exactly have the patience for that. (Though I did buy one a couple of Januarys ago; it was half-price in the stationery shop up on the Broadway. I started out OK, prattling on about *what* I'd done that day and *what* I was feeling and *what* we'd had for tea, but by January 10th

1

I was just doodling flowers on the page. And the entry for January 15th just said "BORED, BORED, BORED", so I kind of chucked it in after that.)

So this time, I think I'll do it like an essay... Only it might be a bit on the long side. You know what I'm like. Remember that last report you saw when I was at primary school? *"Ally is very bright and imaginative, but her mind does tend to wander..."* Hey, guess what? Nothing's changed. It's like Grandma says, I'd get twice as much done if I stopped wittering for five minutes. Which is sort of true, I know. And which is what I'm doing now, I suppose...

OK, so back to my plan.

I think I'll do it like I'm writing it for some stranger to read, 'cause – sorry, I don't mean to give you a hard time about this – it might make me too sad if I just set it all down for you. I suppose that's because I know it's not exactly likely that you're going to come walking through the door in the next two minutes or anything, and beg to read this...

But then, if – by some mind-blowing magic – you did, you'd have all our pictures and things to look at, *and* be able to read all my stories about what's been going on with me and Linn and Rowan and Tor. And, of course, Dad.

Speaking of Dad, I think I'll start with his fortieth

birthday, 'cause that was when Kyra turned up, and when – don't panic – we nearly lost Tor…

Love you lots,

Ally

(your Love Child No. 3)

Chapter 1

WELCOME TO MY (WEIRD) WORLD...

Look at a map of the world, and find Britain (small, jaggedy, sort of in the middle).

Look at a map of Britain and find London (big blob, down in the south).

Look at a map of London and find Crouch End (weird name, nice place).

Look for Palace Heights Road (number 28, to be precise).

When you find number 28, stand on the pavement opposite and look at the terraced house with your eyes half-crossed (all fuzzy like that, it seems almost as posh as the ones on either side of it. *Un*cross your eyes and you'll see that it's actually pretty tatty round the edges).

I'm Ally Love, and this is where I live with my dad (Martin), a power-mad control freak (my seventeen-year-old sister, Linn), a complete airhead (my fifteen-year-old sister, Rowan) and a space cadet (my seven-year-old brother, Tor).

OK, so now look up, past the big bay living-room

window, past the first-floor bay (my sister Rowan's room) until you see a tiny window at the top – my attic bedroom.

That's where I've woken up nearly every morning for all of the thirteen years I've been on this planet, and where I'm normally very happy to wake up. Except for one particular morning…

It was weird – for some reason, my whole head was vibrating.

But then, there are plenty of weird things in this world. Like nose hair. I mean, if the point is that it's there for protection, then why doesn't it grow in your mouth too? (Blee…)

And electricity. It doesn't matter how many times the principle's explained to me, I still don't get it. But don't get me wrong, I am pretty *pleased* about it. Dad sometimes likes to light these big, fat, coloured candles we have in the living room, but until they invent a candle-powered TV (that would need a *really* big, fat candle, I guess), I'm OK with electricity, however weird it is.

Of course, plenty of people – including my oldest sister – think our parents are weird for giving their kids odd names (me, I got off lightly out of the four of us), but I think it just goes to show that some people have no imagination. And anyway, when they get to know the story behind each name, they usually think it's pretty cool after all.

Oops, there I go. Getting sidetracked by weird stuff when I was supposed to be talking about the head-vibrating thing. But I do that a lot (get sidetracked, not have a vibrating head) – so get used to it.

Anyhow, it was a Sunday morning when I felt my head vibrate. At first I didn't panic; I just told myself that there must be a giant articulated lorry parked in the street outside, its engine throbbing so hard that it was shaking the house from the foundations right up to my little room under the eaves. That, or maybe it was a low-flying plane, rumbling through the skies above our house, sending tremors from the roof tiles down.

Then I noticed something else – one side of my face and neck were as hot as a very hot thing. A vibrating head *and* a burning-hot face...

OK, so *then* I started to panic. Compared to people like my airhead sister Rowan and my ditzy best mate Sandie, I know I come over like I'm confident and logical. But underneath, I'm basically a world-class worrier...

What had they told us at school about meningitis? Did the telltale signs include victims hearing a persistent droning noise that made their heads vibrate? Was it a common sign to feel one side of your face burning up? I couldn't remember.

Then all of a sudden, the noise and the vibration stopped. In its place, there was silence, broken only by one small noise.

"Snurph."

My eyes flicked open. I was awake, and instantly flooded with relief.

I didn't have the first warning signs of meningitis.

I wasn't about to be carted off to the Whittington hospital down the road.

I turned my head on the pillow and found myself nose to nose with Colin.

"Don't mind me," I muttered, as he moved in his sleep, settling himself more comfortably in the cosy pile of people fur that he'd come across.

As I tried to pull my long, brown hair slowly out from under him, he gave another snuffly cat snore and started off with his loud, droning purr again.

Freeing myself, I flung back the duvet and left Colin to it. I padded over the old, worn carpet and did the morning ritual I've done ever since I was tall enough to reach the ledge on my tiptoes – staring out of my tiny window at the view of the Palace, perched on top of one of London's only proper hills.

"Well, Ally Love," I said to myself, "You could

have been famous; you could have gone down in medical history as the first person to suffer from Vibrating Head Syndrome."

I shot a glance backwards in the direction of Colin, who was now sprawling his whole body and three legs (hey, I'll explain later) across the whole pillow.

Then I thought of something *truly* weird: do cats' heads vibrate when they purr?

I walked back over to Colin, and clamped my fingers round his face.

"Yeee-oow!"

My scientific experiment didn't prove the vibrating theory. What it did do was show that cats really, *really* don't appreciate having their heads squeezed when they're sleeping.

Trust me, I've got the bite-marks to prove it.

Now that I knew I wasn't going to die (well, eventually, yeah – but not right that *second*), I should have been skipping down the stairs to breakfast with a stupid grin of relief on my face.

But I didn't. Mainly because my fear of immediate death had been replaced by an ominous feeling that I'd forgotten something...

Uh-oh.

Chapter 2

LINN'S LOUSY IDEA

"What's up with your hair? You look like you've been dragged through a forest backwards," said my big sister Linn, staring up at me and wrinkling her nose.

"A cat slept on my head."

"Oh," shrugged Linn, carrying on buttering her toast. "Which one?"

"Colin," piped up my little brother, as I sat down at the kitchen table beside him.

"How did you know that?" I asked, rubbing at my nose where it was tickly with stray cat-hairs.

"Ginger fur stuck on your face," Tor muttered, reaching over and pointing his finger right into my cheek.

"Oh."

"And that – that's Colin's teeth-marks."

"Thank you, Pet Detective," I mumbled, looking down the hand that Colin's fangs had dented.

Here's the thing: I close my door every night before I go to bed, but always in the morning some animal's worked magic and wangled its way in (but usually into some cosy corner – getting comfy on my head doesn't happen too often). And I include my little brother Tor in that. It's pretty sweet, actually – whenever Tor has nightmares, which isn't often – it isn't my dad, or Rowan, or Linn he scampers to. It's *my* bed he ends up curling up at the bottom of, like one of the army of hamsters and gerbils he's got stashed in cages all around his own room.

"Rowan up yet?" I asked, helping myself to orange juice from the sticky carton in the middle of the table.

I still hadn't figured out what the thing was that I'd forgotten. Maybe when I was more awake it would come to me...

"You're joking, aren't you? Haven't you noticed it's only half-nine?" mumbled Linn with her mouth full. "The Queen of the Night won't be gracing us with her presence for ages yet."

That was true – Rowan never got up much before noon at the weekends, much to our grandma's disapproval, *and* Linn's. But then Linn gets snippy and grouchy at Rowan pretty easily.

Honestly, my two sisters are about as different as people can get and still be related. Linn is seventeen and sensible, and likes everything neat, tidy, organized and lined up with a set square (believe me, she *would* if we let her). Which is a bit of a shame for Linn, since she has to live in a wonky, ramshackle house like ours. And our whole family's pretty ramshackle and wonky too, when you think about it, and that doesn't please Linn too much either.

You should see her room – it's on the other side of the attic from mine. Where mine's painted sky blue (kind of fitting for an attic, don't you think? The room closest to the real thing?), with posters and pictures and my big old map of the world covering most of the wall space, Linn's is the exact opposite. Everything's so white and streamlined and minimal you'd think she'd ironed it all, from the carpet to her textbooks. Sometimes I catch Linn in there, sitting on the window seat and staring out at her view of central London sprawling away in the distance (approximately eleven and a quarter kilometres, fact fans). At times like that, locked away in her little oasis of calm and non-clutter, I get the feeling that the one thing she'd love to do is get away from sleepy Crouch End – and us.

Now take Rowan's room. You think our living room's bad, with those canary-yellow walls and the navy woodwork? (Mum's choice, by the way, like every other colour scheme in the house except our own bedrooms). Well, Rowan's room is something else. At the moment she's painted it raspberry, and it's like an explosion in a fairy-lights factory. She's got them draped everywhere: round the bay window, along the shelves, the wooden bedhead, and, once, even round Tor.

Rowan had just taken a photo of him all decked out in blinking lights, when Linn barged in and yanked them off him, accusing Rowan of trying to electrocute our little brother. Of course, she was totally right, in a strictly speaking, safety-conscious way, but sometimes I think that Linn doesn't know how to have fun. After all, Tor *did* look pretty cute (and bemused) in the photo, and he didn't seem to mind too much. But then Tor never grumbles about anything. Mainly 'cause he never says much, ever.

If Rowan could get away with wearing fairy lights, I think she'd do it. She's fifteen now, but ever since I can remember, show her anything that twinkles and glistens and she's completely sold on it. It's like with her clothes – ages ago, she bought all these little-old-lady beaded cardies for about zero pence from jumble sales and second-hand shops and wore them all the time. She got loads of weird looks and sniggery comments for it, and then BLAM! everyone from Miss Selfridge to New Look starts selling them.

And you should see the piles of fashion magazines she's got in her room. One stack of *Elle*s comes up to my waist practically, and they've been sitting there so long she's stuck this mad old tasselly table lamp on top.

So, my two older sisters have got different tastes, but that isn't the main reason Linn gets bugged by Rowan. The main reason is that Rowan insists on doing the one thing that no one else does – she calls Linn by her full name: Linnhe.

Boy, does Linn hate that name. I remember her blowing up at my dad once, saying it was cruel of parents to give their kids weird names. I can't remember how Dad reacted – he probably just nodded and agreed with her. It's his usual way of avoiding arguments. But I'm with Rowan on this – not that I'd dream of saying so to Linn. I think Linnhe (think: Linny) is really pretty. Still, Linn hates it so much that she changed it to the more normal sounding Linn. She even went so far as to try and change the spelling to Lynne, but it got too complicated; her name was spelt the old way on everything from her school records to the "Property of Linn Love" notes that she sticks on everything she owns. Including her favourite yoghurts in the fridge. Honest – I'm not joking.

"So, where's Dad?" I asked Linn, sloppily

spreading some peanut butter on my toast.

"Out getting a newspaper," said Linn. "And listen, speaking of Dad, I'm a bit worried…"

I paused – was my forgotten thing something to do with Dad? Nah – that didn't feel right. I carried on with my peanut butter.

"Worried? How come?" I asked her, through a mouthful of toast.

"Well, we have a problem…" she sighed.

"Houston, we have a problem…" muttered Tor in a fake American accent.

He watched a programme about rocket launches the night before with Dad, if you want an explanation. But then Tor and his little ways don't need explaining, if you just grasp the single fact that he's a bit of a space cadet in general.

For example, at that moment, I noticed he was drawing a smiley face with his finger in the margarine on his toast, which was completely normal. For *him*, I mean, not necessarily for *every* seven year old. But *our* seven-year-old brother has the habit of moulding *all* his food into some kind of artwork before he eats it. He's very good with scrambled eggs – makes them look like clouds in the sky on his plate. That's why he hates soup; it's really hard to do anything artistic with a bowl of mushroom soup. Try it if you don't believe me.

"What kind of a problem?" I asked my sister dubiously.

The reason I felt a bit dubious is that Linn sees practically *everything* as a problem. Tor merrily announcing that he's found a new walking-wounded, stray animal to clutter up the house with is a major problem. Me leaving my homework till Sunday night is worthy of a drama. Rowan sitting daydreaming instead of taking her turn doing the dishes is virtually an arrestable offence.

Linn gazed at me in despair; I was obviously meant to *know* something, or be *aware* of something. Oops. Since I hadn't a clue what that might be, I just gazed back at her, wondering how she always managed to look so unnaturally together first thing in the morning. It wasn't fair. Her blonde-ish fair hair was dragged neatly back into a ponytail, and unlike me and Tor – who were still in our pyjamas (me: baggy, drawstring-waist trousers and an old T-shirt; Tor: a Wallace & Gromit number) – Linn was already dressed in her regulation black trousers (she has about seventeen thousand pairs, I swear she does) and zip-necked top.

My eyes dropped – as they often do – to the outline of her perfectly formed boobs in that tight top. I was thinking – as I often do – how was it that fate gave her a proper-sized chest, as *well* as everything else, when all *I* got from the Love family gene pool was two mini-mounds that have trouble filling a double-A bra? ("Plenty of time for them to grow!" Grandma always trots out whenever I moan about it. Well, I'll try to be patient – but I won't hold my breath…)

"Don't you realize the date?" Linn said wearily, making me flip my gaze back up to her face smartish. "It's Dad's birthday two weeks tomorrow – and it's his fortieth. What on earth are we going to get him?"

"Uh … a present?" I ventured, knowing I was probably saying the wrong thing.

Tor must have thought so too – he stopped what he was doing and eyed us both warily. Out of the corner of my eye I could see that he was obviously inspired by my encounter with Colin. Beside the smiley face he'd traced in the margarine, he'd been moulding a wobbly, vaguely cat-shaped dollop of gingery marmalade.

"Yes, I *know* we've got to get him a present," said Linn irritably – still, not as irritably as it could have been, knowing her. "But what *kind* of present? I mean, it's got to be special, since it's his fortieth. And it's up to us to make it special; after all, who else will?"

I knew what – or rather who – she was getting at: Mum, of course. But I wasn't in the mood to get into all that.

"Mmm, it *would* be nice to do something special…" I agreed non-committally.

Agreeing with Linn is always the easiest way to go. Like I said, even *Dad* knows that.

"Well," she said, suddenly losing the anxious look, and seeming quite chuffed with herself. "I've had an idea."

"Oh, yeah?"

Me (doing the talking) and Tor (just listening) were both on tenterhooks waiting for this. Whatever was coming wasn't just an idea that we could all kick about and discuss. Whatever Linn had thought of was probably going to happen.

"I thought," she began, a conspiratorial grin breaking out on her face, "that we should … have a surprise party for him!"

Right away, I knew I needed to set her straight, remind her that sweet, shy people like our dad don't really respond to the whole "Oh my goodness – all this for little old *me*?!" centre-of-attention thing. And I needed to remind her that after four years of looking after us on his own (with a little help from Grandma, of course), he hadn't exactly got a lot of time for keeping up friendships. The surprise was, who exactly was she planning to *invite* to this surprise party?

But of course, I am speaking about my sister Linn – She Who Must Be Obeyed – here.

"Yeah! That sounds like a great idea!" I lied through gritted teeth.

Chapter 3

SENSIBLE ANSWERS ONLY, PLEASE

Considering that my friends' houses are all magnolia-painted neat, with matching towels and plate sets – and chairs, for that matter – it's quite reassuring to know that there's another building in the area that's as beautiful, but as crumbly round the edges as my house.

I ended up thinking just that, sitting on a bench in the park surrounding Alexandra Palace and gazing up at the huge Rose window of the Palace itself. I'd come to the park with the dogs after my conversation with Linn about Dad's birthday present. Walking clears my head, and right now, I knew I needed to come up with an alternative plan to Linn's – and quick.

But so far, of course, all I'd done was daydream.

See, Alexandra Palace is this stunning, big building from a distance, but up close, OK it's *still* amazing, but it's sort of tatty round the edges. One side of the building's semi-restored and shiny, and the other is semi-smoke-damaged and boarded up. It's really sad when you imagine how awesome it would have looked (all sandstone and glass domes) when it was first built back in 1800-whenever. But then not a lot of people ever had a chance to see it that way – the whole place caught on fire sixteen days after it was finished. What a bummer.

Not that I'm saying a fire or anything that drastic has ever happened to *our* house. It's just that, while it's a really comfy, pretty place to live in, there's loads wrong with it. It's the kind of house where there's always handles falling off the kitchen cupboards and window frames with big, breezy gaps in them and pipes in the wall that sometimes gurgle like they're about to throw up. That's not even *starting* on stuff like the sofa my dad brought home after he "salvaged" it from a skip (it was so full of fleas that the *cats* refused to sit on it), or the ominous cracks in loads of the walls and ceilings that keep getting bigger and bigger ("Subsidence," my grandma occasionally points out darkly). But I wouldn't swap our house – even though it does look like a cross between a craft fair and a second-hand shop – in a million years. (Linn, of course, *would* – in a *micro*-second.)

So, it was late morning on Sunday, and I was sitting staring at the stained glass of the Rose window, views of distant high-rises in central

London behind me, when this frenetic barking started up.

Rolf (our big, hairy dog) barks at anything – the postman, the gate-post, traffic cones, blades of grass, you name it – but the fact that Winslet (our small, hairy dog) was barking too meant only one thing: Billy and Precious were on their way.

I was glad – I wanted to sound out Billy, since he was a boy, about any ideas he had for a good present for *my* dad. OK, so Billy is my age and twenty-seven years *younger* than my dad, but they're both males, so I figured he might come up with *something* useful. I knew I was clutching at straws, but I was desperate to go back home with at least *one* alternative suggestion to Linn's rotten surprise-party idea.

"Hi!" I waved at him, as he stomped over the grass towards me.

"Hi, Ally!" Billy grinned, flopping down beside me on the bench.

Billy's my mate; we've known each other since we were – ooh! – *that* high. I sometimes don't see him too often during the week since he goes to a different school from me (Muswell School for Boys), so whatever we're doing, we always try to meet in the park on Sunday mornings to catch up. He comes over from his side of the Palace

(Muswell Hill), I wander over from mine (Crouch End), and we meet in the middle, on the grass just downhill from the Rose window.

"So how's it going?" Billy asked, keeping one eye on the typical mayhem going on in front of us.

All three dogs were tearing round in a big blurry bundle, playing their favourite game, which involves lots of running in circles, barking and occasional growling (Winslet). Translated into people speak, the game is called "Aw, Go On – Let Me Smell Your Bum!", and the object of it is for Billy's small, white, irritating poodle to attempt to sniff the bottoms of *my* dogs, while Rolf and Winslet do everything short of biting Precious to get him to stop. Personally, I think they're both too polite.

"I'm OK," I shrugged. "What about you?"

"Yeah, great," said Billy unconvincingly. "Except for the fact that I failed two tests at school this week, everyone gave me a hard time 'cause I let in three goals at five-a-side yesterday afternoon, and that really pretty new girl that's just moved in on my street still doesn't know I exist."

At the mention of school, I immediately felt that faint, worrying flutter at the back of my mind again. What *was* it I'd forgotten? I waited for a second, giving my brain a chance to explain itself, but when nothing happened, I turned my attention back to Billy.

"But you said that girl looks about eighteen," I pointed out, knowing I was about to burst his bubble. "She's not exactly going to be tripping over herself to talk to you, is she?"

I'd been starting to notice that Billy was getting a bit predictable lately. We used to have these great conversations about life, PlayStations and everything, but nowadays, he'd always work the conversation round to girls, sooner or later. He was desperate for a girlfriend (that much was obvious), and kept asking me for advice about how you get together with someone and what you do once you *are* together. Like I was some big expert or something. I've only ever been out with one boy – Keith Brownlow – and that only lasted a few dates. (What a disaster my love life is – just don't get me started, OK? I know eight year olds who've had more snogs from boys than me...) Anyway, if you must know about Keith Brownlow, well, *I* decided to chuck *him* when he kissed me right after he'd finished a can of Coke.

(Hot tip, boys: belching in a girl's mouth is *not* too gorgeous.)

"Just kick me now, why don't you," mumbled Billy, pretending to be hurt at my home truths about his chances with the hot-chick neighbour.

"Don't tempt me," I said, aiming a trainer in his

direction. "Anyway, there's something I need your help with. It's my dad's fortieth birthday soon. What do you reckon we should get him?"

"A Zimmer frame? Grey hair-dye? Ouch!"

I didn't kick him hard, really I didn't. But boys are such drama queens, aren't they?

"Billy! Stop mucking about and help me out!" I nagged him.

"*I* don't know what you should get him, do I?" Billy mumbled, rubbing his shin. "I mean, he's *your* dad. *You* should know what he wants."

"Well, if I did, I wouldn't need to ask *you*, would I?"

It was my own fault. I should have known it was a waste of time bringing up the subject with him. Billy can quote huge chunks of dialogue out of movies and could tell you the name of every weird alien in every series of *Star Trek*, but he's pathetically hopeless at anything remotely normal and useful.

"What about your sisters?" he asked me. "Doesn't Linn have everything organized? She usually does…"

Billy's pretty intimidated by Linn, and you can't really blame him for that – I think she'd be capable of intimidating the Prime Minister if she was in the right mood (make that *wrong* mood). Whenever Billy comes round to my house for tea he goes really quiet in front of her. But then, he's kind of funny about Rowan and Tor too. He thinks they're weird; Rowan 'cause of the way she dresses and everything, and Tor (Billy calls him "Spook Kid") because he just sits and stares silently over the table at Billy, which is what he tends to do with *any* of the friends we bring home. (Tor even does it to his *own* little buddies, but I guess they mustn't mind, 'cause they still want to hang out with him.)

"You don't want to hear what *Linn*'s thought of. C'mon, Billy – what would be your dream present?"

"Dunno, really," he replied, frowning. "But this morning, I was thinking how cool it would be to own a life-sized cardboard cut-out of Lara Croft."

"Billy, a life-sized cut-out of Lara Croft would be about ten centimetres high. Get it through your head – she's not real. You're in lust with a very small character in a computer game. No wonder you can't get a proper girlfriend!"

I could see that he was struggling with a smart comeback line, but bless him, Billy's not really great at sparkling wit. I mean, he's got a great sense of humour and everything, but he's no match for me. Which is fun. For me.

Not that I can talk, of course, considering the only boyfriend I've got right now is Billy – and that's "boy" and "friend" with a very *big* space between both words…

"Oh, yeah? Yeah?" he fumbled around, hoping vainly that something smart and cutting would come to him. "Well Lara Croft *isn't* just a computer character. What about the *Tomb Raider* movie? She's in that!"

"The thing about the *Tomb Raider* movie," I sighed, "is that it's a *movie*. It's not real life – and just 'cause some actress is playing Lara Croft doesn't make her real either!"

"I know that!" said Billy defensively.

It was a stupid conversation, but then it's pretty typical of the stupid conversations we have. Sometimes Billy drives me crazy when we end up yakking round in circles like this, but most of the time it's kind of fun, actually.

I was just about to tell him that even if Lara Croft suddenly did come to life, he had a better chance of going with one of the Teletubbies than her, when we got disturbed by a sudden kerfuffle.

"Precious!" Billy yelped. "Oi! Precious! C'mere! Oh, God – he's off. Hold on, Al, I'd better go and grab him."

I watched as Billy hurtled down the hill to where the pint-sized poodle was trying to do slightly *more* than sniff the bums of two puzzled Dalmatians. The guy who owns those Dalmatians isn't exactly the world's biggest smiler at the best of times. A small yappy dog trying to ram its nose up the bottoms of his prize pooches was definitely *not* going to bring a warm, sloppy grin to his face.

And poor Billy – no wonder he let three goals in and couldn't get a girlfriend. Just watching him run, watching the way his long, skinny legs and arms loped about all over the place, you could tell that he was a complete stranger to the art of coordination. That's the thing: Billy is *almost* what you could call good-looking, but he's such a clumsy geek that no girl in the Western Hemisphere is ever going to mistake him for Brad Pitt in a hurry.

"Precious! Come here! Precious – heel! Now!" I heard him yell to a totally oblivious dog.

Precious. Can you *believe* that Billy's mum came up with that name for their dog, knowing that her poor son was going to have to use it every time he took the thing for a walk? I'm sure there must be a clause in the Children's Act somewhere that says it's cruel to make thirteen-year-old boys shout "Precious!" loudly in a public place. What was the woman thinking of?

I mean, shouting "Rolf" and "Winslet" gets you the odd look from people in the park – people whose own dogs must be called Dullsville stuff like "Spot" or "Rover" or something – but it's a thousand times better than "Precious". Who is, in fact, about as precious as a flu virus.

Both my dogs suit their names, I reckon. Rolf – a pedigree mongrel from a long, distinguished line of mongrels – was our first ever pet; Dad got him from Wood Green Animal Shelter as a distraction for Tor when our little brother suddenly clocked that our mum wasn't around any more. Since it was his dog, Tor was allowed to name him. And since his favourite programme in the world used to be something called *Animal Hospital*, presented by a beardy bloke called Rolf Harris, Rolf it was.

We ended up with Winslet a couple of years ago when Rowan and Tor found her wandering about in the park, dishevelled, hungry and grumpy (her natural state, we found out later). They did the right thing and took her along to the police station, where Dad inevitably ended up ticking the box on the details form saying we'd take her if she wasn't claimed. She wasn't. So, since Tor already had built up quite a little menagerie at our place by this time, all of whom he'd named, the honours went to him again. He'd just seen *Titanic* and had a huge crush on Kate Winslet, so Winslet she became. (Actually, it was Kate at first, but somehow "Kate" didn't really suit a small, hairy, grumpy dog too much.)

Billy came plodding back up the incline,

an indignant poodle writing in his arms, and breathlessly plonked himself back down next to me.

"You know, if you want to get your dad something special," he panted (Billy, not Precious), "then I think you should get him something original, something he'd *never* think of…"

"Yeah? Like what?"

I was intrigued. It sounded like Billy might just be a lot less useless than I'd thought.

"Huh?" he blinked at me, trying not to lose his grip as Precious wriggled around, trying to escape. "I dunno. That's as far as I got."

"Billy," I said wearily, "your *dog*'s smarter than you."

As if to show off how smart he was, Precious attempted to lunge enthusiastically towards me.

I jerked back, just out of licking range.

There was no *way* Precious was getting within half a metre of my face. Not knowing where that nose had been last…

Chapter 4

SANDIE AND HER AMAZING WRIGGLING HAIR...

All the way home, I racked and racked my brains for some amazing present idea, but I think I'd used up all my energy for the day. Me and Billy had walked the dogs till *they* were tired, *we* were tired, and every other dog-walker in a hundred-metre radius was tired of Precious lungeing his small self at their pets.

My eyes were glued to the pavement, like that might help my concentration or something, when a few doors down from our house, I heard Rowan. She'd got these new mules in a sale, and you could recognize the *flippety-flap*, *flippety-flap* of them three streets away.

"Rowan!" I called after her. My sister's mind works in mysterious ways – if anyone could come up with something unusual and special for Dad, Rowan could. "Where are you going?"

"Just up to the shop," she called back, holding up her hand to shield the sun from her eyes, the multi-coloured Indian bangles she wore jangling down her arm. "We're out of loo roll."

See, that's Rowan for you: who else goes to the corner shop for loo roll in red velvet mules?

"Uh, OK – I'll see you in a bit."

I'd catch her later, I decided, and pick her brain. Tor's too – just 'cause he was little didn't mean he couldn't come up with a smart idea.

Thinking so much about Dad, I jumped guiltily as I walked in the front door and came face-to-face with him.

"Hi, babe! Been walking the mutts, then?"

He's so laid-back and nice, my dad. I know people are meant to love their parents, but I sometimes think they don't seem to *like* them all that much. But with my dad, I think I'd like him even if I was just meeting him for the first time.

My best friend Sandie, she's kind of proof of that; she's round at our house *all* the time, and is always saying how cool my dad is. It's actually a bit of a joke in my house how often Sandie comes round. She does this thing where she seems to leave another bit of clothing or another CD every time she's here; Dad says he thinks she's trying to move in without anyone noticing.

"Hi, Ally!" said Sandie, appearing from the kitchen, a cup of coffee in her hand.

See what I mean?

"Listen, Ally Pally—"

That was my dad. He always calls me that.

"—I'm going along to the workshop for an hour. A whole load of spare parts came in yesterday, and I want to get them sorted out before I open up tomorrow."

"OK," I shrugged and smiled at him. It was perfect, really; if he was safely out of the house, I'd have the chance to talk to Rowan and Tor and even Sandie about ideas for a present without worrying that he'd overhear.

But hold on – the Ally Pally thing. Maybe you'll want to know what that's all about. And if I tell you that, I guess I might as well tell you about all our names while I'm at it. Basically, while my dad had a hand in them, they're all Mum's fault. Which I'm pretty glad about.

So, when it came to naming their Love children (as Mum and Dad liked to call us), it happened like this...

First up, there's Love Child No. 1: Linnhe. Mum and Dad were young, happy, but skint, and had borrowed my grandma's car to go on a camping holiday in Scotland. The plan was to see as many castles and lochs as possible, and the day they checked out Inverlochy Castle on Loch Linnhe was the day my mum sussed out that she was pregnant. When my sister was born, my folks were reminiscing about the trip to Scotland, and it just kind of seemed perfect to call her Linnhe. Linn might not agree, but I think she should count her blessings. The day before, they'd been camping beside Loch Fyne. With a name like Fyne Love, you could imagine the stick she'd get from lads at school. Mind you, it would have come in handy if she'd chosen a career in X-rated videos, I suppose.

Rowan, Love Child No. 2, was due to come along next, and by this time my parents (still skint) and Linn (now two) were living in a grotty and minuscule rented flat in Finsbury Park. The landlord didn't allow them to redecorate, and he also didn't allow children. The children thing, they could get around; every time he was due to visit, they'd frantically hide every toy and kiddy-sized pair of sandals under the bed, and Mum would take the evidence (item 1: Linn; item 2: her own growing tummy) around the block till the coast was clear. The other no-no was a bigger problem. Living in a house with walls that were decorated in depressing "mushroom", with furniture in shades of dull brown, dull-ish brown and *very* dull brown, just about sent my artistic mother round the bend. She told me she bought yards and yards of cheap sari material from the Indian shops up in Turnpike Lane and draped them over everything, but it didn't do much good. She said the only thing that cheered her up was looking through the bars of their basement-flat window at the rowan tree that dripped its red-berried branches over the neighbouring wall and into their bare little backyard. And so, Rowan got her name.

Next, things got a little better for my parents. Dad had worked in bike shops for years (the hardwork, pedal kind of bike, if you were wondering), when he heard about this old guy who was retiring and wanted someone to take over the lease of his small bike workshop in Crouch End. Cue, my dad. It wasn't too long after that that my folks spotted this genteely crumbling Victorian house around the corner from the workshop. Because it needed vats of work doing to it, it was dirt cheap, so they gave up their squashed rented flat for a big, falling-down house, all for the sake of their two small daughters and one big bump (me, Love Child No. 3). On the day they moved in, Mum took one look out of the front attic-bedroom window (my room) and copped a load of Alexandra Palace, and that sealed my fate. Alexandra Love is on my birth certificate, but my dad soon gave me the same nickname as my namesake: Ally Pally.

Three explanations down, one to go.

So, Dad had his business, and we had the house,

but my parents were still what can be technically described as skint. Because of that, the family tradition of camping holidays continued, and one rainy summer, when I was six, we found ourselves stomping up the slopes of Glastonbury Tor in Somerset. It's supposed to be this really mystical place (which, of course, is why my mother wanted to go), but I tell you, it doesn't feel too mystical when you're getting soaked by persistent heavy drizzle and your mum's stopping to throw up halfway to the top. But there you go. That holiday had its good points – well, one, anyway. Mum realised that Love Child No. 4 was on its way. And, in due course, there was a baby, and that baby was Tor (minus the Glastonbury bit, thank goodness).

Sandie loves the stories behind our names; she thinks they're terribly romantic. And you can't blame her. Her parents didn't exactly exert their imaginations when they came up with Sandra, which is what her mum is called too. She was thrilled when I accidentally called her "Sandie" once – after we'd just begun to get friendly last year, when we both first started at Palace Gates comp – and it's all she's let anyone call her ever since.

So, anyway, here we were in our hall – me, Dad, Sandie and two muddy-pawed dogs.

"I was taking a DVD back to the shop for my mum and dad," Sandie smiled, sticking her thumb back in the direction of the kitchen, where she must have left the disk. "Do you fancy watching it together this afternoon before I drop it off?"

"Yeah, OK," I said, trying to find space on the overcrowded coat-hooks to hang up my jacket. "What is it?"

It was funny, but right at that moment, just looking at Sandie, I got another flutter of that worrying feeling that I'd forgotten something...

"Don't know. It's something with Nicole Kidman in it, so it should be all right."

"Cool," I nodded.

Then I noticed Sandie was doing something weird with her eyes, making them go wide and then darting them to the side.

Normally, I'd say that Sandie's eyes were the nicest thing about her; they're blue and round and pretty, kind of like a character's out of a Disney movie. (Tor thinks her eyes are exactly like his rabbit Cilla's – and I guess he's got a point. She does tend to do that startled, bunny-in-headlights thing a lot.) But today, rolling them around like she was doing, she looked downright deranged.

Dad was still milling about between us, searching for his house keys and the set for the workshop, so

I guess she was trying to let me know something without alerting him. But what it could be, I hadn't a clue.

Looking slightly frustrated at my lack of psychic power in figuring out what she was on about, Sandie dumped her coffee cup down on the hall table and stomped up the stairs.

"Going to the loo," she said needlessly, stepping over a snoozing cat (not Colin) and throwing one of those bizarre boggly-eyed looks at me over her shoulder.

"OK," I shrugged, passing Dad as he pulled his coat on and giving him a peck on the cheek bye-bye.

Then, heading along the hall to the entrance to the kitchen, I suddenly remembered what Rowan had gone out for.

"Hey, Sandie!" I bellowed after her, loud as an alarmingly loud foghorn. "There's no toilet pap—"

It was then that I saw what Sandie was trying to signal with her eyes.

There, sitting at the kitchen table, gently brushing another cat (also not Colin) off the Sunday supplement in front of him, was Alfie.

Alfie.

With my mouth still hanging open where I'd forgotten to finish my sentence, I stood rigid in the kitchen doorway, wondering if it was possible to rewind my life by ten seconds so I wouldn't look and sound like such a dork.

"Hi, Ally…" he said, glancing up at me from the magazine he was – cat allowing – trying to flick through.

It was hardly even a glance – more of a glancette – but the merest eye contact with Alfie tended to have the most traumatic affect on me: I stopped speaking English and started to speak gibberish.

"Huh – uh, hi," I mumbled, stepping forward awkwardly into my own kitchen.

I was walking with these funny bobbing little moves, like an insecure chicken.

"Uh … where – where's Linn, then?"

"Linn?" he repeated gently, like he was talking to someone who wasn't quite all there. Which I wasn't, in his presence. "I'm just waiting for her. She's on the phone, I think…"

Alfie looked back down at the magazine, which was perfect. It gave me a second to gaze at him, take in the gorgeousness of him, uninterrupted. His short, messily spiky blond hair; those spookily pale, grey eyes; that heart-bursting smile that stretches so wide you can sometimes see the gold tooth he has on one side; that cute leather strappy bracelet thing he wears round his wrist; those skinny but muscular tanned arms... Hey, tell me when you've got an hour. I've only fancied him for ever, so the full list of his many charms tends to run on a bit.

"So," I squeaked, deciding that I should try and squeeze a conversation out of him while I had him all to myself. "What are you two ... guys up to to-to-today?"

For some reason I was stammering, which I never normally do. And for some reason, I'd adopted a faint transatlantic twang to my voice, and believe me, I don't make a habit of acting like an extra out of an American teen show too often either.

He gazed up at me, and I knew my face must be practically *luminous* pink. My cheeks felt so hot you could fry an egg on them. Except for the fact that it'd keep slipping off them, since I was standing...

Getting sidetracked by the logistics of the egg-frying stuff *might* sound insane, but believe me, having a mind that regularly wanders off on garbage like that really helps sometimes. Like right then – it distracted me from my total and utter fluster and I instantly felt the furnace in my face fade away.

"We're just going into town... Check out Carhartt and that in Covent Garden..."

He spoke in this slow drawl of his, which *just* delicious. Course I didn't have a clue what he was on about, but I just nodded knowledgeably anyway. It had to be some trendy clothes shop; he was really into labels and stuff.

"Ah. Right. Well … um … don't do anything I wouldn't!"

OK, so *now* I knew I'd morphed into some seedy and deeply corny bloke off a building site. I could sense that this was *not* going too fantastically well, and I was considering faking a faint just to put an end to my agony when a blood-curdling scream erupted from somewhere upstairs.

Alfie looked shocked.

"What was that?" I yelped, turning and hurrying out into the hall, hoping the relief I felt at the diversion wasn't written *too* obviously all over my face. I mean, for all I knew, something truly terrible could have happened.

But of course it hadn't.

"Sandie!" I panted, after leaping up the stairs two at a time and staring into every room to find the source of the scream.

Sandie was sitting on the edge of Tor's bed, rigid with fear. If I thought her eyes were mad earlier, it was nothing on the I've-just-seen-an-alien! boggling they were doing now.

"What the hell—" barked Linn, appearing at my side, along with Alfie, who'd followed me up the stairs.

But it wasn't her stare or her gritted teeth that was the freakiest thing. It was the fact that, for some bizarre reason, Sandie had all these *twigs* in her hair.

And, uh-oh…

They were moving.

Chapter 5

ONE SURPRISE, WELL AND TRULY SCUPPERED...

"You shouldn't have done it."

"Why?"

"Because it wasn't nice."

"Why?"

"Because you scared her."

"Why?"

"Why *what*?"

It's hard having a conversation with Tor sometimes. As he's a boy of very little words, it sometimes gets kind of tiring trying to read between his (short) lines.

"Why was she scared of them?" Tor asked, gazing at me across the table, all doe-eyed confusion.

"*Because* when Sandie said she'd like to see them," Rowan explained, as she passed a plate under our little brother's nose, "she didn't think you were going to put the stick insects *on her head*."

Earlier in the afternoon, Linn, Alfie and I were still trying to figure out the best way of removing Tor's latest additions to the household from Sandie's hair

– with Tor anxiously watching and wailing at us not to damage their little stick legs – when Rowan came back from the corner shop. Luckily for the general health of the stick insects, she came up with the smart idea of wafting a lettuce leaf over Sandie's shaking head, enticing them away from the aroma of Head & Shoulders and up on to the safety of much healthier vegetation.

Now, his tea sitting untouched in front of him, Tor blinked and said nothing, but you could tell by the look on his face that he was highly disappointed in Sandie's reaction.

He's always deeply suspicious of anyone who doesn't display at least one hundred per cent adoration for animals*, and when he'd hijacked Sandie on her way to the loo to show off his new pets, the last thing he'd expected was for her to act like she did. (*The one exception to Tor's suspicion list is Grandma. She's not at all fond of the animals, but she's very fond of Tor. And Tor is very, *very* fond of his grandma.)

"Rowan, what exactly *is* this?" demanded Linn, staring at her plate in open disgust.

"Well, remember Dad said we should eat more fish…" said Rowan plaintively, her bracelets jangling as she sat down in her own seat.

She looked hurt, but I don't know why. Linn

always has a pop at her efforts every time it's Rowan's turn to cook, so you think she'd be used to it by now. Linn, Rowan and Dad take turns to cook at the weekend. Not Tor, thank God, or we'd probably end up with a tin of cat food, Hula Hoops and hamster mix. (Grandma comes round and cooks tea for us during the week, since us girls are all – ahem – busy with our homework.)

"Yeah, so we should eat more fish. But *this*?"

Linn wasn't being very nice, but then – if I'm honest – neither was our tea. Potato waffles, coleslaw and … kippers. I rest my case.

"Well, it was really busy in the fish shop yesterday and I just got a bit flustered!" Rowan tried to explain herself. "I just … panicked and pointed to the nearest thing when it was my turn!"

If you ask me, the reason she got flustered is 'cause there was quite a cute Saturday boy working in there.

"I'm sure it'll be lovely," Dad interrupted diplomatically. "Thanks, Rowan!"

Rowan gave Dad a grateful smile and reached over for the tomato sauce. Smart move – smothering everything (including coleslaw) in tomato sauce is just about the only way to get through one of Rowan's meals.

"So, Dad…" said Linn, gingerly picking at the

fish. "I was thinking, it's your birthday soon. And last year, we all went out for a pizza, didn't we? But this time round, why don't we stay home and cook something special here?"

"Will Rowan make it?" Tor piped up, with a panicky expression on his face.

"No. Definitely not," Linn reassured him, ignoring Rowan's disgruntled tutting.

My heart sank – I knew what Linn was up to. As far as she was concerned, the surprise party was All Systems Go, and making sure Dad didn't want to go out was just Phase One of her masterplan.

"Stay home? Fine by me," shrugged Dad. "You know I don't like a fuss."

See? I felt like yelling at her, *he doesn't like a fuss!*

And correct me if I'm wrong, but you don't get much more of a fuss than a surprise party.

"Speaking of fuss; poor Sandie," Dad laughed. "She must have been so embarrassed today."

He was right there. Poor Sandie. She's a total sweet pea – you'll never find anyone more trusting or kind – but on a one-to-ten shyness scale, Sandie's a nine-and-a-half, no problem, which makes me pretty protective of her actually. She was so traumatized by the stick-insect incident that she just spent the whole Nicole Kidman movie quietly groaning to herself; and even though I kept zapping the pause button and asking if she was OK, all she'd say was that she was fine. But put it this way, she kept covering her face with her hands so often, she couldn't have seen much of the film.

"Yes, she *was* pretty embarrassed," I nodded, wincing inside for her. I mean, *I* wouldn't exactly like to have someone cool like Alfie seeing me in such a total state.

"I can't blame her," my dad continued. "Being stuck in a room with everyone staring at you and *only* you – that's my idea of a nightmare, that is."

My hand froze as I lifted a forkful of fish to my mouth (well, any excuse not to eat it), and threw a glance over the table at Linn.

She'd gone momentarily rigid too.

I flicked my eyes across to Dad, who – unless I'd gone mad (possible) – gave me the tiniest of winks.

Did he know? Had he overheard somehow? Had he suddenly developed psychic powers and sussed out what Linn had in mind for him? Or was what he said just a timely fluke, and the wink was just a twitch?

I didn't know, and I didn't care. All I *did* know was that the stupid surprise-party idea was well and truly dead.

Long live the next idea.

Whatever that was.

Chapter 6

HEY! LET'S BE FRIENDS! (NOT...)

I was bumbling along the road on my way to school, half expecting to hear the familiar cry of "Allllllllllleeeeeeeeeee! Wait for *meeeeeeeeeeeee*!" from Sandie, but it didn't come. We never plan to meet, it's just that we often do anyway. My sisters go to Palace Gates too, but we all go out of our way not to walk to school together. That would be *so* not cool – for any of us.

Since I was on my own, I guess I should have been doing something constructive with my thoughts – like dreaming up an amazing present for Dad, or maybe even trying to figure out what that I've-forgotten-something feeling I'd had all week-end was about – but instead, inevitably, I thought about Alfie.

More specifically, I was thinking for the millionth time how Linn could honestly be Just Good Friends with someone as totally, omigod beautiful as him. I've never been able to figure it out – what does she see when she looks at him? Doesn't she just want to pounce on him? But, you know, I don't think she does. I've studied her sometimes when she's with him and nope, there's not a trace, not a *hint* of attraction going on there at all.

Same goes for him (I'm glad to report). But that's not to say Linn isn't pretty; she is. (And don't I know it...)

She's more like Mum than the rest of us. She's got Mum's almost blonde-ish wavy hair – not that you can see the waves, since she religiously blow-dries it straight every day – and almond-shaped eyes. (And those perfect boobs, of course.) Me, Rowan and Tor all take after Dad: straight, brown hair and matching Malteser-brown eyes. Of course, the one thing that would make Linn really, *really* pretty is if she smiled more.

Yeah, like *that's* going to happen in a million years.

But with the Alfie and Linn thing, it's not as if I think a girl and a boy can't be friends – I've got Billy, after all. But then, Billy is just, well, *Billy*. And Alfie is just ... *phwoarghhhh*.

Anyhow, I headed into the yard at Palace Gates comp and over to the main entrance, feeling pretty happy after my Alfie daydreams, even though it was Monday morning and I had a whole five days worth of school gaping out in front of me.

And there was still five minutes till the first bell – five minutes to hog a radiator and drool over Alfie in the privacy of my mind.

Or maybe not.

"Ally? Can I have a word, please? My office – now."

It was Mrs Fisher, our Year Head. We got told at the beginning of the school year that we had to look on Mrs Fisher as a friend, as someone we could talk to if we had problems. You know – her door was always open, blah-de-blah.

As *if*.

It took just a couple of gullible pupils to test *that* theory out for the rest of us to know that if ever we had a problem, we'd be better off talking to the janitor, the school nurse, or a random passing stranger about it than Mrs Fisher. I don't know what side of herself she showed off to Mr Bashir the Headmaster to get him to think she had it in her to be this compassionate advisor, but it *sure* wasn't the side we got to see. When it came to irritants like us, she was from the "Don't be silly – pull yourself together!" school of non-sympathy.

Needless to say, my good mood evaporated mighty quick as I obediently and silently followed her along the corridor and up the stairs to her office.

"This," she said, sweeping her door open and wafting her hand impatiently at someone sitting in a chair, "is Kyra Davies. And this—"

She wafted her hand vaguely in my direction.

"—is Ally Love. Ally, Kyra has just joined the school today, and she's going to be in your form class – therefore, I've decided to assign you to look after her for her first week. Show her about. All right?"

All right? I suppose it was. At least I wasn't in some terrible trouble over something I had no memory of, like I'd dreaded when Mrs Fisher had first summoned me. But now the relief that I wasn't about to be hung, drawn and quartered for some unknown misdemeanour was over, I got my first proper look at who I was going to have to babysit.

And I wasn't sure if I liked her.

Kyra Davies was sitting slouched in the chair, an arm sprawled casually along the back of it. She was chewing gum with her mouth open, eyeing me up and down quite blatantly, like I was a sack of potatoes she was trying to guess the weight of.

I tried to brazen it out and stare back at her, but I'm not great at that kind of thing; I don't have the bottle to act that hard (since I'm about as hard as mashed potato). I did stare enough to decide that she was Mediterranean-looking, or something.

She was quite pretty – apart from her sticky-out ears that looked glaringly obvious because of the way she'd dragged her dark, curly hair back into a top-knot – but she had this really kind of arrogant manner.

"Well, what are you waiting for, girls?" Mrs Fisher frowned. "The bell just went. You'll be late for your History class, if you don't hurry."

Chop, chop, go, go – that was Mrs Fisher's duty done, as far as she was concerned.

Kyra languidly stood up, hoisting her bag on to her shoulder, and blasted a teeth-baring, obviously insincere smile in the Year Head's direction.

"Thank you *sooo* much, Mrs Fisher," she said in a saccharine-sweet voice just dripping with sarcasm.

"Goodbye, Kyra," muttered Mrs Fisher in response, shutting the door firmly behind us.

"What a frigid old cow!"

I couldn't believe Kyra had the nerve to say that so loud, and right outside Mrs Fisher's door. And I couldn't believe that I suddenly found myself jumping to Mrs Fisher's defence.

"She's all right," I shrugged, walking off in the direction of the History class and just presuming Kyra would follow.

"Not from where *I* was sitting," Kyra snorted, falling into step beside me.

Maybe with someone else I'd have agreed with them straight away, but there was just something about Kyra's cockiness that bugged me, somehow. She'd only been at Palace Gates five seconds and she was mouthing off her opinions. It was a bit much, if you see what I mean.

"So, when did you arrive in Crouch End, then?" I asked, trying to change the subject.

"Last week," she replied, yawning.

I mean, *yawning* – how rude is that?

"Do you like it?"

"Don't know. Looks a bit boring. I told my mum and dad that we should live in south London, not north London, if we were going to move here at all."

"Oh?" I answered through gritted teeth, stomping along the corridor faster.

I know it's crazy, but I really love where I live – I'm really proud of how green and leafy and historic it is, and how many cool shops there are, and how comfy and trendy it is at the same time.

"Yeah – Brixton's much more happening than *this* place."

I couldn't say anything for a second, I was too annoyed. But I tried; I'm not into being rude. Even if Kyra was.

"So whereabouts are you living?"

"Cranley Gardens. The place we're in is a pit."

"Uh-huh."

Cranley Gardens is the sort of place that the local estate agents go all poetic over. It's a "highly desirable turning", apparently, and the way they tell it, every house is "luxurious". But not Kyra's, it seemed. God, just how spoilt was this girl?

"Mmm. So where did you live before?" I asked, relieved to see the door to Miss Thomson's History class in the not-too-distant distance.

"Rye. It's this little place down in East Sussex."

"I know it. We visited once when I was little."

"Total dump, isn't it?"

"I thought it was nice," I found myself protesting. "All those old, cobbled streets…"

"Yeah? And boring as hell."

Everything was a dump or boring, as far as this girl was concerned. Her boredom was boring me already.

"How come you moved?" I asked, out of politeness rather than actually wanting to know the answer.

"We move a lot. My dad's an assistant bank manager. We get around," she yawned again.

"And your mum?" I asked, eyeing up the approaching doorway.

"She's a professional drinker."

I shot Kyra a shocked look, and her face broke

into a lazy grin.

"Only joking…" she sniggered.

What a horrible thing to joke about, I frowned to myself.

But then I guess I'm pretty super-sensitive about stuff to do with mums.

At last, the doorway to the bright, white classroom loomed large.

Everyone was still drifting in, shuffling noisily into their seats. Over by the window, Sandie was already sitting in our usual spot; she shot me a questioning look. From the back of the room, where Chloe and Jen and the others sat, I could practically feel their eyes boring into my head, wondering what the deal was with the new girl.

"Hello, Ally. So this must be Kyra?" smiled Miss Thomson.

"That's me!" trilled Kyra, *really* insincerely.

I groaned inside. Being facetious with Mrs Fisher was one thing, but Miss Thomson was something else. She's too nice and reasonable to muck around with. Actually, she's my favourite teacher at school.

"Right, let's see… Do you want to sit yourself here for the moment, Kyra, and I'll come and chat to you in a second?"

With an almighty sigh Kyra flopped down into

the seat at the desk that had been pointed out to her.

Miss Thomson gave me one of those looks that, like my dad's the night before, *could* have meant something and then again might not. But from where I was standing, her eyebrows definitely shot up and down, as if to say, "*She's* going to be a pain, isn't she?"

But that was me guessing. Or wishful thinking. What Miss Thomson *did* say kind of took me by surprise.

"So, Ally, I was just in the middle of asking Sandie how you're doing with your project."

Our project.

Oh. My. God.

You know that thing I'd forgotten? All of sudden, I hadn't forgotten it any more…

Chapter 7

MORE STRESS? YES, PLEASE!

I'm not mean. Honest I'm not. Well, OK, I've been known to be a *bit* mean to Billy, but that doesn't count. He knows I'm only joking.

Hopefully.

But that Kyra – I was sick to death of her by the end of the day. It was absolutely zero fun, having to drag her around every class, and hear her slagging off the school all the time. (I got a break at lunchtime – I went home to my own place, as usual, after pointing her in the direction of the dinner hall.)

The world according to Kyra went like this: all the teachers she'd met at Palace Gates so far were morons; she was too smart for most of her old teachers and that's why they didn't like her; everybody in her last school was a total nerd; all her old schools were trash, but our school beat them all; everything about Palace Gates was scuzzy, especially the toilets.

Big wow – the toilets! What was she expecting? Fake-fur-lined seats and toilet-paper monitors handing out individual sheets to everyone entering a cubicle? Get real.

But if I'm honest, Kyra was just an irritation. The *real* problem that was doing my head in was our history project, and the fact that me and Sandie had done precisely nothing about it.

"I can't believe it's come up so fast!" I moaned, as the two of us mooched miserably out of the school gates on this Monday afternoon.

Trying to keep up with homework was one thing; trying to cram a project we'd had six weeks to do into the remaining two weeks was something else.

"I know," nodded Sandie.

"I mean, where's the time gone?"

"I know," Sandie sympathized.

"It's a disaster – we haven't even thought of what we're going to do!" I whimpered.

"I know," Sandie agreed.

We'd been told about this joint Drama and History department project a couple of months back. To celebrate our school's fiftieth birthday, the Drama crew were going to be putting on a play for local primary schools, based around what Crouch End was like fifty years ago. Us lot in the History department had been split up and given different tasks to do: some were helping with research for the play itself, while others – like me and Sandie – were supposed to be coming up with fascinating visuals on a wide variety of subjects to a) decorate the hall outside the auditorium, and b) expand the minds of the visiting small primary kids.

Back when Miss Thomson first told us about it, it had seemed about a hundred kilometres into the future. But now... *uhhhhhhhhh*.

"How could we have just forgotten about it?" I moaned, miserable at my own crapness. It was my leaving-homework-till-Sunday-night outlook to blame, I guess.

"Mmmm."

It slightly jarred that Sandie had stopped saying "I know". What was "Mmmm" supposed to mean?

"Mmmm?" I repeated, staring at my best friend.

"Well..." said Sandie sheepishly.

"Well?" I asked.

"Well ... *I* remembered."

"Remembered what?"

"Um, about the project..."

"You remembered about the *project*?!" I yelped. "All this *time*? Why didn't you *say* something?"

"I was waiting for you... I thought you were thinking up an idea!"

Sandie blinked at me with those blue, saucer-like eyes of hers.

She does this *all* the time – waits to see what I

think about something before she says or does anything. ("That girl's got no gumption!" my grandma said once, when Sandie was prannying about at my house as usual, saying, "Oh, I don't know! *You* decide!" when we were working out what movie to go and see at the Muswell Hill Odeon.)

I know what Grandma meant, but it's pretty hard to stay mad at Sandie. She's the kind of friend who's good to have around; she's got a brilliant sense of humour (even if she doesn't have the confidence to be funny herself), and she's so honest that she'll always tell you things straight (but she's also smart enough to know when to tell a little white lie – like saying I look fine when I have the biggest spot in the cosmiverse erupting on my chin).

But you know something? Just this once, I was *really* mad at Sandie. I couldn't help it; it could land us in real trouble. I mean, I know I was a doughball (double doughball) for forgetting about the project, but it was pretty stupid of Sandie not to have said anything about it earlier.

I suddenly felt a bit sick. It was all such a total disaster. Then, just when I thought the moment couldn't get any worse, I heard a sound that made my heart bounce off the pavement.

"Hi, guys," said Kyra, very casually strolling up beside us.

But she didn't fool me – she must have had to run to catch us up, 'cause there was no one behind us a minute ago when I looked back as we were crossing the road.

"Hi," I said half-heartedly. "So … what did you make of your first day, then?"

"Bo-*rinnnnnngggggggg*. That teacher, Mr Horse Arse—"

"Horace. Mr *Horace*," I corrected her, quickly.

I was well aware of what all the boys in our class called him. But we'd been taught by him for ages, and since Kyra had sat through one measly class with Mr Horse Ar—, uh, Mr Horace, it did seem kind of cheeky of her to get so casual with his nickname already.

"Yeah, whatever," shrugged Kyra. "Anyway Mr Whatshisname is a complete plonker. He's the worst so far."

I'd had it. If I heard one more whinge about our school and everything in it, I'd have to kill her.

"Um, don't you live over *that* way?" said Sandie tentatively, pointing at the other side of the road we'd just crossed.

I could have kissed my best mate then and there. For once Sandie wasn't just letting *me* do all the talking. And it was a fair point anyway – what *was* Kyra doing coming creeping after us when she lived in the opposite direction?

"I was just ... going ... to the post office."

No she wasn't. I heard that little hesitation in her voice, and saw her glancing ahead quickly to see where she could pretend to be heading for.

"Oh, right," said Sandie, giving me a quick nudge with her elbow. Looked like she'd sussed out Kyra's porky-pie too.

"Well, bye!" I said cheerily, as we approached the door of the post office.

"Yeah, bye. So I'll see you at the main entrance tomorrow, then, Ally?"

Deep gloom. Being Kyra's school babysitter for the week was just too annoying to contemplate.

"Uh-huh. See you tomorrow," I mumphed, forcing a half-hearted smile.

"God, what's she *like*?!" whispered Sandie, glancing behind to check that we weren't being followed again.

"Like the most pushy, irritating, whining person on the planet?" I suggested, loud enough for anyone in the vicinity – possibly even in the post office – to hear me.

OK, so now I had *three* things to stress over:

1) The fact that the wind was blowing through the vast, empty wilderness of my imagination every time I tried to come up with an idea for Dad's

birthday. At this rate, Linn would be trying to force Very Bad Plan No. 2 on us any second now. And I dreaded to think what *that* could be.

2) The wind was *also* blowing through the vast, empty wilderness of my imagination when I tried to think up some super-amazing idea for the History project too. Not that it had to be super-amazing. An averagely dull idea would have suited me fine by this late stage.

3) And I had this miserable feeling that Kyra was going to be a bit of a cling-on. I worried that she would try and tag along with me and Sandie as the only possible options open to her. After all, from what we'd seen (and heard) of her, people at school weren't exactly going to be queuing around the block to become big buddies with her.

I'd left Sandie a few streets back – both of us vowing to come up with some project ideas overnight (i.e. she'd wait and see what *I* came up with and then agree enthusiastically) – and was quite glad to see my familiar front door looming up in front of me.

Then, walking up the garden path, I heard raised voices coming from inside my house and wondered if I'd done something particularly awful in a past life to deserve such an annoying day.

"What's everyone yelling about?" I asked, stomping into the living room and taking everyone by surprise.

Tor was sitting cross-legged on the floor, petting a cat that wasn't Colin, while Rowan, Linn and Grandma were standing, hovering in a circle around him. From their body language, it looked like my sisters were in the middle of some strop, with Grandma acting as referee.

"Ally, dear, we are *not* yelling," said my gran, contradicting what was so clearly true. "We're just having a debate, that's all."

"OK," I said, chucking my school bag on the sofa and plonking myself down beside it. "So what's everyone debating about?"

"Dad's birthday," Linn replied snippily, settling herself down at the other end of our vast, squishy, old sofa.

It groaned gently as she did so, like a long, low fart, completely ruining her air of superior snottiness.

I threw a glare at Tor that said, "Don't you dare giggle at her – it'll make things worse!" But Tor was smart and knew that already; he'd yanked the black and white cat up into his arms so he could bury his face – and giggles – in it.

"Rowan has had this *stupid* idea," Linn began,

ignoring the sofa squelch, "that we should get Dad a session with a feng shui expert for his birthday!"

I glanced around our sunshine-yellow living room – at the old sofa and chairs with their throws, mounds of cushions and magazines and papers spilling off them, then at the fireplace, at the shelves and surfaces, all covered in pictures and ornaments and bric-a-brac and books and plants and candles ... a feng shui expert would walk in here and collapse with clutter-overload.

"I thought that would be right up your street, Linn," I suggested, suddenly remembering I'd forgotten to include assorted pets in the living room inventory. "Getting minimal and everything..."

"Minimal!" squeaked Rowan in alarm. "I thought feng shui people brought you luck by moving the furniture around a bit and sticking a couple of wind chimes up!"

Poor Rowan obviously hadn't swotted up on her suggestion properly. But then, speaking before she put her brain in gear was her speciality.

"I wouldn't mind *any* excuse to get this tip sorted out," sniffed Linn, gazing round the room dismissively, "but it's not exactly something Dad would be into, is it?"

And neither is a surprise party, I thought silently, finding myself irritated with Linn turning up her nose like that. After all, most of the paintings and bits of pottery in here was stuff Mum had made.

"Well, at least I tried to come up with something special," Rowan huffed, the bangles on her wrists jangling with irritation. "At least it's not *boring*, like Linn's idea!"

"Now, girls!" Grandma interrupted, holding a hand palm up in the direction of each of my sisters.

"So what was your idea?" I asked Linn, kicking off my school shoes as I talked.

"Go on! Tell her your idea and see if she falls asleep!" Rowan said stroppily.

"I thought maybe a watch – with a message engraved on the back," shrugged Linn, turning round on the sofa to face me and studiously ignoring Rowan.

"But he's already got a watch – the one Mum gave him," I replied automatically. After all, I couldn't see Dad parting with *that* in a hurry.

"*See?*"

"Enough, Rowan," muttered Grandma. "All this silly bickering over your dad; he would be very upset if he thought you girls were falling out over him."

Nobody said anything then – we all knew she was right.

"Anyway, I thought I might have a suggestion for

you," said Grandma, folding her arms across her chest.

"What?" I asked bluntly.

"Well, the most important thing to your dad is all of *you*," she began, now unfolding her arms long enough to point a finger at each of us in turn.

We waited wordlessly, all privately hoping Grandma was about to solve our problem for us.

"So, why don't you give him a family portrait of you four children? That photography shop on Crouch End Broadway always has *lovely* photos in the window of families they've snapped in their studio. They're—"

"Oh, Grandma, *no*!" exclaimed Rowan, looking as horrified as if the government had suddenly announced a ban on the year-round use of fairy lights. "Those posed photos are *awful*! They're *so* naff! All soft-focus and cheesy smiles!"

Grandma frowned at Rowan, then glanced round at the expressions on the rest of our faces.

Even Linn, who was Grandma's right-hand girl, couldn't hide the fact that she thought it was a deeply corny idea.

"Right! If you don't want to listen to my advice, then fine!" said Grandma sternly, turning and heading out the door. "I'd better get started on tea anyway…"

Uh-oh – major huff alert.

Grandma tells *us* lot off for bickering or sulking, but boy, can she do a mean teenage strop when she wants to….

Chapter 8

HACKED OFF...

A word of warning: never, *ever* try to cut your fringe when you're in a bad mood.

I gazed at my reflection in the toilet mirrors while a bunch of girls who were in the year below me charged about screaming and giggling about something or other in the background.

Hopefully, it wasn't my hair, but I couldn't have blamed them if it was. One single, solitary chunk of fringe was cut so high that a big, shiny patch of forehead positively *gleamed* at me in the mirror. My fringe would've looked better if I'd just let Tor's hamsters *gnaw* on it for a while.

You see, Grandma usually trims my hair for me – it's just past my shoulders, with a fringe, so it's not like I'm any challenge to a hairdresser – but last night, she was still huffing too much for me to ask for hair-snipping favours, so I did it myself. In fact, Grandma was huffing so much that she didn't even stay for tea with us like she normally does; as soon as Dad came in she was off, saying there was a programme on telly that she really wanted to catch, which sounded like a flimsy excuse to all of us. Not that any of us let on to Dad that there was a problem – that would have been giving the game away.

So, today, I could add a new dollop of stress to my stress mountain. I had a non-existent History project (no overnight miracles there), no idea about Dad's dumb birthday present, Kyra still bending my ear with her moaning between classes, and now there was Grandma going all grumpy on us.

Oh, and a hairdo from hell.

"No! Don't! No! *Nooooooo!*" shrieked the girls behind me. They were really irritating me – I felt like explaining that it was still possible to laugh without doing it at a level of decibels that burst eardrums. But I was just in a bad mood.

Back to Grandma: she might come over all strict and everything but, underneath, she's a total softie. She tuts and gripes a bit at the state of the house (her flat is like one of those show homes – not a crumb or a speck of dust to be seen. You see where Linn gets it from...), but she's always been there for us. Well, especially since Mum and everything. A couple of years back, she even sold her house up in Barnet and moved to a flat round the corner from us, just to help out more. So even if she was a bit serious and not exactly the kind of person you could kid around with, there's no way I – or any of us – would deliberately want to hurt her feelings. But it looked like we'd managed to...

"Come on! That's the bell! Quick! A prefect might come in an' catch us!"

I moved my eyes away from the vision of hacked hair in front of me in the mirror, and watched the posse of giggly girls tear out of the loos.

I couldn't resist it. I had to have a nosey at what they were all in a tizz about. They'd seemed to be hovering around the cubicle behind me; I stepped across the scuffed vinyl floor and peered in.

Their art teacher wouldn't exactly have been proud of what they'd been doodling on the wall in thick black marker pen. (*I* certainly don't remember any diagrams like that from the sex-education talks Mrs Fisher gave us.) And their English teacher wouldn't have been impressed with the sort of stuff they'd been writing either. I mean, if you're going to scrawl obscenities on the toilet walls, you should at least spell them properly, shouldn't you?

"Nicole is a hoe," I read aloud. "A '*hoe*'?"

Not much of an insult, is it? Comparing a person to something that sits next to the spade in a garden shed, I mean.

But staring at the handiwork of a bunch of girls without a brain cell between them, it did suddenly occur to me that Kyra was right for once: the toilets at Palace Gates *were* pretty scuzzy.

Thinking of Kyra, I breathed a sigh of relief. I'd managed to shake her off at the beginning of the afternoon break, fifteen minutes before, and hadn't seen her since. Could it be that she was as bored as *I* was of us trailing around together? Could it be that at least one of my stress-factors was finished with?

I gave my hair a quick, useless ruffle in the mirror, and hurried out into the corridor.

Where I bumped slap, bang into Miss Thomson, my History teacher.

"Ally!" smiled Miss Thomson. "I've just been talking about you!"

"Oh?" I replied, wondering what was coming next.

"Yes – remember that you told me yesterday in class that you and Sandie were a little behind with your project?"

A little behind? Try four weeks behind...

"Well, I just had a surprise visit at the beginning of breaktime – from someone who could lend you a hand..."

I didn't have to listen as Miss Thomson finished what she had to say. All I knew was that me and

Sandie had just found ourselves with a little helper that we most definitely didn't want.

Kyra 'in-yer-face' Davies.

Chapter 9

SMART IDEAS, WORSE LUCK...

A cat that wasn't Colin started sniffing at the tuna sandwich I'd just made.

"Oi!" I yelped, rushing back from the fridge with a bottle of low-fat salad cream in my hand (it had a "Property of Linn Love" sticker on it, but I was doing my best to ignore that).

The cat that wasn't Colin jumped off the work surface and walked indignantly across the wooden kitchen floor with a clickety-click of its claws. I peered after it, and saw from the funny bend in its tail that it was Frankie. That's the only way I can identify the cats that aren't Colin; by the broken bits on them. Tor, of course, knows every cat by the sound of its purr or the flick of a whisker, but it's harder for the rest of us. It's just that, apart from Colin (being ginger and having only the three legs), our other four cats are all a universal black and white. From a distance, or when they're snoozing in a tight cat-curl, it's hard to tell the difference. Up close, it's easier: Frankie has the wonky tail, Eddie has ears that are so fight-chewed they look like they're lace-edged, Derek is very cross-eyed, and Fluffy makes Frankie look good – he's got no tail at all.

"Your house is amazing! I love all the colours, and all the pictures and stuff!"

I didn't particularly like Kyra, I *definitely* resented having to include her in mine and Sandie's (invisible) History project, and I wasn't exactly *thrilled* at the idea of having to invite her back to my place this Wednesday lunchtime so we could go over our "plans" for the project.

But, hey, I'm shallow enough to appreciate a compliment when it comes my way.

"Thanks," I nodded, handing her a plate with a tuna sandwich on it.

The one Frankie had been sniffing at, of course.

Kyra pulled out the nearest chair, which was directly opposite Sandie, who was already halfway through her sandwich and had been flicking through a mag while Kyra was upstairs in the loo.

"Listen," said Kyra, peeling back the top slice of bread to inspect what I'd given her, "what's going on in the room at the end of the hall upstairs? I heard all these *noises*…"

I hesitated for a second as I blobbed a dollop of Linn's personal low-fat salad cream on my own sandwich, and tried to figure out what she meant. And then I realized – Tor's bedroom is a den of tanks filled with fish, stick insects, lizards and a variety of small things whirring round in wheels.

"Was it squeaking and scrabbling type noises?" I asked.

"Yeah!"

"That's my brother's hamsters and stuff."

"Wow – and you've got those two dogs too?"

Rolf and Winslet had been very excited by the sudden activity in the middle of the day. Normally it was just me and Rowan who were home at lunchtime (me, 'cause I like the peace, and Rowan 'cause – to be honest – she hasn't got any friends at school to hang out with in the dinner hall).

"Yes, and we've got five cats too," I said, yanking out another chair from the long wooden kitchen table and settling myself down.

"Yeah?"

I half-expected Kyra to come out with a sarky comment about smelly animals or something, but she didn't. I was surprised. But not as surprised as what she said next.

"So who's the freak-show sitting in your living room?"

I twitched. How dare she speak about Rowan like that? Although – as much as I didn't want to –

I had to acknowledge (only to myself) that Rowan *had* gone for a very odd look today. She'd twisted her dark hair into all these tight little bobbles on her head, like Björk used to do (which was weird enough as it was), and then tied tiny pieces of ribbon around each bobble. It must have taken her ages to do, and to be honest, the effect wasn't quite worth it.

Still, that *was* a member of my family she was talking about.

"That's her sister!" said Sandie, leaping to mine and Rowan's defence in the face of Kyra's tact-free comment.

"Yeah? Poor you!" snorted Kyra.

I was just about throw a very sarky comment Kyra's way (if I'd been able to think of one fast enough) when she went all gooey all of a sudden.

"*Oooooh! Bab*eeeeeeee! What happened to you?"

From nowhere, Colin hopped up happily into her welcoming arms and set up a rattling purr that would have rocked the foundations of the house ... well, in my dreams anyway.

"You mean his leg?" I said, obviously. "He had an argument with a car, and lost."

"Oh, my God, you must have been so upset!" Kyra exclaimed, stroking an ultra-content Colin.

"Nah, it happened before we got him," I shrugged.

"We inherited him from a friend of a friend of my gran's – they were moving away and couldn't take him."

But then that was the story of all our pets' lives; every one of them was wonky and shop-soiled in one way or another. Like Winslet; apart from her old-lady grumpiness, we also realized when we found two sets of keys, a hairbrush, a hot-water bottle and Dad's favourite jersey hidden under the doggy blanket in her bed that her kleptomaniac tendencies had probably helped lead her to be abandoned in the first place.

And the cats; well – apart from Colin – we inherited Frankie and Derek from nearby neighbours who'd moved in for four months and done a runner in the night, abandoning their four-legged furrballs, while Eddie had just been a stray we'd started feeding. Fluffy is the bad-tempered, feline equivalent of Winslet, who'd had her tail amputated after it was bitten by the Doberman she lived with. In the circumstances, Fluffy and the Doberman couldn't live together any more and, rather unfairly, their owners (people who worked in the grocer's next to Dad's workshop) decided that Fluffy should get herself a new home. Which happened to be ours.

"You're so lucky," murmured Kyra, nuzzling

Colin's head with her nose. "We've moved around so much we've never been able to have any pets…"

I sneaked a look at Sandie, who was sneaking a look back in my direction. If I read her mind right, I knew she was thinking, "What's with *her*?" – same as me.

It was hard to keep up with Kyra's changes of character. In the two and a half days we'd known her at school, she'd been the Snarl Queen. In the five minutes we'd been sitting in the kitchen, she gone from praising my house, to dissing my sister, to practically drooling over my cat and getting embarrassingly slushy over animals in general.

"So, this project," I said, trying to drag Kyra's attention away from Colin before she stroked the fur off his back. "To be honest, we haven't got very far with it."

"Oh?" said Kyra, gazing up at me.

"We haven't done, well, *anything*," Sandie shrugged, nervously scraping her fine, fair hair back behind her ears.

She had little pink spots of guilt on her cheeks too, I noticed.

It's not Miss Thomson we're having a tuna sandwich with! I felt like saying to her. *What are you blushing for?*

"Good!" exclaimed Kyra, puzzlingly.

"Don't mind me…" Rowan's voice drifted into the kitchen. She padded over to the fridge and was about to help herself to some orange juice when her hand hovered over a carton of raspberry yoghurt drink, which she picked out instead. It had a "Property of Linn Love" sticker on it, I noticed.

"Why's that good?" I asked Kyra, turning my attention back to her.

"'Cause I've had this brilliant idea!" she replied. "Well, it's a rip-off of something I did at one of my old schools, but I think it'll work OK."

"Go on…" said Sandie, leaning her elbows on the table and narrowing her big, blue, Disney eyes at Kyra.

"Well, you've got a local historical society here, haven't you? It's just that I bet they'll have maps about where bombs fell in this area during World War Two," explained Kyra, still busily fondling Colin's ears. "At my old school, we did these big posters, showing where the bombs fell, and showing photos from the time, with arrows and stuff pinpointing them on the maps."

"That sounds brilliant!" said Rowan suddenly, a pink yoghurt moustache noticeable on her upper lip. "People are always nosey about stuff like that, aren't they? Trying to see if the street *they* live on was affected!"

"Exactly!" agreed Kyra.

I looked from one to the other. Weren't they both forgetting something?

"Er, hello? Remember us?" I waved at my sister. "Thanks, Rowan, but it's up to me and Sandie to say if it's a good idea or not."

"Well, you haven't *got* an idea, have you? So you haven't got much choice," said Rowan curtly, looking a little hurt.

But then I felt a little hurt myself, with her having a dig at me. As if I didn't feel useless enough when it came to the project.

I watched as Rowan stomped out of the kitchen, back to the strains of some Aussie soap starting up on the telly in the living room.

I sighed to myself. If there's one thing I really hate it's when people are right about something you wish they weren't right about. If you see what I mean.

"So, what do you think?" asked Kyra.

"Mmm," I nodded reluctantly. "Sounds good. Let's do it."

Well, let's face it – it was do Kyra's idea or leave the country before Miss Thomson found out the truth...

Chapter 10

ALL THAT GLITTERS (IS IN ROWAN'S ROOM)

You know that Friday feeling? When it's like you've been set free for a whole, delicious weekend, starting as soon as you get out of the school gates at four?

Well, I didn't have it. Or at least I had it for fifteen whole minutes, till I got home in time to see Rowan storming up the stairs, hiccuping with tears, while Linn was shouting, "Oh, for God's sake, Ro, stop being such a baby!"

"What's wrong now?" I asked Linn, following her back into the living room.

"Ask *her*! I was just trying to have a discussion, and she flounces off. As usual."

Linn flopped down on the sofa and picked up a copy of some magazine. From the way she was holding it up in front of her face and angrily flicking the pages, I could tell I wasn't going to get any more out of her.

I turned and walked out of the room, into the hall – its lilac walls looking more bruised purple as the strange stormy light poured in through the glass panels on the front door – and headed into the kitchen.

"I'm keeping out of it," said Grandma, anticipating what I was going to say.

Beside her at the kitchen table was Tor, sucking unhygienically at the end of his pencil, a notebook with scrawled sums open in front of him.

"But, Grandma, what are they—"

"Ally – Tor and I are too busy doing his homework to worry what silly girls are arguing about. Aren't we, Tor?"

My little brother nodded.

"And silly girls like that would be better off getting *their* homework out of the way on a Friday afternoon instead of bickering, wouldn't they, Tor?"

Tor nodded at Grandma again and looked back down at his sums.

Compared to his sisters, Tor might have been in Grandma's good books for now, but he wasn't all sweetness and light. I could see the slight bulge in the top pocket of his school shirt, and I could see it was moving. Since it was only a small pocket, I guessed that one of his white mice must have been chosen to come down and be his maths muse. If Grandma spotted that she would *not* be amused.

If Linn and Grandma weren't going to tell me anything, then there was only one person who would. And she was upstairs snivelling.

"Rowan?" I said softly, knocking at her door.

There was no reply.

"Ro – it's me, Ally!" I called a little louder, in case she thought it was Linn coming to continue their fight, whatever it was about.

"Mnnnumph!"

I took the trumpeting of her nose to be a yes, and walked in.

It was only twenty past four and shouldn't have been so dark outside, but the purply-orange storm clouds lay low and ominous outside the big bay window. Because it was as if twilight had landed early, Rowan had already switched on her collection of fairy lights and charity-shop lamps. With all her trinkets twinkling in shades of pink and green, red and yellow, the effect was beautiful. Her whole room was beautiful, in an over-the-top, brain-dazzling way. Everything was beautiful – except for the hunched-up girl perched on the bed, her mascara smeared and her nose immersed in a snotty white tissue.

"That's new," I said, pointing to a kind of collage thing on the wall.

It was a sugar-pink fluffy heart mounted on a big

piece of baby-blue art board. All round the edge of the board and the heart, multi-coloured sequins were glued, and in the centre of the fluffy heart itself was a tiny doll, wearing what looked like a little tutu.

"I made it last weekend," sniffed Rowan, blowing her nose again. "Found the doll in a junk shop on Saturday and decided to do something with it."

She seemed a bit happier already – talking about the pictures and stuff she made always cheered her up. Linn maybe got Mum's looks, but Rowan definitely got our mother's love of all things arty-farty. Me, I didn't inherit either Mum's blondey-fair hair or her arty-fartyness. I don't know if I inherited any of her traits at all, really; sometimes my memory of her is a bit hazy. Which is a pretty weird feeling...

"Nice," I commented, though I wasn't sure if I'd have fancied something like that up on my wall.

"Thank you," said Rowan, uncurling her legs from under her and starting to look more composed.

"So, what were you and our lovely big sister arguing about?" I asked, lowering myself down into her green blow-up chair. It was on the semi-deflated side – my bum was just about touching the floor – but it was still kind of fun to sit in.

"Oh, her!" sighed Rowan, throwing a theatrical

glare at the ceiling. "Linnhe is so bossy it makes my blood fizz!"

Now if I was Linn, I'd have been correcting her at that point, telling her the word she was looking for was "boil", not "fizz". But I didn't bother – that's just the sort of thing that Rowan comes out with and I always find it quite entertaining. My favourite thing is when she's singing along to the radio in the shower or the bath – she warbles along really enthusiastically, but *always* gets the words wrong.

"What's she bossing you about for?" I quizzed her.

"You'll never believe it," said Rowan, her eyes wide and comical with all the black mascara smeared round them. "She's only just gone and decided that this family photo of Grandma's is a good idea after all!"

"What?" I yelped, nearly bobbing out of the inflatable plastic chair in surprise. "How come?"

Rowan flopped back on to her squashy rose-covered duvet.

"That's what I tried to ask – before she bit my head off!"

"What did she say?"

"She said that since me and you hadn't bothered coming up with anything, Grandma's idea was probably the best we were going to get and we should just go for it."

I felt a twinge of guilt at that. Like with the History project, I'd been spectacularly bad in the inspiration department.

"Then I tried to say that I didn't want to do it," Rowan continued, "and Linnhe tells me to shut up unless I had something useful to say!"

I couldn't see Rowan's face at that point, since she was lying on her bed and I was practically down at carpet level, but I could tell she was going all snively on me again.

"Don't let her get to you!" I said lamely, as I struggled to get out of the wobbly seat.

There was only one thing for it, I decided: I had to try to come up with a better idea for a birthday present before Linn went and booked an appointment at the photographer's. Linn and Rowan were going to come to blows soon if things went on the way they were, and I didn't suppose Dad would be all that chuffed with a grinning portrait of his family, with his two oldest daughters showing off the black eyes they'd given each other.

Speaking of Dad...

"Hey, Ally Pally! Come to make sure your old dad gets home safely?"

Dad had stuck his head out of the back workshop at the sound of the bell above the door, and I squelched my way in, trailing wet footprints across the lino.

"Well, you're always reading about old people getting mugged in the street these days..." I grinned at him.

An oily rag came whizzing in my direction.

"What did I say?" I jokingly protested, ducking sideways and letting it fly clean past me.

"Give me a minute – I'll wash my hands and then I'll be ready," he called out, disappearing further into the workshop. "The rain's really hammering down out there now, isn't it?"

"Yep. So, been busy today?" I yelled above the sound of running water in the sink.

"Not really," he yelled back. "Pretty quiet for a Friday. I sold one kid's bike though."

Dad didn't just repair bikes, he sold second-hand ones too – in the teeny-tiny front shop I was now standing in, dripping.

"So, what's brought you round here, Ally Pally?" Dad's voice drifted through.

"Don't know – just felt like a walk," I shrugged to myself.

What a joke. If I'd wanted a walk I'd have grabbed Winslet and Rolf and gone up to the Palace or to Queen's Woods – not just tootled five minutes around the corner to Dad's shop. And moseying out for a stroll isn't the first thing you generally think of doing when a storm's just broken and the rain's bouncing in sheets off the pavement.

No, I didn't just fancy a walk: unknown to Dad, I was on a spying mission...

"So," said Dad, appearing in his red checked shirt and jeans in the doorway of the workshop, drying his hands with a towel, "you haven't come round to pick my brains about what I want for my birthday?"

Damn. Guess the FBI wouldn't be calling to recruit me soon.

"How did you know?" I asked, slouching in defeat.

"Oh, I overheard Linn talking to Rowan about it last week," he grinned at me. "Tell me, Linn's not still keen on that surprise-party idea, is she?"

"No," I reassured him, remembering that look I thought he'd thrown me across the kitchen table a few days before. "You managed to put her off on Sunday, when we were talking about Sandie and what had happened with the stick insects."

"Good," he smiled, chucking the towel over an old stool and pulling his worn denim jacket off the hook on the door. "I don't want any big fuss. I'm just happy to have all of you guys – I don't want anything fancy."

It was one of those lump-in-the-throat moments. I knew he was thinking of the one person who was missing from the equation, and *he* knew that *I* knew what he was thinking. I blinked hard and tried to say something funny before I started the waterworks like Rowan.

"Don't let on to the others, but keep an eye on things, will you, Ally?" said Dad, sliding his taut, muscular arms into his jacket.

"Sure," I gulped, still feeling that lump in my throat, especially now that Dad had trusted me with his thoughts.

"Maybe you could try not to let things get out of hand," he continued, patting me on the shoulder.

"No problem," I reassured him. "So, no fanfares; no cheerleaders; no ticker-tape parades..."

"Exactly!" laughed Dad, coming and putting his arm around my shoulders and ushering me out the front door.

OK – so now I knew what he *didn't* want. But it still hadn't got me any closer to figuring out what he *did* want...

Chapter 11

CHEEK, AND PLENTY OF IT...

"Ally – look!"

Now, Tor isn't one of those annoying kids that goes loopy in toy shops. You know, the type that just start grabbing anything within a metre radius, whining "Can I have this? Can I have this? Can I have this? Can I have this?" over and over again like a jumping CD.

Nope. I can safely say that I could take Tor into the best toy shop in the world, and he wouldn't twitch. But take him to the local pet shop, and that's a different kettle of gerbils altogether...

"Ally – it's pretty isn't it?"

Tor's brown eyes were gazing up hopefully into mine. We were here at the pet shop doing our regular Saturday-morning stint, stocking up on hamster bedding, fish food and whatever little extras Tor managed to wangle out of our budget.

"Uh, yeah, I suppose it's quite pretty," I nodded, peering at the small sponge ball covered in soft, glittery, tinsel spikes. It looked like a strange mating between a hedgehog and a Christmas decoration. "What is it?"

"Cat toy," said Tor earnestly, pointing at the display box full of glitter-spiked balls he'd plucked it from.

"Mmm. Looks more like a Rowan toy," I commented, thinking how much our sister would like something that sheeny-shiny and stupid.

Tor giggled.

It's great having a kid brother sometimes; it doesn't matter *how* lousy your jokes are, they always laugh.

"Better not tell her about these, Tor," I said to him, all mock-serious. "She'll be in here buying the whole lot, and end up glueing them round her headboard or something."

Tor giggled some more. And then he stopped.

"Can I get one, then?" he blinked up at me. "Please?"

He doesn't miss a trick; really he doesn't.

There he was, luring me into a false sense of security, pretending he thought what I was saying was funny and everything, and then *wham* – just when my guard's down, he hits me with the wide-eyed pretty-pleases.

"Well, if we buy this, then we can't go for a hot chocolate…" I warned him.

That's part of our Saturday-morning ritual too –
going for a hot chocolate at Shufda's, a little egg 'n'
chips caff a couple of doors up from the pet shop.
Unless, of course, we end up spending our "treat"
money on stuff like sponge glitter balls.

"That's OK," he shrugged. "The cats'll like it."

So, we headed home early, armed with pet bits
and cat toys. With just me and him and no one else
around, I felt it was time to pick Love Child No.
4's brain.

"You heard Rowan and Linn fighting yesterday,
didn't you?" I asked, as we trudged along the busy
pavements, sharing a consolation Kit Kat (well,
even if we didn't get our hot chocolate, we still had
to keep our sugar levels up...).

"Yep," said Tor, leaning sideways with the weight
of his shopping bag.

"It didn't upset you, did it?"

"No."

"Did you figure out that they were arguing about
what to get Dad for his birthday?"

"Yep."

"So, what do you think, Tor? Do you think
Dad would like a big framed picture of the four
of us?"

"Nope."

Like I say, he's a boy of few words. But you always get his drift pretty easily.

"What do you think *would* be a good present for Dad, then?"

Tor looked up at me, his eyes squinting against the sun.

"The zoo..."

"The zoo? Well, I know we want to get Dad something good, Tor, but I don't think even all our pocket money clubbed together is enough to buy the whole of London Zoo..."

"No!" he said, whacking me on the arm with his half of the Kit Kat. "A day out! All of us! And Grandma!"

Ooh, I could just see Grandma there, pulling a disapproving face at the sight of the baboons and their obscenely red bums. Or Linn yawning and looking at her watch. And considering Dad had taken Tor to the zoo one Sunday last month, I didn't think he'd particularly think it was some big-wow birthday treat to go and count the penguins yet again, quite so soon.

"Right, fine. Thanks, Tor – that's, er, another idea to think about!" I lied, as we took the turning into our road.

"Who's that?"

Tor was pointing his chocolate bar into the

distance.

"Who's that where?" I asked, peering down the street to see what he could see.

"At our door," said Tor, now nibbling distractedly at his Kit Kat, like one of his hamsters let loose on a carrot.

Fleetingly, I just made out a figure – a dark-haired girl – being let in our front door.

"Wasn't that Von?" I suggested.

Von is one of Rowan's best buddies; one of her two best mates (the other one is a monosyllabic guy called Chazza) who our gran strongly dis-approves of. Mainly because they're quite a bit older than my fifteen-year-old sister (Von and Chazza are both eighteen) and pierced (in Von's case it's her nose, in Chazza's it's his eyebrow), and because Grandma really has a thing against nicknames (Von is short for the hard-to-get-your-head-around Irish name Siobhan, Chazza is playground mumbo-jumbo for Charles). Can you imagine my uptight grandma giving it the old "So, how are you … Chazza?" It doesn't come naturally, I'll tell you that. But what choice does poor old Rowan have? All the people in her year give her a pretty hard time, since they think she's so weird and everything, so if Von and Chazza think she's cool, who cares if they're older, pierced, or in possession of rubbish nicknames?

"No – it wasn't Von," Tor said definitely.

"Was it one of Linn's mates?" I suggested, wracking my brain. "Mary? Or maybe Nadia?"

"No."

I frowned. Who was wandering about in our house right now? If that girl wasn't one of Linn or Rowan's mates, then who was she?

"She had big ears," said Tor simply.

He's a bit spooky sometimes, my brother (no wonder Billy calls him Spook Kid). He has this thing where he hones in on details other people just don't get…

"You couldn't have seen her ears from all this distance away!" I laughed, as we trudged along the pavement.

But as soon as the words were out of my mouth, I remembered someone who did have big ears, when her hair was pulled back tight in a ponytail.

It suddenly occurred to me who the girl in my house really was. And she wasn't a friend of *mine*.

The cheek of Kyra Davies…

Chapter 12

WHOSE HOUSE IS IT ANYWAY?

Rowan was sitting at the table, her knees tucked up inside her white, cotton, Victorian-style nightie. From where me and Tor were standing in the kitchen doorway, it made her look like she had enormous matronly bosoms.

She was still sleepy from her long lie-in – you could tell by the way she was yawning and the way her hair was sticking up at one side. Lucky for her, someone was filling the kettle to make her a cup of coffee.

"Oh, hi! I just got here," said Kyra, ever so casually, as she plugged the kettle in. "I woke Rowan up ringing the doorbell, so I'm making her a coffee to make up for it. Do you want one?"

It's weird seeing someone you don't know or like very much making themselves at home and rummaging about in your kitchen cupboards for mugs. Not just weird; downright INFURIATING!

"Uh, Kyra – wasn't I meant to phone you later, about meeting up?" I said, hoping she'd get my point.

She didn't.

"Oh, it's no problem," she shrugged, clattering cups down on the work surface. "I've already been to the Historical Society – I've got everything we'll need."

Now, you see what I mean about the girl? How presumptuous was that? The plan was supposed to be that I'd call Sandie and Kyra around lunchtime, and work out a time to go to the Historical Society *together*, so we could research and pick out all our reference stuff for the project *together* … and now look what she'd gone and done. She obviously had some kind of difficulty understanding what "together" is supposed to mean. Like, it doesn't mean "Never mind anyone else; you just go on and do whatever you fancy…"

I was so mad, I couldn't think what to say.

"Yeah, I got up early this morning and was just a bit bored," Kyra blithely continued, turning and placing a cup in front of Rowan.

"Thanks," muttered Rowan sleepily.

"No problem. So I thought I might as well go along and get everything we needed. What do you take in your coffee, Ally?"

I still hadn't said anything, and I was still hovering uselessly in the doorway, carrier bags in hand.

"She takes milk. And one sugar," yawned Rowan, doing my talking for me.

"Well, are you going to sit down?"

I'm an idiot sometimes, I really am. This bossy, pushy girl tells me to sit down in my own house, and what do I do?

I sit down.

"Look, this is what I got," Kyra continued, settling herself into a chair and pulling copies of photos and maps out of a white plastic bag. "All we need to do is get these blown up to poster-size first – does the office at school have a good photocopier, or are we going to have to go to a specialist copying place?"

"I … I don't know," I shrugged stupidly.

"Oh, wow – look! This is Von's street!" said Rowan, suddenly springing to life at the sight of the first photo on the pile.

"Yeah – see this house here? It's completely gone. That's where the bomb fell," Kyra explained.

"Gee, this is going to be really interesting for everyone, seeing if their street was bombed…" mused Rowan, riffling through the other photos. "This must have taken you for ever to sort out!"

"Yes, it did. But the two women down at the Historical Society were brilliant, helping me go through everything."

Do you ever get times where you feel surplus to

requirements? That's how I felt right then, watching my sister and this practical stranger sitting with their heads together, cooing over *my* project.

And it was about to get worse.

"Do you like hamsters?" said a small voice.

Because I'd been so stunned at the sight of Kyra Davies swanning round my house like she was my lifelong buddy, I hadn't noticed Tor disappearing from my side. And I hadn't noticed him reappearing, sidling up to Kyra with a handful of fur, teeth and claws.

"Yes I do!" said Kyra, turning and attempting to stroke Mad Max.

"Don't – he bites!" warned Tor.

Too right Mad Max bites. Tor had inherited him a few weeks earlier from the reception class at his school. Instead of being this sweet, fluffy creature for the little kids to cuddle and love, it turned out that Mad Max was the Rottweiler of the small-mammal world, merrily biting children and teachers at every possible opportunity. If Tor hadn't taken him, Mad Max was destined for a one-way trip to the vet...

I got quite chirpy at that point. Tor was testing Kyra; forcing her to come face to face with his scariest pet, and see how she'd react. Good lad.

"He won't bite me!" said Kyra assuredly, scooping

Mad Max right out of Tor's hand and cuddling him to her chest.

Come on, Max, I thought to myself. *Do your stuff!*

"Prrp! Eeeeee!"

"He likes you!" chirped Tor, grinning in delight.

Great.

I couldn't even trust a hamster to be on my side…

Chapter 13

KISSING BILLY (YEAH – LIKE, RIGHT!)

The grass was a little bit too damp to lie on, but I didn't care.

Staring straight up, I watched little, ripply clouds wisp their way across the blue, blue sky. Then, accompanied by a far-away roar, a large plane came streaming over the top of Alexandra Palace, its silvery wings glinting with reflected sunlight.

I love skywatching. It chills me right out. Whenever my head gets in a knot, or if I just fancy a daydream, I come and flop down here at the top of the hill and gaze into space. The best part is when the planes swoosh past though – I love imagining who's sitting up there, eating free peanuts, as they gaze down on the amazing aerial view of Ally Pally (the building) and maybe the less impressive and much smaller Ally Pally (me) – if their eyesight's sharp enough. I always wonder where they're going and what their lives are like...

That Sunday morning, I'd happily have swapped places with anyone on the big silvery plane up above me. It wasn't as if anything dramatically *bad* was happening in my life, but I *was* feeling well and truly fed up by how irritating and complicated things can get.

Like the business of Kyra turning up unannounced the day before, and half my family falling for her. I tell you, I'd decided that it was the *last* time I'd take Rowan's side over Linn's, and the *last* time I'd go shopping for spoilt cat toys with Tor...

If only I was on that plane, going somewhere far away... I wished to myself, watching it fly off towards the horizon. *Anywhere that wasn't here would do...*

You know how some people have recurring dreams? Well, I have a recurring fantasy. It goes like this: I'm sitting on a plane that's headed for somewhere tropical and warm and beachy (this week's choice of imaginary destination was Sri Lanka – I'd seen it on a travel show and checked out where in the world it was on the big map on my bedroom wall). Anyhow, I'm on this plane, gazing out of the window at these great, fat clouds below me, when someone asks if I'd mind them sitting in the empty seat next to me. And my heart skips a beat or three, 'cause I recognize that slow, lazy drawl, and I turn round to find Alfie, smiling his gold-toothed smile at me...

Good fantasy, isn't it? Lying up there on the hill, I often try to edge it on a little further than that; you know, start imagining me and him hanging out on the beach together at whatever's my Destination of the Week, rubbing SPF15 on each other's bodies... But somehow, I don't tend to get that far. Mainly because – back in the real world – Winslet will end up padding over and licking my face, just to check I'm not dead or anything. Or Rolf will come and drop a drool-covered plastic disk on my tummy, so that I know that I'm neglecting my Frisbee-chucking duties.

"Yip! Yip! Yip! Yip!"

Winslet had just finished slobbering her dog-food-scented tongue all over my mouth and nose, when I heard her growling at the incoming dog.

"Hi!" said Billy, staring down at me, and blocking out the sun with his back-to-front baseball-capped head. (The baseball cap was back-to-front, not his head. Though with Billy, it's hard to tell sometimes.)

"Out of the way," I replied, motioning him to move over. "I'm trying to beam myself on board that plane, but your big head's between it and me."

Billy lifted his hand to shield his eyes and stared into the sky.

"What – *that* one?" he asked, pointing to the plane as it headed into the distance, above the skyline of central London.

"Yep," I nodded, pushing myself up on to my elbows.

Further down from us on the grassy slopes, Precious was doing his level best to shove his precious nose exactly where my dogs didn't want it.

"What do you want to be on that plane for?" asked Billy.

"I'm bored of the petty irritations that make up my life," I moaned. "I want that plane to take me away to somewhere exotic…"

"What, Gatwick airport?"

"Huh?" I blinked at him.

"Well, with *that* flight path, and at *that* height, I'd say it's about to land at Gatwick airport," said Billy, crouching down beside me.

Billy doesn't have a romantic bone in his body, he really doesn't. Which is another reason he doesn't have a girlfriend. I mean, I'm not saying he was wrong; it's just that he never knows when a girl doesn't want to hear cold hard facts about flight paths and unglamorous local airports and needs some sympathy and understanding instead.

"Anyway, I don't know what you're on about –

you've never even *been* on a plane," he pointed out unkindly. "You don't even know if you'd like it."

"So?" I answered defensively.

But he was right. It's just kind of embarrassing sometimes to admit that your family can't afford to take you on flash holidays. I'm not knocking the camping stuff we've always done (well, I *do* when it rains...), but it can still make you feel like you're missing out compared to other people.

"You all right?" he asked, suddenly noticing my grumpy expression.

"No."

"What is it – your hair?"

I'd tried to brush my fringe into some kind of side parting, but it obviously hadn't covered up my hack job.

"No," I protested, running my fingers through it again, like it would help.

Ha.

"So what's up, then?"

I sighed at the grating memory of Kyra getting cosy in our kitchen with Tor over a packet of milk-chocolate Hobnobs.

"There's this new girl who's started at school this week – and I might end up having to strangle her with my bare hands."

"How come?" frowned Billy, pulling his cap

round the right way. "If she's annoying, why don't you just ignore her?"

"Ignore her? Huh!" I snorted. "That's kind of hard, when she's already been helping herself to tea and biscuits at my house!"

I didn't want to ruin another day of my weekend by talking about Kyra, but you know how it is – you have to have a moan. And Billy is quite good to moan to, and knows me better than most. I guess I'm closest to Sandie, because she's a girl and because we go to the same school, but like I said before, Billy's my oldest friend.

We got to know each other when our mums took us to the same playgroup. I liked Billy straight away because he was the only kid who was willing to let me bury him in the sand pit. (He's a very trusting soul.) Oddly enough, my mum and his got to be pretty good friends too. It was odd because his mum's this real neat fiend, who dresses in matching shoes and handbag just to go to Tesco's, whereas Mum was more of a long, baggy skirt and hand-knitted jumper kind of person. And when we were small, Billy's mum would be all uptight, bleaching and disinfecting every surface and every toy in case a stray germ dared to infect her precious little boy, while my mum horrified her by claiming that if everyone licked the kitchen floor each day we'd all be so toughened against germs that we'd never need antibiotics. (We never did though. Lick the kitchen floor, that is.)

Although I played round there a lot when I was small, I don't much like going round to Billy's house now – his mum always gives me these really pitying looks and asks how we're all coping...

Anyhow, that day, Billy ended up sitting on the grass beside me just long enough to hear my whinge about Kyra and to get a wet bum, courtesy of the damp grass.

"And what's she like in class?" he asked, once he'd got the whole story.

"She does that thing where she's totally cheeky to teachers," I explained, "but she does it so subtly, they can't get her for it."

"Like how?"

"Well, you know – they'll ask her a question, and she'll tell them the right answer, but with this really *booooorrred* tone in her voice. Or say 'Yes, *Sir*' or 'Yes, *Miss*' but with this *sneer* in her voice."

"I'd love to meet her."

You could have knocked me down with a sparrow's feather then. After everything I'd said, after explaining how my family seemed to be taken in by her, Billy'd let me down. His girl radar had gone up, and he'd blanked out all the bad bits I'd told him.

"What?!" I yelped.

"Well, I'd like to meet her – just so I could snub her. Show her she's no big deal."

Right then, I could have put my arms around my best mate Billy and given him a great, big kiss.

If the idea wasn't so totally icky.

Chapter 14

GOOD VIBES AND BIG MOUTHS…

"You know, I think it's growing in already," Sandie lied sweetly.

I knew it was just Sandie telling one of her occasional morale-boosting white lies – bless her – so I didn't bother to contradict her, even though my reflection was telling me something radically different.

I rifled around in my bag for the butterfly clips I knew were in there somewhere. My fringe was going to get clamped off my face until it had reached a decent length to be seen in public again.

The reason I decided not to tell my friend that I knew she was spinning me a line was that I'd made a decision; and that was to stop being a moany git.

After I'd seen Billy the day before and sounded off all my woes to him, I'd gone home and idled the rest of my Sunday away, mooching around miserably. There was nothing worth watching on telly in the evening, so I decided to stomp upstairs to my room and dig out my most depressing CD to listen to. But as soon as I walked into my room, before my hand automatically went to flick on the light switch, I saw out in the dark night the glowing vision of Alexandra Palace (don't worry – it wasn't on fire again).

Normally, as soon as darkness falls, you can hardly make the Palace out, but now, all lit up at the top of the hill, it almost looked like it was some fantasy fairytale castle, floating in mid-air. Spotlights shone the length of the Palace's yellow brickwork, the stained glass of the vast Rose window was illuminated like a giant version of something you'd find eating up the electricity bill in Rowan's room, while white streaks of lasers whizzed from the parapets up into the night sky.

OK, so I knew that the Palace must have all lights blazing because they were holding some big corporate do there, but even if this magical apparition was down to the Chartered Surveyors Annual Chartering and Surveying Awards or whatever, the startling prettiness of it still shook me out of the rotten mood I'd been slithering into all week.

Suddenly, I realized that being grumpy was boring me to death.

From tomorrow, I vowed, kneeling on a chair and staring off at the stunning sight of Ally Pally, *I will stop whingeing and whining, and be calm and positive. Hopefully...*

So, here I was, being calm (etc.) first thing on Monday morning, standing outside the main entrance to school, and about to explain my new approach to problems (i.e. Kyra) to my best mate (i.e. Sandie).

"You know something, Sandie?" I said, struggling to get my butterfly clips to stay put.

"What?" Sandie replied, holding up her pocket mirror so I could see what I was doing.

"We shouldn't let this stuff with Kyra wind us up," I mumbled, holding a purple clip between my teeth.

"Yeah?"

"Yes. I've been thinking: we can't get out of doing this project with her, so I think we should just ... grin and bear it and make the best of it."

"Oh, OK," nodded Sandie. "And I suppose we've got to feel sorry for her too. Being new and everything..."

See? Sandie always tries to be nice. But sometimes she's *too* nice. Well, she's a lot nicer than *me*, anyway. I was still grumpy with Kyra for doing all that stuff without us on Saturday.

"But Ally..."

Uh-oh – was I wrong? Was Sandie going to have a bit of a moan about Kyra?

"What?"

"Well, I'm confused…"

"What about?"

"Uh, does that mean we are going to be proper friends with her … or not?"

"No, it doesn't mean we have to be *friends* with her," I tried to explain. "It just means that me and you are mature enough to work with her for the next week without any hassle – and then once the project and the play and everything's out of the way, we start trying to shake her off. Gently."

"Oh, OK – I get it," nodded Sandie.

While we'd been talking (and hairstyling), the area around the main entrance had started filling up, full of people like us who were dawdling around, chatting, delaying till the very last moment taking that first Monday morning step into the school buildings.

"Hi, Ally, hi Sandie…"

It was Chloe Brennan, along with Salma and Jen and Kellie. They're like my second-division mates, after Sandie and Billy.

"Not hanging out with your new best friend, then?" Chloe grinned at me.

I like Chloe, but she's a bit mouthy, a bit cheeky

sometimes. Sometimes she winds me up, if you want to know the truth. And twenty-four hours before – when I was feeling all bitter and spiky – that dig of hers would have really bugged me. But now I was calm and serene, and no digs about Kyra Davies were going to get to me.

"No – I just had to show her around for her first week. Thank God."

Oops, that came out a bit spiky and not too serene.

Must try harder...

"She's a real show-off, that Kyra, isn't she?" said Salma, yawning.

You'd like Salma; she's got this laid-back way about her – as if her natural habitat is lazing on one of those posh, slinky chaise-longues sofas, doing nothing more energetic than chatting to mates down the phone all day. Sometimes the things she says would sound sarky coming out of anyone else's mouth, but when she says stuff, you know she's only trying to be funny.

"Yeah, she's got a right attitude on her. Did you hear her in French class the other day?" chipped in Kellie.

Kellie's cool, but she's a total gossip queen.

"Oh, yeah!" Jen giggled. "She started arguing with Mr Matthews, didn't she, when he tried to correct her pronunciation!"

Jen's a real giggler – she does it at the most out-of-order moments, like in assembly, or when there's a sad, slushy, romantic moment in a movie.

"It's like she wants to be the centre of attention all the time, isn't it?" Salma commented. "Silly cow…"

Ouch. Maybe Salma wasn't just being funny, for once. Still, at least, it wasn't *me* who was being bitchy. Even if I couldn't help smiling.

"Oh, hey, Ally – did you know that new horror movie's out this week?" said Chloe, suddenly changing the subject.

I knew what was coming next. Chloe is very popular within our little crowd – her dad runs this grocery shop that does a sideline in DVD rentals, and every time a new movie comes out that we want to see, Chloe can always get her hands on it a couple of days before it's officially meant to go on the shelves. And then that's where *I* come in – all of us take turns having everyone over for a girlie DVD night once in a while, and it looked like right now, it was my turn to turf the family out of the living room and let my friends invade.

"Cool," I nodded. "Do you want to come over at the weekend to watch it?"

"Nah – it's got to go out on the shelves on Friday, so we'll have to do it before then."

It's stupid, I know, but it's a bit of a buzz for all of us, getting to see something before anyone else, so I had to come up with a better offer.

"OK, Wednesday, then?"

They all murmured and ummed and ahhed, but eventually everyone settled on Wednesday being film night.

BRRRRRRIIIIIIIIIIIINNNNNNGGGG!!!

Big mistake – we were standing right under the bell.

"Fantastic!" I grinned inanely at Sandie once the shrill sound had faded. "The start of a whole new week at school! I don't know about you, but there's nowhere *I'd* rather be!"

Sandie grinned back, knowing exactly how I felt. That is, about as pleased as if someone had suggested superglueing my eyelids together...

Me and Sandie had just turned to follow Chloe and the others up the couple of steps to the main entrance, when I felt this weird sensation, like a stare was burning into my head.

I flicked my eyes to one side, and across a crush of people I caught sight of Kyra, hurriedly averting her gaze to the tarmac. Strangely, in that split-second, I noticed her ears – not 'cause they were big (that goes without saying) but because they looked deep pink against her light-brown skin.

("Ah! Ears burning – it's a sure sign someone's talking about you!" Grandma's words rattled round my head. She's very matter-of-fact, my gran, but she still likes to trot out ye olde worlde superstitious sayings from time to time.)

Urgh, I thought, my heart suddenly sinking with guilt. Was Kyra standing anywhere near us while everyone was talking about her? Had she heard?

Call me a hypocrite, but I hated the idea that she might have caught any of that, and got hurt by it.

Ally Love – you are a hypocrite.

There, I've said it myself.

Chapter 15

SISTERLY LOVE (DON'T LAUGH...)

"No! Don't you dare!"

At Linn's barked command, Rowan stopped dead, her hand hovering over the saucepan on the cooker.

"But it needs it!" whimpered Rowan. "It'll be really boring on its own!"

"Spaghetti bolognese does *not* need curry powder!"

"But—"

Rowan was a braver girl than me (and madder – I mean, curried spaghetti bolognese?). Linn was looking particularly frosty-faced, and arguing with her when she was wearing that expression was just pure insanity.

"Ally – *tell* her, before I ram this spoon down her throat!" Linn beseeched me, waving a tomato-sauce-stained wooden spoon ominously in the air.

"Um," I muttered, hovering in the kitchen doorway.

Both Linn and Rowan were staring at me, waiting for my verdict.

I wished Grandma had been able to make the tea as usual, instead of having to pootle off early to get ready for a someone's wedding-anniversary party this Tuesday night (partying on a Tuesday night? Our gran had a better social life than us...). Then there wouldn't be a battle for cooking supremacy going on between my two sisters, and I wouldn't be stuck in the middle as an unwilling referee.

"I think..." I said slowly, stalling for time. "I think curry is *brilliant*; but I quite like spaghetti bolognese just the normal way."

There – was that tactful enough to satisfy them both?

Nope.

"You *told* Ally to say that, Linnhe!" Rowan burst out.

"*When?*" gasped Linn, laughing at Rowan's plainly ridiculous accusation. "You mean, when I sent her an extra-sensory, telepathic message as she was walking through the hall two seconds ago? Oh yeah, you are *so* right, Ro!"

"There you go – twisting everything round so you look like you're *so* smart!" Rowan snapped at her, blinking hard like she might be on the verge of tears.

"Yeah? Well, looking smart's not hard, when I'm anywhere near *you*..."

"Shhh!" I hushed them, wide-eyed. From where I was standing, I'd heard the telltale creak of the stairs, even if they didn't.

Linn suddenly turned her attention to stirring the spaghetti, while Rowan grabbed the sponge by the sink and started wiping the work surface.

"Mmm, that smells good," smiled Dad, walking into the kitchen. "Anyone seen my specs? I'm supposed to be helping Tor with his homework, but it might help if I could read what the heck he's supposed to be doing..."

"Oh, they're here, Dad!" said Rowan cheerfully, handing Dad the glasses he'd left lying on top of the breadbin.

"Thanks, Ro. So, you girls all right?"

I knew then that he'd heard the raised voices on his way downstairs from Tor's room.

Me and my sisters, we've got this unspoken rule: never to let Dad catch us arguing. It's not fair to him, you see. He's had such a rough time with what happened with Mum and everything, that he would just get really flipped out if he thought we were ever falling out with each other. So, rows, bickering, disputes ("Debates", as Grandma would say), whatever; they're all kept well away from Dad.

"Yes, we're fine!" I said, probably a little too

brightly to be convincing. "Those two were just moaning a bit because I was reminding them I've got my mates coming round tomorrow night!"

"Oh, Ally – don't be silly! You know me and Rowan don't mind!" smiled Linn, playing the part.

She's very good at pretending her and Rowan get on. The only time she lets her true feelings show in front of Dad is when she's confronted by Rowan's terrible attempts at cooking on her nights in charge of the kitchen. But, well, people do have their limits...

"Yeah! I was just reminding Ally that she better remember to tidy up when they've gone – last time her mates came round, Rolf and Winslet were eating spilt popcorn off the floor for weeks! Weren't they, Ally!"

Rowan was positively twittering now. She's a born actress, she really is. Over-acting a speciality.

"Good. Anyway, I better get back up to those multiplication tables!" smiled Dad, as he pushed his specs on.

The three of us girls stood like statues, stupid grins fixed on our faces, till we heard Dad clomp back up the stairs and listened to the creak of him opening and shutting the door to Tor's room.

Then World War Three started again.

"You are so *bossy*, Linnhe! You think you can tell

all of us what to do and think!" Rowan hissed.

She was furious with our eldest sister, that was for sure, but considering she had done her hair in these two stubby short plaits, Rowan looked more like she should be going out to milk the cow in an ancient episode of *Little House on the Prairie* than arguing over curry powder in the middle of a kitchen in Crouch End.

"What's this got to do with anything?! What are you having a go at me for?" barked Linn, her green eyes blazing. "And for the ten thousandth time, my name is *Linn*, not *Linnhe*!"

"For one thing, you – you still want us to do this stupid family-portrait thing, even though me and Ally and Tor think it's a totally rubbish idea," Rowan railed at her. "And another thing, you can change it as much as you want – you can say you're name's *Bob* if you want – it doesn't change the fact that Mum gave you the name Linnhe, and that's who you are!"

It went strangely silent again at that point. Linn looked weird at the mention of Mum, like she'd been slapped in the face or something. Rowan looked upset at being forced to bring it up.

I didn't feel too good either, being reminded of the big, yawning gap in our lives. But I remember that Dad once said that your brain has an amazing capacity for protecting you from pain. And right at that moment, my brain obviously decided that it was going to distract me from sad, longing thoughts of Mum by giving me the giggles.

Suddenly, I found myself just struggling not to laugh out loud at the idea of Linn being called Bob...

"If you *must* know," Linn said huffily, pulling herself together and turning her attention back to her stirring, "I don't think we *should* do the family-photo thing now..."

A cat that wasn't Colin swooped round my ankles, alerted by the smell of cooking.

"Why not?" I asked, picking up the battered black and white moggy and identifying it by its crossed eyes as Derek. "I thought you were dead keen on the idea."

Linn pursed her lips.

"That was before I found out how much it costs..." she mumbled finally.

Ah-ha, so *that* explained her frosty features.

Rowan had a triumphant little grin on her face. She was about to say something that would end up with both my sisters yelling at each other again, I could tell.

"How much *would* it cost?" I leapt in, before Rowan could.

"More than we could afford," Linn said firmly.

Rowan was itching to speak.

"OK," I said a little too loudly, anticipating a vindictive outburst from our in-between sister. "So let's think of something else, then..."

"Like what? You haven't come out with any useful suggestions so far!" Linn said to me, pointedly.

Derek was wriggling to be free. He could sense the sisterly tension in the room and, smell of food or not, he was keen to be out of the kitchen and cuddling up somewhere more chilled-out.

"Well, why don't we all go to Camden Market this weekend?" I suggested, letting Derek bounce down on to the floor. "If we can't find something unusual for Dad there, then we'll never find it anywhere."

I don't know if you've ever been to Camden Market, but it's absolutely amazing. It started off years ago as a little patch of stalls in some old buildings by the canal in Camden and it's been expanding ever since, taking over every dilapidated old factory and building in the area. The stalls sell weird, wonderful and bizarre stuff, from clothes to food (OK, so neither of those sound particularly bizarre, but you haven't seen what some of them are like), to clocks carved out of driftwood, knitted pot-plant ornaments and wind chimes made out of old forks. Weird, I know, but good. Trust me.

Linn and Rowan glanced briefly at each other. Without saying anything, it seemed like something had been decided.

"OK," nodded Linn, for both of them. "Let's go to Camden at the weekend."

Phew.

I'd stopped them rowing.

Even if it just meant they'd be saving their worst quarrels for when they tore each other's hair out at the market on Saturday.

Still, Camden Market's so full of buskers and street entertainers that people might watch Linn and Rowan fighting and just presume it was performance art.

I could stick a hat in front of the two of them and see if any tourists chucked money into it...

Chapter 16

OH, THE HORROR...

"Present for you!" giggled Jen, standing on my doorstep.

"Jen! It's fabulous! You shouldn't have!" I fooled around, taking the tube of Pringles she was holding out towards me. "Come on in – everyone's here already."

Letting her close the front door behind her, I zoomed back into the living room and leapt into the one free armchair.

"Hey, where am I supposed to sit?" Jen protested, looking around at us all.

Chloe had bagsied the beanbag and was lolling on the floor, while Salma and Kellie were both stretched out, at either end of the sofa, like Siamese bookends.

Sandie, meanwhile, was sitting scrunched up to one side of the other armchair from me, looking not entirely comfortable. Rolf's gangly-limbed, furry body took up the rest of the space, his head lounging, *very* comfortably, in Sandie's lap.

Jen stuck her bottom lip out and did a very passable impression of someone who was three years old and about to have a major blub.

A Wotsit came flying through the air and hit her on the face.

"Oi!" she yelped, and took a dive at Kellie – the Wotsit-chucking culprit – tickling her mercilessly till Kellie had wriggled over enough to leave a reasonable gap on the sofa between herself and a cackling Salma.

Jen spotted the space and jubilantly parked her bum there.

At the same time, Rolf – sensing food on the loose – bounded off the chair he was sharing with Sandie and gave chase to the rogue crisp, utilizing her stomach as a handy launchpad.

"Rolf!" I snapped at him, as Sandie grimaced at the sudden impact of a dog diving off her abdomen.

"No, it's all right! I'm OK!" gasped Sandie breathlessly, waving one hand in the air and trying to smile.

She hates "being a bother", as she calls it. If she'd been playing the Drew Barrymore part in the film *Scream*, she'd be lying in a pool of blood at the end of the scene whispering, "No, I'm fine. Honestly! It's just a scratch!"

"Right, chuck me the disk, then, Chloe, and I'll

get the movie on," I said, pushing myself off the chair and kneeling down by the DVD player. "So, how scary is this one meant to be?"

"Worse than the *Blair Witch Project*, my dad says," Chloe replied. "But wait a minute, Ally – you never answered my question."

"What question?"

My mind was a bit of a muddle; it had been all go since I finished school for the afternoon. First I'd had to go shopping and buy enough crisps, dips and Coke to keep my mates happy for the evening, then I'd had to stop my family from eating or drinking any of it before my friends actually arrived. And despite the fact that my dad is very fair about us all getting a "turn" to have the living room to ourselves like this every once in a while, it had still been a nightmare to shoo them all out before Sandie and Chloe and the others rang the doorbell.

"Before Jen arrived – I was asking about Kyra, remember?" said Chloe. "How it's going with her and the History project?"

Urgh. *That*.

It was all right for Chloe, Jen, Kellie and Salma. Right at the start, they'd been excused from doing anything for the History project, because they'd offered their services in the make-up and wardrobe departments for the play itself. Cushy, if you ask me. Whereas me and Sandie, we had to endure Kyra at close quarters, spending our History lessons stuck exclusively with her and our pile of posters. The Drama group were performing their play starting on Monday, so it was all hands on deck to get everything finished; which is why Miss Thomson had given us class time – and a note to our other teachers to let us have the whole of Friday afternoon off – to get everything finished.

"It's going … all right," I shrugged non-committally, without catching Sandie's eyes. I knew she'd be thinking I couldn't be telling less of the truth. "But, hey, let's not speak about boring stuff like that. Let's get the movie on!"

"Aw, come on, Ally," said Kellie. "Spill! We already told you how much she was bugging us today in Mr Matthews's class, when she started putting on that stupid over-the-top 'haw-he-haw' French accent."

"Oh my God, yeah!" Jen half-gasped, half-giggled. "Was she taking the mick out of Mr Matthews by doing that, or did she genuinely think he'd be impressed with it or something?"

"Come on, Al," Chloe cajoled me. "You and Sandie have seen more of her than we have. You've even had to put up with her coming round here to work on your project, haven't you? So what's going on with that girl? Is she a big-head, or is she just totally mad, or what?"

"Listen, I can't really be bothered talking about her," I mumbled.

I also didn't want to give up on my own personal resolution not to moan.

"Oooh, are you getting all protective of her?" Kellie sniggered. "Is Kyra your new best friend, then?"

"*Her*? You *must* be joking!" I barked. "I'd rather clean the loos at school with my toothbrush than be friends with Kyra Davies!"

So much for my resolution.

"Who are you whinging on about now, Ally?"

Linn stood in the living room door, looking at me in her best snooty and superior older-sister manner.

God, you know, it *really* bugs me when Linn does stuff like that. For one thing, I thought she'd gone out already (Rowan was upstairs in her room listening to music and creating her next junk master-piece, while Dad and Tor were doing some father and son bonding, watching a repeat of *ET* together on the old portable telly up in Dad's bedroom). For another thing, Linn always seemed to save that snooty and superior older-sister malarkey for when my friends came round. And most annoying of all, it was easy for her to make a glib comment when *she* hadn't had to spend the last few days in enforced close contact with Kyra Davies, getting told "No, Ally, that photocopy's too blurry. Do it again" and "Give those scissors to me, Ally, you're not cutting it straight" and "Don't tint that photo that colour, it looks crap!"

And I'd been good and patient and non-moany, just like I'd promised myself, even though Little Miss Know-It-All was working my nerves so much that she was in danger of finding her *face* getting photocopied.

"I'm not whinging, I'm debating," I tried to say calmly, borrowing that favourite saying of Grandma's.

"Yeah! Like, *right*!" snorted Linn, pulling her jacket on.

I suddenly had a vision of my perfectly featured sister with *her* nose squashed sideways on a photo-copier too.

It made me feel marginally better.

"That'll be Alfie…" Linn muttered out loud to herself, as the doorbell shrilled.

My tongue was totally tied and I could feel that my face was about one million degrees hot – partly through my anger at Linn sounding off and showing me up in front of my friends, and partly because

Alfie was in the vicinity…

Then I found myself distracted and infinitely cheered up by the sight of Chloe pulling a face and silently mimicking my sister's nagging. But she soon stopped *that* in a hurry as Linn reappeared in the living-room doorway.

"Another one of your lot," she announced, before breezing off.

Sandie, Jen, Chloe, Kellie, Salma … there wasn't any more of "our lot" to come.

"Hi. I haven't missed the start, have I?"

Six mouths fell open at the sight of Kyra Davies and her bare-faced cheek.

Chapter 17

I HATE HER, I HATE HER NOT...

The young guy with the naff blond-dyed hair job was *not* having a good day. First, he'd fallen out with his girlfriend, *then* he'd gone round to her flat to apologize, only to find that she wasn't up for listening (mainly because she was a tiny bit dead). And now – thanks to the neighbourhood's local friendly axe murderer – Blond Bloke was wearing most of his insides on the outside. And *boy*, that wasn't a good look.

Normally, with horror movies, I'm a total wuss – I watch them from behind cushions, like that'll protect me or something. But this night, I ended up watching the random delights of gore, suspense and more gore with the sort of blank indifference I usually save for the gardening shows my dad regularly tunes in to.

Of course, it wasn't blank indifference I was feeling; it was complete shock. Kyra turning up like that – as if she'd been *asked*, for God's sake – was just so mind-blowingly cheeky that I didn't know what to say to her. Obviously, she must have overheard us all talking about having a girlie film night the other morning outside school, and just … well … decided to include herself in the invite.

You know what I said when she asked if she'd missed the start of the movie? OK, before you guess, here's a random selection of things I *should* have said. If I was the kind of girl to have the bottle. Which I'm not.

1) "What gives you the right to turn up here just like this, Kyra? You're *bang* out of order…"

2) "Missed the start? You're going to miss the whole movie, girl. Turn round and leave where you came in…"

3) "*Hellooooo*? Earth calling Kyra! Let me explain: down here in the *real* world we have this cute little custom where we actually *invite* people to come to our houses, not just have them turning up on our doorsteps like *psychos*!"

See, any of those – though not very nice – would, in the circumstances, have been reasonable responses.

But, oh no; Kyra Davies turns up unannounced at my house (for the second time) and, in answer to her question "Have I missed the start?" I faff about and say, "Umm … no", then watch helplessly as she gazes around the room and settles herself on the floor, leaning her back up against the chair Sandie's sitting on.

"Brought these!" she'd said, opening a white plastic carrier bag and chucking several bags of tortilla chips, kettle crisps and dry roasted peanuts on to the coffee table where the other bowls of nibbles already sat.

Everyone was too stunned to say anything – maybe, since it was my house, they were waiting for me to blast off at her, but I didn't.

Instead, I – oh, the shame – told her to help herself to the two-litre bottle of Coke perched on the table, and immediately pressed play on the remote.

The plot of the movie hadn't even sunk into my frazzled brain, when suddenly a wizened hand burst out of the ground, where the landslide had put an end to the terrible reign of the axe murderer by burying him in choking mud (except it hadn't – you could sniff a sequel coming a mile off).

"What a load of *pants*!" snorted Kyra, as the credits rolled up.

It was a typical Kyra comment, at least from what I knew of her from the last couple of weeks. It didn't make it appropriate though.

"Excuse me?" Chloe bristled, staring across the carpet at Kyra.

Since the DVD was from Chloe's dad's shop, and it was her little kick to give us the treat of seeing it before any paying customers, she wasn't too thrilled with criticism.

"Come on, it *was*!" protested Kyra, wide-eyed.

In one hand, she held a mound of popcorn; in the other, a full glass of orange juice; and in her lap was a snoozing cat that wasn't Colin.

"And you're some fancy film-critic, are you?" snarled Chloe.

"Don't have to be," shrugged Kyra. "Any moron could see that that was pants. I mean, that bit when the girl feels sorry for the killer and starts singing him a lullaby – no wonder he ripped her head off!"

Actually, you know something? The film *was* pants.

Kyra had the judgement to see that. Sadly, she didn't have the judgement to see that she was getting so far up the noses of everyone in the room that she'd need a native guide to get her back out...

"And that bit when the blond guy saw his girlfriend splattered round the room – couldn't he have at least *tried* to act like he cared a bit more? I mean, has he even *been* to drama school, or did he just walk into that part off the street?" Kyra continued her critique, ramming some popcorn in her mouth after she'd made her point.

"Are you for *real*?" Salma suddenly asked, with this really disgusted look on her face.

OK, so now you're seeing the other side of laid-back Salma. She's quite pretty – she's part Portuguese, or Brazilian or something, I forget – but when she's really hacked off, you'd think from the look on her face that she absolutely despises you. But she doesn't – it's just a momentary thing and it's just the way her face is.

Kyra wasn't to know that. But while anyone else would have spotted Salma's expression and shut up, Kyra didn't seem to notice and went merrily on...

"And the guy's mum!" Kyra carried on, regardless. "Were we really supposed to believe—"

"Erm," interrupted Jen, staring her small, but intense eyes like a shoot-to-kill laser beam at Kyra. "Do you want to shut up for five seconds?"

And for once, Jen *wasn't* giggling.

"What?" said Kyra, furrowing her brow. "Aren't I allowed to have an opinion?"

I felt these prickles at the back of my neck. This was getting really uncomfortable. I was starting to wish I'd never bothered having this film night. I could tell the others were staring at me, expecting me to say something, but I just couldn't think what.

"Well, you *might* have been allowed to have an opinion – *if* I'd invited you here tonight," I suddenly heard myself squeaking.

"Yeah, tell her, Al!" Kellie encouraged me, clapping her hands together.

"What's this got to do with *you*?" Kyra snapped at her. "It's not *your* house, Kellie!"

"No – it's Ally's!" Chloe barged in to the conversation again. "And she didn't ask *you* here tonight, did you Ally?"

I looked across at Chloe, perched forward agitatedly on the beanbag, and nodded, feeling a trickle of sweat tickle its way down my forehead. God, I really *hated* when things got all, y'know, *prickly*.

And it was about to get even *more* prickly...

"What's this got to do with you, Ginger Nut?" snapped Kyra.

Ouch. Double ouch. Chloe didn't mind if you called her a redhead, or auburn or copper or what-ever other attractive name you find on the side of hair-tint boxes to describe her natural hair colour.

But start in with the ginger jibes, and you were dead.

"Tell me something," said Chloe, leaning

ominously close to Kyra, her almost transparent white skin even more blanched than usual, "were you born mean, or did you have to practise for a really long time?"

Kyra stopped chewing on her popcorn and stared at Chloe.

Something had hit home.

A split-second later, Kyra scrambled to her feet – surprising the cat that wasn't Colin from his slumber and out of her lap. Two seconds later she'd stormed out of the room and through the front door, letting it crash closed behind her.

As the bang of the door was still reverberating, we all gazed at each other in shock.

"Well," said Chloe finally, a small smile of triumph creeping on to her face. "That showed her!"

She was right. Kyra had overstepped the mark by several large, bounding steps, that was for sure.

But you know the weird thing? And this will sound weird – I felt kind of sorry for her...

Chapter 18

DON'T TRY THIS AT HOME

I was late back from lunchbreak, but that was the joy of having Friday afternoon off to finish our History project – I could wander into the empty art classroom we'd been assigned without worrying that I had to explain myself to a teacher.

Mind you, it didn't look like Sandie and Kyra had exactly hurried themselves either. All I had for company was a spooky stone angel statue that some of the Art classes must have been drawing. It looked like it should be smothered in ivy and mouldering away on top of a Victorian grave, not hanging about in a modern school, watching me with its blank eyes and giving me the willies.

Trying to ignore it, I started pushing back tables and chairs to clear a space on the floor: we had six big display posters to finish off, and it seemed like a good idea to get them all laid out together, so we could see what still needed to be done.

If Kyra ever turned up with them, that was. And where was Sandie?

Feeling slightly breathless after dragging and shoving furniture about, I perched myself on the nearest table, and gazed idly round the room. There were paintings and drawings displayed on every available space, as well as some weird and not-especially-wonderful collages made out of what looked like chicken wire and tissue paper. On top of the waist-high cupboards that ran around the perimeter of the room were dozens of half-made papier mâché ... well, *blobs*, and loads of wobbly pottery ... *things*. It kind of reminded me of home. All this room needed was a couple of cats padding about and a large hairy dog skidding across the lino floor and it would've been a dead ringer.

Thinking of home, my heart sank – a vision of our prickly encounter with Kyra on Wednesday night flashed into my head. Since then, I'd given up taking her to and from classes (she pretty much knew where everything was around school by now anyway), and we'd both done an excellent job of avoiding eye contact with each other. Chloe and Kellie and the others were ignoring Kyra too. Even Sandie said she was, but I don't think she was very happy doing it. Sandie's not very good at being mean to people. Even people who deserve it.

And now, I was about to spend a whole afternoon with Kyra. Was she going to mention anything? Or was she just going to pretend it never happened? I hoped so – it's what I planned to do, if I could get away with it. (I know, I know – I'm a coward. You don't have to tell me.)

God, I wished Sandie would hurry up. The idea of facing Kyra and having to make conversation with her on my own didn't exactly make me feel too fantastic.

My heart did a quick couple of star-jumps as I heard footsteps echoing along the corridor towards the classroom door.

Then I heard giggles.

Giggles?

Picture this: my best friend Sandie joking and chatting with Kyra Davies, as she helped her carry in our pile of posters.

Seeing me sitting on the table, Sandie's smile sank like a stone.

Kyra, on the other hand, was as bright and breezy as you like.

"Hi, Ally! All by yourself? Me and Sandie have just been having a *great* laugh about Mrs Fisher, haven't we, Sandie?"

"Mmm!" squeaked Sandie, looking wildly uncomfortable.

I said nothing as the two of them placed the posters on the table beside me and Kyra began unrolling them. But between you and me, I had this funny lump in my throat. I know it was stupid to feel so betrayed, but I did.

"We passed her in the corridor a minute ago and she's got herself the most *terrible* new perm, hasn't she, Sandie?"

Ah, *now* I could see what Kyra's game was: trying to make out to me that her and Sandie were such big mates and make me feel excluded.

That was her revenge for what had happened at my place on Wednesday night.

"I mean, what was it like, Sandie?" Kyra prompted her, acting all chummy.

"Uh ... bad," mumbled Sandie, her cheeks flushed pink.

"God, it was worse than *bad*," Kyra twittered, spreading all the artwork out across the table. "She looks like a sheep, doesn't— Oh, what a pain! I forgot to pick up all the sheets of paper with the captions printed on them! Hold on – I'll have to nip back to Miss Thomson's room for them..."

No sooner had Kyra darted away along the corridor, her top-knot of dark curls bobbing as she ran, when Sandie started blabbering.

"I haven't been hanging out with her, Ally; it's just that I bumped into her coming into school, and that's when she asked me to give her a hand bringing the posters and stuff along here and—"

"It's OK! It doesn't bother me!" I stopped her, even though that wasn't exactly true.

So far Kyra had sucked up to my sister and my brother, even our *animals*, and now it looked like she was doing her best to suck up to my best friend too.

Kyra was like my own personal vampire – sucking my life out from all around me...

"You know, she's all right, really," Sandie blinked her eyes beseechingly at me. "Before we saw Mrs Fisher in the corridor, Kyra was talking about what happened on Wednesday night and saying how embarrassed she was about just storming out like that..."

"Embarrassed about storming *out?*" I said, incredulously. "Shouldn't she be more embarrassed at turning up in the *first* place?"

Sandie shrugged and wrinkled her nose up.

"I know, but I feel sorry for her, Al," she carried on, peeking out of the door to check that Kyra wasn't on her way back already. "She started to tell me that she has a really hard time at home with her mum."

"Like what?" I asked.

I didn't sound too sympathetic, I know I didn't. But I was deliberately being like that; it was all just because Kyra was totally confusing me. One minute she was bossy, aloof and slagging off anything and anyone in her line of vision, the next she was going gooey over my three-legged cat and turning up on my doorstep like my long-lost best buddy. Someone being two-faced, I could just about handle. Somebody having about seventeen faces I couldn't get my head around.

"I don't know *exactly* what's happening with her mum; she never finished telling me, 'cause we caught sight of Mrs Fisher," Sandie explained, making curly-wurly circles with her fingers around her head. "But she *did* say that when Chloe called her mean, it really hurt her, 'cause her mum calls her that too! Can you believe that? Her own *mum*?"

My first thought? I was shocked – how could someone's mum say things like that to their face? And then I had a second thought... Maybe Kyra was making it all up, y'know, just for attention or something.

If that was true then it had worked. Sandie had completely bought the story – great big squashy softie that she was.

"You don't honestly think—"

A tip-tap of approaching feet stopped me where I was.

"Right, that's everything!" said Kyra, slapping the stack of paper and a pair of scissors down on the table beside me. "Shall we get started?"

The rest of the afternoon wasn't exactly awash with pleasant conversation, which suited me fine. Kyra spotted a paint-splattered radio on the windowsill, and tuned it into Radio One. Apart from that, there was too much glueing and sticking and finishing off to do; so if we weren't talking about who was doing what, we didn't talk at all.

One thing I couldn't get over was that Kyra didn't once try to bring up the subject of Wednesday night with *me*, even though she'd been more than happy to with Sandie earlier on. It just made it more obvious in my mind that she was deliberately trying to get some attention from Sandie after all. That all this sob story about her mum was just made up. It had to be. Didn't it?

But I tried not to let the whole thing wind me up – we had to get this project finished this afternoon, in time to fix it up in the hall first thing on Monday, ready for the Drama department's first performance on Monday afternoon.

Just get through the next few hours as painlessly as possible, I kept reminding myself, as the hours ticked away, *and that'll be you finished with Kyra Davies...*

* * *

"There!" I said, sticking the *final* caption on the *final* poster.

I stood up straight, and surveyed our handiwork, all laid out on the floor in front of the three of us.

"Looks nice!" said Sandie brightly.

The posters definitely did look "nice". In the centre of each large sheet of artists' card was an A3 enlargement of a section of map, with bomb sites circled in red, and long, thin red lines trailing off to accompanying prints, enlarged from old photos, of what the individual streets looked like pre-war, along with a few images of what they looked like now.

I had to hand it to Kyra: she'd come up with a really good idea. Even if she was a pain-in-the-neck, conniving weirdo.

"Hmm, I'm not sure…"

"Not sure of what?" I asked, finding myself frowning at Kyra.

"It needs something else … it looks a bit boring like that."

Was she joking? Our project was done, wasn't it? It was twenty to four on Friday afternoon, i.e. twenty minutes to the official start of the weekend, and there was no way I wanted to start faffing about with these posters now.

"What do you mean, *boring*?" I quizzed her, stunned.

"I just think the maps don't stand out enough as a main image," she mused, infuriatingly. "I think maybe they need a border round them or something."

"Mmm ... maybe," Sandie half-heartedly agreed, before I got the chance to shoot her a shut-up look.

"Kyra, they're fine the way they are!" I protested, but she'd already walked over to the cabinets closest to us and started riffling through them.

"I know, but they can be *better*," she said brightly, pulling a big roll of masking tape out. "Look – if we paint lengths of this stuff black, it'll dry really quickly, and it'll be easy to cut it to the right length to frame each map. Sandie – see if there's any black paint ready to use in those containers over by the sink, otherwise we'll have to mix some up..."

"Kyra – what's the point of going to all this trouble?" I asked, fuming at the sight of Sandie meekly trotting off sink-wards. "It's not a competition. And anyway the only people who are going to be looking at it are the primary-school kids coming to see the play!"

"So?" shrugged Kyra. "I still want our project to look better than anyone else's. Oh, good, Sandie –

you got some!"

"Yeah, there's loads here," said Sandie, walking back towards us with a square plastic container of black poster-paint, left over from someone's artistic efforts that morning.

"See?" Kyra flashed her dark, almond eyes at me. "It's all ready for us – all we have to do is paint the masking tape and tidy away all our rubbish and we'll be done!"

I felt bubbles of irritation rise in my chest. She was just so pushy!

Just be patient for a little while longer, and you don't have to have anything to do with her again... I reminded myself, as my teeth ground together.

"Right! Fine! You know best!" I barked, trying to sound tough, but feeling a choke of angry tears making my voice wobble. "Here, give me the paint, Sandie – I'll do it!"

"Oh, no, you won't – since you seem to think it's such a lousy idea!" snapped Kyra, yanking the plastic container forcefully out of my hands.

Only I hadn't touched it yet.

It wasn't a particularly big container that Sandie was holding out – just about the right size to have held a family-sized chunk of raspberry ripple ice-cream in it (hey, I didn't guess that; the remnants of the label were still visible on its side) – but it sure held enough paint. Enough paint, that is, to send a mini tidal wave swooping up into the air.

It's amazing how far flying paint can fan out, it really is. I'd say try it sometime, but you'd have to be really stupid to give it a go.

Kyra – looking stunned – was left untouched, still clinging to the now empty plastic container. Me, Sandie, even the spooky statue watching over us were, however, covered in what might be described as *ebony* ripple.

Oh, and of course, our project certainly wasn't boring any more. Now, instead of trying to identify their own streets from the posters, all the visiting primary kids could have fun trying to guess what exactly the posters were supposed to *be*, under all those plate-sized splodges of black paint...

Chapter 19

ONE FOR ALL, AND ALL FOR ... UH-OH

"Ooooooh – isn't that the most beautiful thing you've ever seen?"

I squinted at the object Rowan was holding up. It was a small, fat, gold-painted cherub, stuck inside one of those domed snowstorm ornaments.

Rowan shook it hard, and instead of the usual dandruffy "snow" wafting down over him, a cascade of twinkling gold bits drizzled over his small, fat features.

"It's, er, cute," I commented, wondering what the gloopy liquid was inside those snowstorms. "But it's not exactly the most beautiful thing I've ever seen..."

No, that honour went to stuff like lightning crashing across the sky behind Ally Pally, or our garden in summer, when the wisteria goes crazy and covers the entire back wall in masses of trailing purple blossoms...

God. Who was I kidding? The most beautiful thing in the world to me was the one, the only (drum roll, please) Alfie.

Sigh.

"What are you looking at?" demanded Linn, appearing at our side.

"Um, this?"

Rowan held up the entombed cherub for Linn to inspect.

"Is that any good for Dad?" Linn asked sternly.

"Er, no," muttered Rowan.

"Well, what are you wasting time looking at it for? If it's not a possible present for Dad, then there's no point, is there?"

Linn should join the army. Sergeant major Love; at your service, *sir!*

The hippie-looking stall-holder stared at Linn, took the ornament out of Rowan's hands, and cradled it protectively to his chest.

"And what's going on?" Linn suddenly barked, scanning all around us.

"What?!" Rowan and I squeaked in unison.

"Where's Tor? Whose turn was it to hold his hand? I *told* you we have to watch out for him. I mean, this is Camden Market – I *told* you he could get lost in a second in amongst all these crowds!"

Rowan and I exchanged panicked glances. Whose turn had it been to look out for Tor? Obviously *she* couldn't remember any better than I could.

That's what an hour's worth of shopping amidst this rabbit warren of stalls and crush of people does for you – you end up suffering from the three Ds: Disorientation, Distraction and Death (by older sister, for failing to do your duty).

"I'm not lost!" came a small voice in our midst.

"Oh, thank goodness, Tor," said Linn, her shoulders sinking in relief. "Where did you go?"

"There!" he said indignantly, pointing to a spot all of twenty centimetres away.

Suddenly a surge of gawping shoppers shoved past, sending all four of us almost crashing into the snowstorm stall.

"OK. Enough. Let's get out of this for a while," Linn announced. "Let's go and get some food."

"Noodles!" yelped Tor excitedly.

"Noodles," Linn nodded at him, and off we all trotted (very obediently) behind her.

You know, it's funny with me and Rowan and Linn; OK, so we might niggle and nark at each other, but, boy, when the Love sisters gang up against the world, the world doesn't stand a chance.

There were only a few picnic-bench-type tables beside the takeaway food stalls, and all of them were full. Carefully selecting our victims (Rowan had raised her eyes and nodded towards the group of tourists sitting hugging their all-but-finished coffees) we moved in. Hovering right beside their table with our tinfoil trays of Thai noodles, we three girls started rabbiting away in the most obnoxiously loud, screechy voices we could. The tourists started twitching. They were on the verge of moving, to get away from our irritating banter, but not quick enough for Linn.

Bending down, she whispered something in Tor's ear.

"But I wan' it!" he yelled instantly. "I wan' it! *Whhhhhaaaaaaa*!"

"No! I told you you can't have it! Bad boy!" I scolded Tor in a pantomime voice, winking at my sisters from the corner of my eye.

"Let me have it! I wan' that *toyyyyyyyyyyyyyy*! *Whhhhhhhhaaaaaaaa*!"

For a boy who didn't like to say much, he could really let it rip.

Loud enough, for sure, to send the tourists scuttling off – leaving the four of us with a roomy place to eat our lunch.

"Good work, Tor!" I grinned, holding my hand, palm-up, just as my sisters were doing.

"High-five!" whispered Tor, grinning as he slapped his small hand against all of ours, one by one.

"Hey, Ally – what's with the black paint in your hair?" asked Linn, twirling noodles round her plastic fork.

"I'm in mourning…" I mumbled, suddenly reminded of the disaster of the day before.

"What for?" Linn asked.

"My History project died."

"What, that thing with the bomb maps and everything?" Rowan exclaimed, raising her eyebrows.

She looked exactly like a movie star when she did that. The only trouble was, it was Minnie Mouse. She'd done her dark hair up in these two twisted knots on either side of her head that looked just like the slip-on ears you can buy in the Disney Store.

"Yes – the thing with the maps. That's the one," I sighed.

"It sounded like it would be really good when your friend … whatshername was talking about it. What happened?" Rowan asked, batting her big, girlie eyelashes at me.

Yep, Minnie Mouse.

"Yes it *was* a good idea. And she's not my friend. And her name's Kyra," I reeled off. "Anyway, it got vandalized yesterday."

"Who by?" gasped Rowan.

"Us," I groaned, slapping my hands over my face. "We were having an argument, and this container of paint flew over everything."

"Is this what you were supposed to be doing for

the Drama department's play?" Linn chipped in, as she worked out what I was talking about.

"I'm coming to see that! With my class!" Tor piped up.

"Are you, honey?" I smiled at him. It hadn't occurred to me that his primary school would of course be part of the audience.

"Well, Tor, you *could* have pointed out your sister's project to all your friends," Linn told him, "but now, you'll just have to point out a big empty space on the wall!"

"Ha, *ha*!" I muttered sarcastically at her, as Tor stood up and tootled off in the direction of the bins with his already empty tinfoil tray.

He's very eco-friendly, my brother.

But Linn was right – there *would* just be a big empty space looming on the wall of the school hall. There wasn't any time to do anything else. And boy, I wasn't looking forward to telling Miss Thomson that, first thing on Monday morning...

"Couldn't you save *any* of it? Was it *all* damaged?" asked Rowan, in-between sucking a noodle up into her mouth.

"It looked totally wrecked when me and Sandie left yesterday, but then we did have black paint dripping in our eyes at the time..."

"Did your clothes get covered in paint too?" Linn

156

frowned.

That would be her worst nightmare: having her neatly washed and pressed clothes *gunged*.

"Yeah – but they came out all right. Grandma soaked them as soon as I got in."

Neither of my sisters had been witness to my humiliation the afternoon before; Sandie and I had left the classroom as soon as we got over the shock of being splattered. I suppose it was a bit mean to leave Kyra to clean everything up, but all me and Sandie could think about was getting out of school and safely home before the four o'clock bell rang and we had a school full of people pointing and sniggering at us. Back at the house, only Grandma and Tor were privy to the state I was in. And by the time Rowan and Linn arrived home, I was in the shower, and more inclined to keep the whole farce to myself than merrily announce it to the world.

"Couldn't you try to do a rush job tomorrow and put something together?" Linn suggested.

She *would*. But how could you cram all that work into one day, never mind get your hands on all those materials? Not, likely, Linn...

"We'd need a miracle and a few extra pairs of hands to make that work," I replied flatly.

"Well, *I* could help, if you want. I was supposed to be seeing Nadia and Alfie tomorrow afternoon, but I can easily blow them out."

I gawped at Linn for a second; it always takes me slightly by surprise when she's nice. And she *is* nice sometimes – very nice. You just tend to forget it when you're used to her bossing you about every five seconds.

Gazing at my older sister in starry-eyed shock didn't last long – not when Rowan suddenly noticed who was missing.

"Er … where's Tor?" she interrupted.

"He's gone to chuck his rubbish away," I replied, pointing over in the direction of the big plastic dustbin.

Which is exactly where my brother wasn't.

Or anywhere else that we could see.

"Tor!" Linn yelled out in her best sergeant-major boom, alarming everyone at the surrounding tables.

This time, there was *no* small voice saying "I'm not lost!"

Chapter 20

SENDING OUT THE SEARCH PARTY

Imagine every neighbour in your street has their window open, and every single one of them has music blaring out. Walking along the pavement, you hear this weird mix of techno thumping, rock blasting, new age plinky-plonking, classical Spanish guitar-twanging and even Gregorian monks *chanting*, for God's sake.

Add to that the sensation of being in a crowd at a football match, only everyone's wearing T-shirts with band names and slogans on them instead of football shirts.

And that's what it felt like, pushing through the hordes of browsing punters in Camden Market, music pumping from ghetto blasters on every stall, it seemed, while I searched hopelessly for my little brother. I could feel my heart whirring at seventy million beats an hour; I was going into total worry overload. But how could I stop myself? I mean, how can you stop yourself imagining scary stuff, like faceless strangers just silently whisking Tor off to God knows where?

I consciously dug my not-very-long fingernails into the palm of my hands so that the pain gave me something else to think about. It didn't work: all that kept repeating through my head was how on earth me and Linn could ever hope to find Tor – presuming he hadn't (please, oh please) been spirited away – in this crush...

Then above all the din, my ears tuned in to a familiar sound.

Flippety-flap, flippety-flap...

I spun round to see Rowan's panic-stricken face, as she pushed and pattered through the sea of shoppers in her impractical red velvet mules.

"Ro!" I shouted at her, waving to get her attention before she was diverted off, down into a maze of stalls selling second-hand clothes.

"Ally!" she yelped, hurrying over to me with a speeded up *flippety-flap, flippety-flap.* "No sign of him?"

"No," I shook my head, noticing how her Minnie Mouse ears were unravelling as she ran. "But what are you doing? Linn told you to wait back at the tables in case he turned up!"

"I couldn't just hang about and do nothing!" she wailed, strands of hair flopping round her face as her knots unfurled. "I spoke to the guy at the noodle bar – I asked him to look out for Tor and get him to stay there if he came back!"

I shrugged. I guessed it made sense to have all three of us searching, but so far, at least two of us had had zero success, to my knowledge.

With that thought in my head, I looked down at my watch, and saw that twenty minutes had passed since we'd started the hunt. It was time to rush back, as agreed with Linn, to our meeting point by the noodle bar.

"Come on..." I motioned to Rowan. "Linn might be there already – and she might have found Tor..."

As if there was some enormous people-magnet lurking somewhere behind us, a wall of ambling shoppers surged towards us, blocking our way.

I'm not a pushy person, but all of a sudden, sheer fear made me develop elbows of steel, and I found myself ruthlessly barging my way into the oncoming crowds, carving a route towards the muddy courtyard that held the food stands.

A hand suddenly searched out mine, fingers clinging round it desperately. For a split-second, I thought it might be Tor, but the hand was too big to be his. I didn't even have to look round to know that my elder sister was relying on me to get us both through this. And right then, I felt a little bit braver, just knowing that poor Rowan was crumbling around the edges and depending on me.

Still pushing through determinedly, I gave Rowan's fingers a comforting squeeze, and felt her squeeze mine back.

Food stalls, noodle bar, Linn.

No Tor.

"What are we going to do?" whimpered Rowan, edging closer to hysteria. "What if someone's taken him?"

"Stop panicking; no one's taken him," said Linn authoritatively, although the slight wobble in her voice gave her away. "We'll split up and have another look round, then … *then* we'll think about calling the police…"

At the mention of the police, Rowan lost it completely. Her bottom lip trembled with a life of its own, and fat, hot tears tumbled down her cheeks.

"It's OK, Ro; he'll be all right," I said softly, wrapping my arms round Rowan, being the big sister to my elder sister again.

"Brilliant," sighed Linn, her voice suddenly laden with irony. "What great daughters *we* are…"

"What?" I mumbled, grabbing a serviette that the guy behind the noodle bar was kindly holding out to help mop up Rowan's tears.

"Well," Linn explained, agitatedly, "the plan today was to get Dad a brilliant surprise, and what happens? The surprise turns out to be us managing to lose his only son..."

Chapter 21

LOST: ONE LITTLE BROTHER, HARDLY USED

London's big. London's *very* big. There are about eight million people living in London – and that kind of blows your head off when you know there are only about five million people in the whole of Scotland. (You've got to let me off if I'm out by a thousand or two; I always *was* better at History than Geography.)

And because it's big, one of the moans about London is that it's impersonal. That you could be being mugged by a bloke on stilts with fairy wings and a Bart Simpson mask and people would pass you by without helping, as if it happened every day.

Well, I don't think that's true. Like the guy at the noodle bar? He was on his own behind the counter, and could have carried on serving the queue of hungry customers hovering around his stall instead of helping us.

"Do you need to make a call?" he asked, after I'd taken the serviette from him – the one Rowan was currently soaking with tears and snot.

Now, he was holding out his mobile phone, trusting that a) we weren't going to do a runner with it, and b) we weren't going to call Australia, peak rate.

"Um, no – not right this second," Linn shook her head. "We're going to keep looking for—"

"Wait a minute – Grandma!" I burst out, gratefully yanking the proffered phone out of the noodle guy's hand.

"Grandma?" Linn furrowed her forehead. "What do you want to call her for? You'll just worry her – we might find Tor if we get out there looking again, and she'll never know—"

"No!" yelped Rowan. "Ally's right! Remember that Dad's always taught Tor her phone number, for emergencies?"

"He might have called her…" Linn finished the train of thought, as I hammered Grandma's number into the phone pad.

"Grandma?"

Linn couldn't help it; her Oldest Sister Instinct took over and she snatched the phone from me as soon as she heard me make contact.

"Grandma? It's Linn. No, that was Ally. Listen, have you— Oh, oh God…"

Rowan was clutching my hand again, so tightly that her purple-painted nails dug right into my skin.

I squeezed her hand back just as tightly. I could hardly breathe for panicking.

Try as we might, neither of us could make out what Linn's expression meant, as she muttered, "When? Is he...? But how... OK... OK..."

As she pressed the End Call button, the noodle guy and most of his customers were on tenterhooks alongside me and Rowan.

"You'll never guess where Tor is..." she said, looking as if she didn't know whether to laugh or cry.

Tor has his own way of working. It might not be the way that me, or Rowan or Linn would handle things, and he maybe isn't too great at explaining his reasoning (since he's not too fond of the old chit-chat, as you know), but whatever Tor decides to do, it always makes *some* kind of sense. Even if it only makes sense to Tor.

So, what had happened was, our kid brother had wandered over to the bin to chuck his rubbish away, when his well-attuned animal radar pricked up. Straight away, he spotted the pigeon – its wing trailing – huddled between two stalls, as it tried to escape the barrage of passing feet.

Without a backward glance at us, Tor went rushing over, pulling off his sweatshirt as he ran. One poorly pigeon found itself safely wrapped up in a green hooded top, and within minutes Tor was speeding out of the nearby exit with it, and straight into a parked black cab that he'd spotted dropping off passengers.

Looking in the rear-view mirror, the cabbie must have been pretty startled to find a seven year old and a pigeon as his next fare.

In fact, he was concerned enough to try to find out where Tor had come from and who he was supposed to be with. But it was no good; Tor kept repeating the same address over and over again until the cab driver decided that the safest thing to do would be to take him there.

Once at the desired destination, Tor had been very apologetic about not having any money, but the cab driver had to understand, he'd said calmly, that it *was* an emergency.

The cab driver had replied that he'd only let Tor off if he gave him a phone number of someone at home…

Smart thinking. Once Tor had reeled off Grandma's number, he'd scrambled out of the car, with his sickly charge still hugged tight to him. And once Tor had scrambled out, the cab driver was straight on his mobile, phoning Grandma.

"She was just about to leave for Harmsworth when I called," Linn explained, to me, Rowan and anyone else who cared to listen. "But I said *we'd* go and pick him up; we're much closer."

"Harmsworth?" repeated the noodle guy, as he took possession of his phone again.

"It's near the Holloway Road. It's an RSPCA clinic," Linn told him – and the hungry customers who were following the saga of our missing sibling.

"It's where they used to film that show *Animal Hospital* – with Rolf Harris," Rowan chipped in.

The noodle guy looked none the wiser.

"If you knew our little brother," I grinned at him, "it would all make perfect sense…"

Chapter 22

HOW TO BE MYSTERIOUS, BY ROWAN LOVE

Rowan added an extra dollop of beans on Tor's plate, right where he indicated.

On his breakfast plate this Sunday morning was a particularly fine piece of food art. A small log cabin (made of toast) sat under a sky full of fluffy clouds (scrambled eggs), with a couple of birds flying high (carved with care from a slice of bacon). Now, Tor was delicately manoeuvring the beans into a radiating sun.

"That's pretty," Linn smiled tolerantly at our little brother. "Now, how about eating some of it?"

She wasn't nagging, though. Her tone was more jokey than bossy. We were all glad to get Tor back in one piece, but Linn especially had smothered him in protective love since we picked him up from the RSPCA centre the day before. And she looked the the most shattered of the three of us after our little heart-stopping adventure; her normally pristine blonde-ish hair was unbrushed and just roughly tucked behind her ears.

I think it was because, being the eldest, she felt very guilty for losing Tor. Course, it wasn't her fault, but *you* try telling Linn something when she's already made up her mind about it. Dad was unbelievably cool about the whole thing and tried to get her to drop the guilt thing too, but I guessed she'd do that in her own time. And in the meantime, Tor was going to have to put up with getting hugged to death by her.

Speaking of Tor, he was fine, if a little quieter than usual. You should have seen his face when the three of us came running into the reception of the Harmsworth hospital; his eyes were like saucers at the sight of these deranged girls descending upon him. Later, he and Dad had a little man-to-boy chat about what had happened, and how while getting the pigeon fixed up was a noble and worthy thing to do, it really would have been better to let at least one of us girls in on the medical drama too.

The pigeon, meanwhile, hadn't broken its wing (much to the relief of Love Child No. 4), but had superficially damaged its feathery bits by doing something unwise like flying into an overhead cable. Its wound had been cleaned, its wing had been bandaged to its fat little body and it was now sitting blinking and looking bemused in the luxurious comfort of our garden shed. (I'd been woken up at six-thirty in the morning – after a sleep filled with nightmares involving Tor going missing in all manner of elaborate ways – by the sound of Tor's bedroom door squeaking open. It turned out he was heading downstairs and out into the garden, off to the shed to check on his pigeon patient for the hundredth time.)

"Hey, about Dad…" Rowan whispered, checking to hear that she could still make out the sound of the shower upstairs.

"Oh, not this business with his present again. I can't think about that. I'm too tired!" Linn whimpered, pushing her hardly touched breakfast away.

She was exhausted. She hadn't had a broken sleep like me – just no sleep at all, after the day's drama.

"But we've got to get him something – and quick," I pointed out. "His birthday's tomorrow!"

What a great day *that* was shaping up to be; a History project with no project, and a birthday with no present. I toyed with emptying my bank account and emigrating, but – sadly – you can't emigrate too far on £33.50.

Linn looked like we'd just asked her to climb up Mount Everest dragging a crateful of tinned beans behind her. Stress and sleep deprivation were playing havoc with her leadership skills.

"Don't worry, Linnhe – I've got an idea for Dad's present!" Rowan hissed excitedly, pulling her antique (i.e. old and holey) kimono dressing gown tighter round her as she sat down.

Linn *must* have been exhausted. She didn't even raise an irritated eyebrow at Rowan for using her whole name. Instead, she just stared wearily at her.

"Uh-huh," she said, flatly. "Hit us with it…"

"Aha! It's a secret! I'm not going to tell you!" Rowan grinned.

"OK, so we're all clubbing together to get Dad a present, but *you're* going to sort it out and keep it secret from us. Is that right?" I asked, trying to spell out to Rowan the ridiculousness of what she'd just said.

"Oh, I don't have the energy to play head games. Just do what you want, Ro, it's fine by me. Right now, I'm going back to bed for an hour," sighed Linn, scraping back her seat and getting to her feet. "And *you*—"

She pointed sternly to Tor, before reaching over and ruffling his hair.

"—stay put! OK?"

Tor nodded, his big brown eyes gazing up at her.

"So, what's your idea? What are you thinking of buying Dad?" I quizzed Rowan, as soon as we heard Linn's tired, slow footsteps trudging up the stairs.

"Who said anything about buying anything?" shrugged Rowan, trying to look mysterious.

Only it was pretty easy to work out what she was up to. If she didn't plan to *buy* him a present, it only meant one thing: she was going to *make* him something.

Uh-oh.

"What are you planning on making, then?" I asked.

Rowan looked a bit miffed that I'd managed to work out her mind-bogglingly complicated conundrum.

"I'm not telling you," she said haughtily. "But I need your help."

I was just about to explain to her that she was facing a no-tell, no-help showdown, when Tor – an eggy cloud stuck on the end of his fork – shushed us, and pointed out into the hall.

Dad was on his way down the stairs, whistling loudly to whatever had been playing on the radio in the bathroom.

"Meet me upstairs; five minutes – your room!" hissed Rowan, getting up and swanning casually out of the room with a piece of toast in her hand.

"What do you reckon, Tor – is she going to make him a bike out of balloons or something?" I whispered. "Or maybe individual zebra-striped, fake-fur covers for his spanners?"

Tor crossed his eyes, cartoon-style.

"Exactly," I nodded at him.

The one good thing about losing Tor (and finding him again – of *course*) was that it had distracted me from the hideous reality of facing Miss Thomson in the morning and explaining *what* we'd messed up and *why* we'd messed up. But then his disappearing act had created another problem in that we'd managed to come home from our shopping trip with a pigeon instead of a fantastic, unique birthday present for Dad. So, as I padded up the stairs to my room a few short minutes after Rowan, I decided that I wouldn't press her to tell me what she was up to, if she didn't want to spill. If she was so keen to solve our hassles and make something, then I should just be grateful, shut up and let her get on with it.

She was sitting cross-legged on my bed, staring up at the big map of the world on the wall above it.

"This," Rowan announced, as soon as she saw it was me, "would look really nice framed."

I shrugged and flopped down on to the bed

beside her.

"But if it was framed, I couldn't stick those coloured pins in it," I pointed out to her.

"Mmm, I suppose..." Rowan muttered, her fingers twirling the little crystal on the end of the silver chain she wore around her neck.

I stared at the pretty piece of rose quartz and felt one of those instant flashback memories fly into my head – suddenly I could picture another set of fingers playing with it, when that necklace used to belong to Mum.

Mum... Most of the time, I only try to think happy thoughts about her. (I know that sounds corny, but it's the only way I can handle it.) But just for a second, I got that ache for her: just 'cause she'd know *exactly* what to do for Dad's birthday. Actually, while Rowan stared at my map, I tried to concentrate really hard, and *will* an answer from her.

But nothing happened. All I could hear was Rowan breathing and my tummy gurgling.

"What do you want me to do?" I asked Rowan, breaking the tummy-gurgling silence. "How can I help?"

"I don't want you to do anything... I just want to have a look in that box you keep. Where is it?"

I knew straight away what she meant. Slipping

off the bed, I walked over to my old-fashioned wooden wardrobe and pulled out the wicker box I kept in the bottom of it.

"Guess I can't ask you what you're looking for?" I said, plonking it on the rug in the middle of the room.

Rowan slithered off the bed and on to the floor, ending up cross-legged again beside the box.

"Don't know myself till I see it," she smiled wryly.

She was coming over all mysterious again, and this time she was succeeding.

Downstairs in the living room is the proper, official record of our family life: a pile of photo albums, with pictures of holidays and birthdays and school plays all neatly stuck inside. But my box is a more random, unofficial record of the lives of the Loves. All the photos floating about in the box are rejects that never made it into the albums: out-of-focus shots of Grandma, taken by Tor, aged three; a selection of snaps of all of us girls, taken in different places and at different ages, but with the same black shadowy thumb effect ruining them all; stupid stuff like the time me, Linn, Rowan and Tor all crammed into the photo booth in Woolworth's and pulled the most horrible faces.

Apart from the artistically lacking photos, there're

school reports in there, and corny stuff like Tor's first baby tooth, all wrapped up in cotton wool in a tiny box. And in there somewhere too is a newspaper cutting; a local actress whose name I forget – who used to be in *EastEnders* or something – was promoting fitness in the borough, and ended up perched on a bike outside Dad's shop, with my dad standing beside her, both grinning cheesily at the camera.

As Rowan rummaged, I saw a Polaroid of myself at the bottom. Pulling it out, I stared hard and didn't know whether to laugh or cringe at the sight of me – aged ten – trying on one of Mum's long, flowery, hippie dresses. It had suited her, but it was so big on me that it was like looking at a picture of a rose bush with a head stuck on top.

"Right – this is it!" proclaimed Rowan suddenly, jumping to her feet and heading out of my room.

Rats – I hadn't even caught a *glimpse* of what she'd picked out...

Chapter 23

WHOSE FAULT IS IT ANYWAY?

There was a gentle snoring coming from the pile of laundry I hadn't sorted out yet in the corner of my room.

Well, at least *someone* was getting a good night's sleep, even if it wasn't me.

Yep, for the second night running it looked like my bed was going to be a snooze-free zone: last night, it was down to Tor's exploits; tonight it was down to sheer unadulterated dread of facing Miss Thomson first thing in the morning...

I propped myself up on my elbows to see which four- (or potentially three-) legged friend had invaded my space, but it was too dark to make out anything other than a cat-sized blob on my discarded white T-shirt.

I'd have seen more earlier; when I'd first gone to bed, the nearly full moon had been streaming a bluey light down through the small skylight directly above my bed. But now, it was gloomsville again, which kind of suited the way I was feeling.

Yeah, I know – I should have stuck my bedside light on and read a book or a magazine for a while till I felt sleepy, but I wasn't in the mood to concentrate on anything except what I do best: worrying.

It's a talent, it really is. There are starving refugees carrying all their worldly possessions and their grannies on their backs just to get to UN food camps. There are volcanoes, earthquakes, tidal waves (or tsunamis – see? I might not be sure of the exact population of London, but I *do* remember *some* Geography stuff!) that people have to live through and deal with (or run away from, very, *very* fast…). Anyhow, you get my drift; out there in the big wide world all sorts of big scary things happen to people on a depressingly regular basis, and all I can lose sleep worrying over is a stupid History project. Or a lack of one…

I'd phoned Sandie in the afternoon to have a moan about it, and immediately wished I hadn't. She didn't mean to, but she just made me stress out more.

"Miss Thomson's going to be so mad with us!" Sandie had whimpered pathetically. "She's going to kill us!"

Sandie was overreacting just a *tiny* bit. Miss Thomson wasn't the *Terminator* or anything.

"Well, I guess she isn't going to give us a hug and a kiss and say it doesn't matter!" I'd tried to joke.

"I feel like staying off sick tomorrow!" Sandie whined.

"Oh no, you don't!" I panicked. "You're not skiving off and leaving me to do this all on my own!"

What a hypocrite I am. I'd let the notion of skiving off drift through my head myself, only an hour before. I was only annoyed because Sandie saying it meant *I* couldn't do it.

"You won't be on your own – Kyra will be there!" Sandie had protested feebly.

"Wrong! *You*, me and Kyra will be there!" I'd corrected her.

What with fussing over Tor and helping Rowan select her Mystery Object from my box, I hadn't made my usual Sunday-morning rendezvous with Billy (and dogs) up at the Palace. So, after my less-than-comforting conversation with Sandie, I gave him a ring – just to see if he had any words of wisdom, any insightful thoughts that might put the whole thing in perspective for me.

Fat chance.

"Sssssssss…"

Billy took a long sharp intake of breath once I'd told him about Friday's fun events.

"What does 'ssssssssss' mean?" I demanded.

"Only one thing for it," he announced.

"Go on, then – what?"

"Pretend you've got chickenpox."

"What?"

"Pretend you've got chickenpox," he repeated, as if it didn't sound stupid enough already. "It's better than an upset stomach; that only buys you a day or two at the most, and you'll *still* have to face the music. But chickenpox is great: you've got a legitimate reason to stay off all week, and the whole project thing will have blown over by the time you go back!"

"OK," I said slowly. "Problem one: how am I meant to convince my family that I've got chickenpox? And problem two: how am I meant to convince my family that I've got chickenpox, since they know I've had chickenpox *already*?"

"People, um, can have chickenpox twice!" he said, unconvincingly. "And, hey, you're a girl; you've got make-up, haven't you?"

"*So?*"

"So, *draw* spots on!"

"Billy," I sighed. "Do me a favour: would you go and bring Precious to the phone?"

"How come?" he muttered, dumbly.

"'Cause Precious might have some useful advice

to give me – unlike you!"

And so, here I was, at three o'clock in the morning, trying to talk myself out of worrying by thinking depressing thoughts of starving refugees and earthquake-ravaged cities (not a whole heap of laughs, I can tell you), while my stomach was merrily clenching with tension.

How did I get in this state? I lay there in the dark, asking myself.

Because the project was ruined, I answered myself.

Why was the project ruined?

Because we spilt paint on it.

How did paint get spilt on it?

'Cause me and Kyra were niggling at each other.

Why were you niggling at each other?

Because she's in my face all the time.

Why is she in your face all the time?

Because she's mad.

Why…?

I gave up there. This mess wouldn't have existed if a certain someone had never turned up at our school to start with.

"Are you listening, Kyra Davies?" I said out loud to the darkness and the contentedly snoring cat. "It's all *your* fault…"

Chapter 24

WHO NEEDS THE X FILES?

It was one minute past nine.

I peered round the classroom door.

No one was there.

"It's empty," I hissed at Sandie, who was hovering behind me in the corridor, biting her nails to oblivion.

It was the eighth Wonder Of The World: our entire History class – plus Miss Thomson – had vanished into thin air. Like the passengers and crew of the *Marie Celeste*, one minute they'd been chatting normally, the next they'd hit some Bermuda Triangle weirdness and had been spirited away to a parallel universe.

"They'll be in the hall – getting everything set up for the play!" said Sandie.

Well, maybe not *quite* a parallel universe.

"Why didn't you remind me earlier?" I asked her, not really expecting to get a sensible answer.

Sandie shrugged and widened her Disney eyes at me.

See? I was right.

"Come on, then," I said, steering my reluctant feet in the direction of the hall and pretending my hands weren't really shaking. "Let's get this over with…"

Trudging along, I pictured my make-up bag sitting temptingly on the chest of drawers in my room. That dark pinky lipstick I'd got free off the front of a magazine … that fine make-up brush (off the front of another magazine) … oh, how easy it would have been to draw on those chickenpox poxy bits…

"Ally! Sandie!" beamed Miss Thomson, suddenly turning out of the hall up ahead and into our path.

I tried to fix something that I *hoped* might resemble a smile on my face, but it probably looked more like I had wind or something.

With every step closer to our teacher and our confession, the knot of dread in my stomach got tighter, and I had this incredible sensation like I was shrinking. At the rate I was going, I'd be ant-sized by the time I'd reached her. Just the right size for her to stomp on me with her heel when I told her what had happened to our project. (And it *would* be me that told Miss Thomson; Sandie would have just opened and shut her mouth like a traumatized goldfish if I'd left it to her.)

184

"Well done, girls!" boomed Miss Thomson as we drew level.

I was confused – did Miss Thomson *do* irony?

"I really like your posters – they work very well!"

I stared at Miss Thomson, waiting for her to bark "NOT!" and burst into maniacal laughter after what she'd just said.

But she didn't.

"Well, hurry along! Better give Kyra a hand putting them up – she's struggling away on her own at the moment!"

And with a bright smile, Miss Thomson was off, leaving us marooned, in stunned surprise.

There was only one thing that could explain it: it was me and Sandie who were in that parallel universe…

Chapter 25

AND HERE'S ONE I MADE EARLIER...

In the auditorium, there was lots of crashing and banging and shouting going on, as actors and technicians lost their rags due to last-minute-rehearsal nerves.

Out in the reception hall, the walls were awash with posters, photos and rambling captions describing life in our little patch of London half a century or so ago. Some of our History class, finished fixing up their efforts, had wandered off to nosey at the drama unfolding in the auditorium, while others were still faffing about, putting up, taking down and generally rearranging their masterpieces.

Me, I was sitting on a hard wooden bench, staring across the room at the six unstained posters of bomb sites.

"I still can't believe it," I said, shaking my head. "They don't look like they've been touched!"

"Well, the third and fourth ones were the worst; I had to bin them and start from scratch," said Kyra, who was also perched on the bench, in-between me and Sandie. "But the others only had the odd spot on them – I managed to wipe off the black paint almost completely. You can still see it faintly if you go up close, though."

"But when did you do it all? When did you have the time…?" I asked, in wonderment.

"Well, after you two left on Friday, I just carried on, till the caretaker came and kicked me out at teatime," she explained, her eyes staring straight ahead at her handiwork. "And I even managed to use the photocopier in the office before they packed up for the day – I re-did all the photos on *that* one and *that* one."

Me and Sandie both stared at the particular posters she was pointing at. "But you couldn't have done all that so quickly!" I protested.

Sandie was saying nothing, I noticed. I think she was still in shock.

"No," Kyra shook her head, her gaze still directed straight in front of her. "I came in yesterday afternoon too. The caretaker told me that the Drama lot were coming in to do a dress rehearsal, and he had to open the school up for them anyway, so he didn't mind if I was here as well."

I felt choked. I'd spent my Sunday getting gloomy and sinking into a pit of pessimism, while Kyra was actually doing something constructive.

How dumb did *I* feel?

"You … you did a really good job, Kyra," I mumbled. "Thanks."

"Yeah!" Sandie sighed in amazement from the other end of the bench.

Kyra dropped her eyeline down to the floor, and scuffed at the faded lino with the toe of her shoe.

"Well…" she shrugged shyly. "I felt like I had to do it, really."

"No, you didn't," I contradicted her.

It was true; she didn't *have* to do it. She could have left the posters in the mess they were in and shared the blame with me and Sandie when it came to facing Miss Thomson. And, of course, being the new girl, Miss Thomson might have given her the easier time and saved the bulk of her scolding for me and Sandie.

"But I had to fix things – it was my fault!" said Kyra, finally staring me in the face with her dark almond eyes full of … what? Embarrassment? Remorse? Guilt?

"It was my fault as much as yours!" I found myself arguing.

"And mine!" Sandie chipped in.

See – I told you Sandie was a sweetie. She wasn't the one who was arguing with Kyra, but she still tried to take a share of the blame. I hadn't even thought of that before…

"I'm just … sorry," muttered Kyra turning away from me.

Suddenly, this close up, I realized what Kyra reminded me of: small face; almond eyes; light-brown skin; a sprinkling of darker brown freckles across her nose; big ears… She was a dead ringer for one of the deer me and Tor go and visit in the deer and donkey enclosure at the back of Alexandra Palace.

"Sorry about what?" I asked, twisting my thoughts back to the project and Kyra's starring role in saving it. "I just said, it wasn't all your fault."

(Yeah, I know – the hypocrite strikes again. That *wasn't* what I'd been saying to myself at three o'clock in the morning…)

"No, not about the project. Well, a *bit* about the project. But I mean, I'm sorry for being … kind of pushy. For turning up at your house when all your friends were there and everything."

Urgh. What do you say when someone comes out with something as honest as that? "Yes – you *were* too pushy, and you *should* be sorry for turning up unannounced that night"? Maybe, but I couldn't be that hard-nosed. So I did a Sandie and just shrugged.

"I *know* I get too pushy sometimes, and I just can't help it..."

"Why not?" asked Sandie, scoring minus five for tact.

But I was glad she said it anyway. Might as well get straight to the point, instead of circling around it.

"It's just a thing I do, every time I come to a new school," said Kyra, her head hanging. "I arrive, and everyone's already got their little crowd of mates. No one's bothered about trying to get to know the new girl, so I just end up thinking that the only way to get noticed is to be sort of ... pushy. And then I realize I've gone too far, and everyone hates me. And then I'm on my own for a while, till my dad changes jobs and we move and it starts all over again..."

A little cynical voice in the back of my head was whispering, "Don't fall for it – she could still be a nutter..." But what the hell. So I'm a big, stupid softie. So what.

"Must be tough," I said quietly.

"Mmm," Kyra murmured in agreement.

"How come your dad switches jobs so much?" asked Sandie, cutting to the quick again.

Kyra gave a wry little laugh, but still kept up her staring session at the floor.

"He doesn't particularly want to. It's more to do with my mum."

"How come?" I asked.

"Have you got three weeks?" she laughed, without sounding particularly happy. "With my mum, it's a long story…"

Tell me about it, I thought.

Mums and long stories … it looked like Kyra and I had more in common than I'd thought.

Chapter 26

EXTRA FEATHERS ON YOUR PIZZA, SIR?

"Look, Ro – across the road – isn't that your mate Von?"

"Where? Where?" said Rowan, scanning the pavements outside the restaurant window.

As soon as Rowan's attention was distracted, Linn gave me and Tor a wink across the table and promptly dived under it. Me and Tor looked at each other, and ducked down too.

"I can't see her…" we heard Rowan's voice hovering somewhere above us. "Where is she, Linnhe? Linnhe? Oi!"

Rowan joined us under the table, just as Linn was pulling the gift-wrapped present out of the carrier bag at her feet.

"Leave it alone!" Rowan snapped, grabbing the present back out of Linn's grasp.

"Aw, come on – tell us what it is before he comes back from the loo!" Linn whined, as we all straightened up in our seats again.

"No! You'll just have to wait!" Rowan chastised

us.

"Can't we just have a feel? See if we can guess?" I suggested, eyeing up the flat-ish, big-ish parcel.

"No!"

"Patience, patience!" grumbled Grandma, with a sigh.

She was sitting at the far end of the two tables that had been squished together for us, while Dad – as the birthday boy – took pride of place at the other end.

We were sitting in our favourite spot in Pizza Bella: right in the window. Not that it had been hard to get – at seven o'clock on a Monday night they don't exactly have queues out the door.

We had been planning to stay at home and order in pizza, but as soon as he'd got in from work, Dad had announced that he'd changed his mind and decided to treat us all instead. We were all pretty pleased, but Tor especially got excited. He's at that in-between age where he seems very thoughtful and grown-up sometimes, and then reverts to being a total kid. And however grown-up he tries to be, we know he still gets a kick when the waitresses in Pizza Bella wander over with a free balloon for him.

"I saw your pictures at the big school today, Ally. Your name was on them," announced Tor suddenly, surprising us all by coming out with two whole sentences at once.

"Did you?" I smiled at him, as he nibbled his way through a straw-thin breadstick. "What about the play? Did you like it?"

He shrugged, which in universal small-boy-speak meant it was OK.

"Hold on; how did Tor manage to see your posters? I thought they were covered in black paint, same as your clothes, after your little accident on Friday," Grandma commented.

"My friend Kyra managed to fix them," I explained.

"Ooh, she's your *friend* now, is she? I thought you said she wasn't?!" Rowan teased me, reaching over to nick a breadstick out of the packet Tor was hogging.

"Well, she must be, to go and do it all herself, if your project was as messed up as you said it was," Linn pointed out.

Over her shoulder, I could see Dad weaving his way back to us through the tables.

"Well, she's not exactly my best mate or anything, but she's all right..." I mumbled, still getting used to how I felt about Kyra now. "Anyway, Dad's coming back – are you going to give him the present now, or wait till the pizzas arrive?"

"Now!" Tor burst out loudly.

"Now what?" asked Dad, sitting down in his place.

"Now," said Rowan, blushing with excitement, "you get your present!"

"Hey! A present!" Dad grinned, taking the package that Rowan was holding out to him. "You shouldn't have – you all gave me cards this morning; that would have been enough!"

"Don't get *too* excited, Dad," Linn laughed. "You haven't seen it yet…"

"Is this from all of you?" he asked, gazing around the table as he tore at the Sellotape.

"It's not from me, Martin; only from the children," said Grandma. "I haven't a clue what it is…"

"Join the club," I mumbled, grinning at Linn.

With a final impatient tug, Dad yanked the paper off, and studied the A3-sized framed picture in his hands.

"Wow!" he gasped, staring with amazement (and slightly twinkly eyes) at the vision in front of him.

The rest of us, of course, couldn't see what it was. All that was visible from our back-view was the blue feathery trim Rowan had edged the frame with.

"Lemme see!" said Tor, lunging impatiently out of his seat and standing by Dad's chair for a bird's-eye view of the present.

"What do you think?!" asked Rowan, looking as pink and shiny with excitement as the bubblegum-coloured balloon tied to the back of Tor's seat.

"Cool!" said Tor.

"Fantastic!" said Dad. "A family portrait! Perfect!"

Me, Linn and Grandma exchanged looks: unless Rowan had drugged us all and taken us round to the photographer's studio without our knowledge, we hadn't *got* a family portrait done.

"Well, come on, Martin," Grandma chastised him with a smile. "Share it with everyone!"

Beaming, Dad turned the picture round for us all to see.

Apart from the feather-boa-style trim, the main image in the frame was surrounded by a border of Rowan's trademark sequins. And the main image?

It was the strip of weeny photo-booth photos – the ones hauled from my box in the wardrobe – enlarged. There was me, Linn, Rowan and Tor in all our glory, pulling faces and giggling our heads off as we squashed together in the tiny space.

"Hey, Grandma – look!" I pointed out. "It's your idea; the family portrait!"

Grandma shot me an I-told-you-so! look, even if she seemed a bit dubious about Rowan's artistic efforts. I think it's safe to say she'd have preferred a nice soft-focus studio portrait from the place up on Crouch End Broadway.

"It's great!" laughed Dad. "It's just so natural! It's just how I see all of you!"

"Yeah, I got the idea of blowing these pics up on a photocopier from Ally's mate Kyra," Rowan explained. "You know how Chazza's mum's a solicitor? Well, she's got a colour photocopier in her office up in Muswell Hill, so Chazza got the keys off her and me and him went up and did this yesterday afternoon!"

I know it's silly, but I felt all choked up then.

For Rowan to go to all that trouble was amazing. And the picture was brilliant; with all of us laughing and fooling around ... well, you know – it was really nice, really special.

And the fact that Kyra had helped inspire Dad's present was kind of cool too.

You don't need to have a brain the size of a Nobel prize winner or anything to work out that I'd had a big change of heart about her since that morning. All that stuff about moving schools and never being able to make friends – that must have been really lonely for her; especially when you think she's an only child too. And though she didn't go into it too much, her mum sounded like *big* trouble. Apparently, that crack Kyra first made to me about her mum – the one about her being a professional drinker? Well, that's pretty much the way it is. At break this morning, after the decorating of the hall had been finished, Kyra told me and Sandie that her mum is more or less fairly normal, but when she starts to drink, everything changes. She said that her dad ends up being embarrassed by her mum so often – with her phoning or turning up at his work sloshed and shouting – that *that's* why he keeps switching jobs so much.

That's all she said, and neither me nor Sandie felt brave enough to push her for any more details. And bad as that story sounded, I get the feeling that there's more to it than that – Kyra did tell Sandie that thing about her mum calling her mean, after all. Well, maybe in time, Kyra will trust us enough to tell us.

And you never know; I might end up liking Kyra Davies almost as much as I *dis*liked her to start with – well, weirder things have happened...

"Happy Birthday, Dad!" Linn burst out, holding up her glass.

"Yeah, Happy Birthday, Dad!" I joined in, raising my glass, along with Rowan, Grandma and Tor.

Crashing our Fantas, Diet Cokes, Cokes and wine together, Dad made a quick speech.

"Thanks, you lot – and cheers to us all!"

A small voice chipped in as the glasses tinkled

again.

"And Mum!"

There was the tiniest hush for the tiniest moment: all three of us girls saw Dad exchange looks with Grandma.

"To your daughter," he smiled, raising his wine in the air.

"To Melanie," Grandma smiled back.

"To Mum!" yelped Tor, throwing his Coke so high that both his straws jiggled out of it.

"Mum!" repeated Linn, Rowan and me; Love children one, two and three swapping small, thoughtful smiles.

Our Mum? Don't panic; she's not dead. You didn't think she was, did you? No, she's fine (we think). That beach on the last postcard we got from her – it looked pretty gorgeous.

You want to know her story? Well, it's like Kyra said – have you got three weeks?

But you know something? Colin's sitting right beside me on the desk in my room just now, purring so hard he's hiccuping, and rubbing his vibrating head on my hand. So I think I'd better give up for now and pay him a bit of attention.

Stuff about my mum, about Kyra – and whether she turns out to be cool or a psycho – it'll just have to wait till another time…

*   *   *

Until then, I'll leave you with my Thought for the Day: always give people the benefit of the doubt. Unless, of course, they're an axe-wielding maniac asking if you happen to be Drew Barrymore.

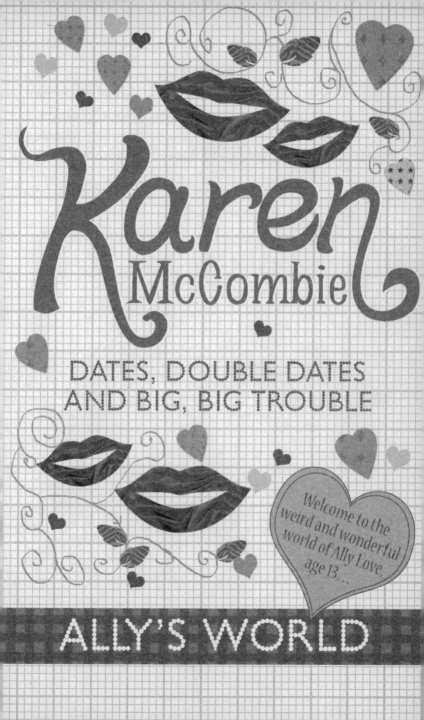

Karen McCombie

DATES, DOUBLE DATES AND BIG, BIG TROUBLE

Welcome to the weird and wonderful world of Ally Love, age 13...

ALLY'S WORLD

Contents

PROLOGUE

Dear Mum,

I came across that photo of you and Dad the other day – you know, the one from your first date. The one where you look a bit weird, 'cause you've just thrown up…

Anyhow, it just reminded me how much I loved it when you used to tell me about how you two got together; all the stuff about how he'd come into the jeans shop in Camden High Street where you worked and try on loads of different pairs every week, just to have an excuse to talk to you. (He never bought any, did he?)

And better than that was how *you* used to spend your lunch-hours in the bike shop he worked in across the street, buying a bell one day, a bicycle pump the next, even a puncture-repair kit.

Then, when he finally *did* ask you out, it wasn't till that first date that he found out you didn't even *have* a bike.

It was so sweet the way you told Dad that you

didn't mind about him getting the cinemas mixed up that first night out together, and taking you to see a horror movie by accident. *Even though* horror movies and the sight of blood usually made you feel ill. And it was *really* sweet of Dad to still fancy you after you threw up on his lap.

True love.

After all that, I guess I wouldn't have been in the mood to hand someone my camera like you did and get them to take a photo of the two of you (I think if it was me, I'd have wanted to forget the whole thing, after puking all over the place). But I'm glad you *did* decide to do it – or we wouldn't have had a record of the time our parents started seeing each other. I don't know if you had a proper kiss that first night (I hope not, under the circumstances), but it's still one of the most romantic stories I've ever heard – even if there weren't exactly string orchestras playing in the background and rose petals raining from the sky.

Hope it happens to me like that one day (but maybe minus the part about being sick).

Not so long ago, I thought it might … and that was also right around the time when me and Linn and Rowan started to realize that Dad had found someone to replace you.

I suppose you'd better hear this from the

beginning…
   Love you lots,
   Ally
   (your Love Child No. 3)

Chapter 1

THAT FIRST KISS (I WISH...)

OK, so when it comes to the whole romance thing, I admit, I daydream about it a lot. And I mean a *lot*.

I daydream about it when I'm walking the dogs up by Alexandra Palace, looking out over the sprawl of London off in the distance. I daydream about it in bed at night, when I lie in the dark and stare out at the stars through the tiny skylight in the roof of my attic bedroom...

So that sounds very poetic and everything. But then, I *also* daydream about all things romantic at distinctly *un*romantic moments. Like during especially boring classes, or when I'm brushing my teeth, or when it's my turn to do the laundry and I'm sorting through my family's dirty socks, or even when I'm helping my little brother Tor clean rabbit poo out of the hutches in the back garden.

I don't think Juliet thought about Romeo when she was cleaning out rabbit poo. Well, when I think about the film, I certainly don't remember seeing Claire Danes in a pair of yellow Marigolds daydreaming about Leo DiCaprio shinning up to her balcony while she was trying to shoo away an irate bunny who's in the mood to bite.

Maybe the fact that I can daydream about romance at really inappropriate times means I'm very imaginative. Or maybe it means I'm a weirdo – I'm not too sure. But anyway, one of my favourite daydreams is That First Kiss. It goes like this…

1) I go to a party and, magically, I look effortlessly cool. (Look, it's *my* daydream, so stuff like that can happen, OK?)

2) The party is amazing, the music's brilliant, and most brilliant of all – I spot *him* across the crowded room. (The *him* part is interchangeable, depending on who I've got a crush on that week. I fall in and out of fancying different boys pretty regularly – but having said that, there's only one boy that I've stayed constantly and truly mad about, and that's my sister Linn's mate, Alfie. Sigh…)

3) During the evening, there's lots of tantalizing staring and looking away going on between us, just to get a bit of a *frisson* going. (Good word, *frisson*, isn't it? Except I said it to my best friend Sandie once, and she thought it was some kind of fish. But I tell you, having a bit of a fish between you *definitely* isn't romantic…)

4) The lights are low and sparkly, my favourite

track comes on (that changes week to week, day-dream to daydream), and from nowhere *he* sidles up beside me and asks me to dance.

5) Right, this is where it gets good... I've got my arms around his neck, and I can feel myself shiver with goosebumps as he pulls me closer to him, his hands on my back. We say nothing, just look into each other's eyes – reading each other's thoughts and knowing instinctively what's going to happen next. In slow motion, we move towards each other, tilting our heads gently as the moment gets closer. I can feel the warmth of his lips even before they touch mine. And then...

I was sitting on the usual bench on Ally Pally, letting my First Kiss daydream drift through my mind, and was just about to melt mouths with Alfie, when the mood was suddenly ruined.

Well, it's inevitable really, when you find yourself in a headlock.

"Billy! Get off me, you total moron!" I yelled, trying to tug his arm away from around my neck.

Out of the corner of my eyes I could see a middle-aged couple walking along the path looking kind of concerned. They probably thought I was being attacked by some lunatic, and who could blame them? They weren't to know that it was just my mate, acting like a complete numpty...

They weren't the only ones looking concerned; my two dogs – Rolf and Winslet – didn't know who to bark at first: Billy, or his yappy little mutt Precious, who was already up to his usual tricks, trying to inspect both their bottoms at close quarters.

"Do you give up?" I heard Billy asking, though I couldn't see him since he was standing behind me and the bench.

He must have been watching that stupid wrestling programme again, I sighed to myself.

"And are you going to give up acting like a six year old?" I managed to growl. "God, no wonder you can never get a girlfriend…"

It was a low blow (Billy's mighty sensitive about his lack of success with the girlies), but still he didn't let go.

It was time to get tough.

I reached back and, after a couple of searching slaps, found his nose and pulled it hard.

"Arghhhhhh!" he whined, letting go of my neck and scrambling over the back of the wooden seat, with me still hanging on to his nose.

The couple walked past at that point, staring disapprovingly at us – a pair of delinquent thirteen year olds spoiling the serenity of their Saturday-morning stroll. They obviously didn't approve of the barking dogs either, eyeing up Precious, Rolf and Winslet like they were the spawn of the devil. (Course, that might be true in Precious's case.)

"Gum on, Ally. Led go," pleaded Billy, nasally. He sounded like he could be in an ad for Night Nurse or something.

But you could tell he was quite enjoying it, since he was now sitting beside me with his hands on his thighs, making no attempt to make me stop.

"You look ridiculous," I told him, as I gave his nose an extra tweak for luck.

"You'll look more ridigulous in a segond when I blow snot all over your hand..."

"You wouldn't dare..." I said, narrowing my eyes at him.

"Wouldn'd I?" he grinned.

He took a big breath, ready for blast-off, when I let go and jumped off the seat.

Rolf and Winslet thought this was a cue for play-time, and bounded over to me, tails flapping about enthusiastically.

"Billy – you are the most disgusting boy I know!" I yelled at him.

He grinned again, put his hand over his nose and made the most grotesque snotty noise.

"And you *laaaaaaaave* it!" he roared, getting up and running straight towards me, holding his hand out like he was going to rub it in my face.

I was pretty sure he'd just blown a raspberry behind his hand, but I wasn't taking any chances, not where snot was concerned. So I did the only sensible thing – I ran.

I wondered what the couple were thinking now, seeing a screeching girl, hurtling down the hill pursued by three mental dogs and a deranged boy in a baseball cap. They were probably thinking that they were glad we weren't *their* kids...

"Gotcha!"

The red gravel path that led to one of the park entrances was just hurtling into view when Billy grabbed me by the waist and rugby-tackled me to the grass.

"Get off!" I yelped for the second time so far, feeling him land heavily on top of me.

"Aha! You will never get away from the evil Hand of Snot!"

Somehow I managed to twist around underneath him, grab the evil Hand of Snot with both my fists and force it *well* away from my face.

"Billy – grow up!" I panted in his face, trying to sound angry – and trying just as hard not to laugh.

"Ooh! Listen to Ally Love! She's *so* sensible!" teased Billy, putting on a dopey voice. "Well, we'll have to do something about *that*..."

With his free hand, Billy started mercilessly tickling me, running his irritating fingers from my waist to my armpit to my neck and back down again.

"*GERRROFFFF!*" I squealed breathlessly, between giggles, but he didn't – not that he'd have been able to hear me above the din of three barking dogs anyway, all of whom thought this was an excellent game.

But somehow, I heard another sound above the racket.

They say mothers can tune in to the noise of a crying baby, no matter how faint it is, or even if it's not their own baby. Well, I managed to tune in to a crunch of gravel on the nearby path, and the rubbery screech of bike brakes (when your dad runs a bicycle shop, I guess it's in your blood). Of course what caught my attention most was my name.

"Hi, Ally…"

As I turned to look at the source of the voice, I tried to brush Winslet away with one hand, but she carried on happily licking my face, regardless. I didn't realize it at the time, but I had my other hand right over Billy's face.

"Whas-going-on?" Billy mumbled, trying to shake his face free of my splayed fingers.

But I didn't answer him – I was too busy staring at

the vision in front of me, perched on his mountain bike.

"Hello, Alfie…" I smiled stupidly, waggling my dog-licked hand at him in a half-hearted attempt at a wave.

Talk about bad timing.

I had why-don't-you-just-kill-me-now-before-I-die-of-embarrassment timing…

Chapter 2

LINN IS WAY, WAY, WAY OFF THE MARK

It's funny how you know when you're being stared at.

"What?" I demanded, catching Linn gawping at me for the seventeenth time in the last hour or so.

We were in the living room – me (on the sofa), Linn (next to me on the sofa), Rowan (on one of the armchairs painting her nails silver) and Tor (on the floor, driving his toy cars over a mountain range played by snoozing Rolf) – aimlessly watching a rubbish quiz show after stuffing our faces, this Saturday teatime.

I'd seen Linn eyeing me up earlier over the kitchen table, studying my face like I'd grown another nose or something. And ever since we'd come through and flopped in the living room, she'd kept up the surreptitious scrutiny, even though she was supposed to be flicking through the work section of the local paper in search of a Saturday job. And here she was, at it again...

"What? I'm not doing anything!" said Linn,

opening her green eyes wide and looking shocked at my accusation. "I'm just reading this!"

"Well, if you're trying to read it, then here's a handy hint: keep your eyes on the paper instead of on *me*," I said, sarcastically. "Anyway, who's going to give *you* a Saturday job?"

To tell the truth, I didn't mean to be so mean. And anyone in their right mind would give Linn a Saturday job; she's pretty, well-presented and polite. (Polite to other people, that is. Not to her sisters…) It was just that I'd got myself in a bad mood ever since Alfie had caught me in a compromising position that morning. And it was all Billy's grandad's fault. Well, what I mean is, if his parents hadn't planned to visit Billy's grandad on Sunday, I could have met up with Billy as usual – instead of swapping to Saturday – and Alfie wouldn't have seen me like that: i.e. lying on the grass with Billy sprawled across me like a wet blanket, and a dribble of dog drool dangling off my face, courtesy of Winslet.

"No need to get snippy with me, just because *you're* in a bad mood…" said Linn, in an infuriatingly righteous voice.

My big sister Linn is an expert in being infuriatingly righteous. In fact, I might be wrong, but I think she's doing it as an A-level…

"I'm *not* in a bad mood!" I said, sinking further into my bad mood.

"Mmmm…" muttered Linn dismissively, flicking noisily through the pages of the paper.

"I'm *not*!" I protested.

"Whatever you say…" shrugged Linn.

See what I mean? It makes me so angry when she goes all big-sister-superior on me like that. It makes me want to … I don't know – ruffle her immaculate hair or go and mess up her colour-coordinated knicker drawer, or something else that would ruffle her perfectly organized feathers.

"Shut up, you two! I can't hear what he's saying!" Rowan snapped at us.

It's not that my in-between sister (in-between me and Linn, age-wise) was particularly wild about corny Saturday-evening game shows; it's just that she's kind of super-sensitive and hates bickering. Even though she and Linn bicker on a practically daily basis.

But, hey – we both shut up. Linn glued her eyes to the newspaper and I stared blankly at the TV screen.

"…*and now, name an animal indigenous to Australia!*" said the cheesy, toothy TV presenter.

"A marsupial!" Tor piped up, not even glancing up from his game.

Rolf snuffled and flicked his tail as a fire engine drove over his furry haunches.

"That's too smart, Tor!" muttered Rowan, fixing the top back on her nail varnish with extended fingers. "All the contestants on this show are picked to be thick, I reckon. They wouldn't be able to *spell* marsupial."

"*Come on, Keith – an Australian animal! You can do it!*" the presenter encouraged, a despairing glint in his eye.

"Duck-billed platypus!" said Tor, as the participant on the screen chewed his lip and struggled to come up with an answer.

"*Still* too smart, Tor," I chipped in, trying to take my mind off Linn and her snide remarks. "All they're looking for is 'kangaroo' or 'koala', and that bloke will win a car. And he can't even get that!"

"*Barrrrpppp!*"

The buzzer meant the bloke on the screen was out of time. Bang went *his* chances of winning some fancy four-wheeled drive.

"*Well, time's up I'm afraid, Keith. Didn't you even have a guess there?*"

"*Um,*" muttered the bumbling bloke on the telly, "*I thought maybe … a sheep.*"

Me, Rowan and Tor burst out laughing – especially

Tor, who saw ignorance about animals as a sign of deep human failing.

But I stopped laughing pretty quickly – as soon as I felt Linn's eyes on me once again…

"What!? What is it?" I demanded to know, swirling my head around quick enough to catch her squinting at my neck.

"Ally, is that a *love* bite?"

"*What?*" I frowned at her.

She'd *got* to be joking. With my track record of pitifully few romantic encounters, there wasn't much chance of me getting something that yucky!

"There!" she said, extending one finger out to touch me on the side of my neck.

"Get off!" I said, echoing my words to Billy from earlier on in the day.

I leapt up off the sofa and hurried over to the mirror by the living-room door. The mirror was almost a piece of art in itself; Mum made it years ago. She'd bought a plain mirror-tile for a few pence, Dad told us, and then added the whole frame of Fimo flowers and elves that swirled and peeped at you as you stared at your own reflection.

I hauled down the neck of my jumper and tried to see what Linn had seen. Sure enough, there was a dark shadow; but on closer inspection, it was easy to see what I already knew – that it *wasn't* a bruise.

"It's mud! That's all!" I exclaimed, licking my finger and rubbing at the smudge of Ally Pally dirt, still in place after Billy's rugby-tackle earlier in the day.

"Dirt?" said Linn, raising her eyebrows at me. "Well, that's not what Alfie said…"

"What do you mean?!"

"Well, Alfie said that from where *he* was standing this morning, it looked like Billy was snogging you on the grass up on Ally Pally…"

I opened my mouth and shut it again. What could I say to Linn that would put that thought right out of her head, without admitting that the only boy I'd happily let snog me was Alfie?

"What? You and *Billy*!" said Rowan in surprise.

Great – now Linn had *her* believing it!

"It wasn't like that!" I yelped to both of them. "We were just mucking about! We *weren't* snogging!"

"Uh-huh," murmured Linn, disbelievingly.

Arrrgh! She was off again…

"Look," I said, struggling to explain myself. "It's ridiculous. It would be like you snogging Chazza, Ro; or you, Linn – it would be like you snogging Alfie!"

Urgh. The very thought…

"Me and Alfie? As if!" snickered Linn. "Anyway, stop trying to hide it. If you and Billy have got something going on, then…"

But I'd stopped listening: my radar ears had now tuned into what was going on out in the hall.

It wasn't the fact that my dad was talking on the phone; it was the fact that he sounded like he was *whispering* on the phone.

"What is it?" asked Rowan, spotting straight away that I wasn't paying a blind bit of attention to Linn's wind-up any more.

"Shhhh!" I muttered, with one ear to the living room door.

The door thunked as Linn and Rowan darted over and barged into me, wanting to hear what I could hear. Even Tor slunk up silently, ducking under our arms and placing his ear at pole position at the tiny gap in the door.

"Yes, it was great, just like old times…" we heard our dad say, sheepishly.

Linn stared hard at me, and over my shoulder at Rowan, who was standing behind me, her hot, anxious breath on my neck.

"It's been a long time, that's for sure…"

"What's going on?" Rowan whispered. "What's he on about?"

Shhh! mimed Linn, with a finger

"…yes – definitely. I would love that…" my dad muttered. And then, with a small, wry laugh, "No, I haven't told them yet…"

Linn fixed her eyes on me, her stare saying exactly what I was thinking. I couldn't see Rowan's expression, but I felt her trembly hand on my shoulder.

"You don't think…?" I whispered.

"Shhh!" said Linn, dropping her gaze downwards to the top of Tor's head.

That was the problem. We'd always protected Tor from stuff, and we couldn't let him know that we were all thinking the same thing.

Was this… Could this be something to do with *Mum*?

Chapter 3

THE TALE OF THE INVISIBLE MUM...

"Ally? It's me – can I come in?" Linn called out softly from the other side of the door.

I'd become very popular all of a sudden. Normally, around eleven o'clock on Saturday night, I'd be the only one in my room (the odd cat included, and *all* our cats are odd), unless Sandie was staying over, which she sometimes did.

But tonight, my room was like a magnet; three (out of five) cats, both dogs and my sister Rowan were taking up space inside my four small walls and under my slanted roof. The cats – Frankie, Colin and Fluffy – were already here when me and Rolf padded upstairs after a non-eventful night in front of the telly with Dad and Tor (my social calendar wasn't exactly packed this particular Saturday night). And Winslet had followed Rowan in when she'd come tapping at my door (Winslet – smart but grumpy dog that she is – obviously sniffing out that this was the place to be).

At this rate, I was expecting to open the door and

see Mad Max the hamster leading a procession of iguanas, white mice and stick insects up the stairs from Tor's room at any second.

"Yeah – come on in!" I replied, keeping my voice low.

I didn't really want to alert my dozing dad that there was a bit of a family pow-wow happening upstairs in the attic.

Linn had only opened the door a crack when a cat that wasn't Colin slithered his black and white body through the gap. He scampered past me and Rowan, who were sprawled on the floor, and leapt – light as a furry feather – up on to my bed. At closer range, I checked out the fight-chewed ears and sussed out it was Eddie. All we needed was for cross-eyed Derek to come scratching at the door and we'd have a full house in the feline department.

"Oh…" said Linn, looking a little put out to see that Rowan had beaten her to it.

"Hey, Linn – how did it go tonight?" I asked our eldest sister. "You're back early, considering you were going to a party."

"I left early – I wasn't in the mood," she shrugged, shutting the door behind her and joining us on the floor. "I kept thinking about Dad…"

I couldn't blame her; I'd spent the whole evening pretending to watch whatever was flickering on the

TV screen, when all that was really running through my head was Dad and that weird phone call.

(Still, imagine being at a party with Alfie and choosing to leave! But then Linn doesn't see Alfie the way *I* do. That girl's *got* to need specs – it's the *only* explanation. Specs, or a brain transplant. One of the two...)

"Me too," said Rowan, running her hands through her dark curls and sending her Indian bangles jangling. "I was round at Chazza's tonight, and he was showing me and Von what he could play on his new guitar—"

Linn rolled her eyes at the thought of how boring *that* sounded, but thankfully, Rowan was too distracted by Frankie padding on to her lap to notice.

"—but I couldn't stop thinking about Dad," Rowan continued. "And what he was saying on the phone and ... everything."

Everything ... meaning Mum. Or at least our suspicions that his conversation had been to do with her.

Or even *with* her.

"So, Ally – did he say anything about it tonight?" asked Linn, leaning back on her elbows on my threadbare carpet, then sitting up again smartish when she felt how uncomfortable that was going to be. "Anything at all?"

"No," I shook my head. "He just made jokes about what was on the telly, then went up and read Tor a bedtime story. The usual."

Me and my sisters hadn't had the time or the opportunity to talk before Linn and Rowan had gone out. For one thing, Tor was there (and we didn't want to set his little mind whirling), and for another thing, Dad came blustering in to the room as soon as he'd finished the call, cheerily demanding to know what rubbish questions he'd missed on the quiz show.

(You should have seen how fast the four of us moved when we heard the phone go *ping!* as he put the receiver down. One second we were behind the living-room door – the next we were all back in our places on the sofa etc., trying *very* hard not to sound out of breath.)

"But once Tor went to bed," Linn continued to quiz me, "didn't he even give you a little hint then?"

"No, he didn't say anything. No hints, nothing."

I'd just been through all this with Rowan, and I knew what Linn's next question was going to be, mainly 'cause Rowan had asked it thirty seconds before Linn came knocking.

"Couldn't you have pumped him for a bit of information?" asked Linn, right on cue.

"No. I thought about it, but I couldn't work out what to say that didn't let on that we'd been listening in on his conversation," I tried to explain.

But it was no good – my two sisters were looking at me with total disappointment. I'd been their only hope to solve the riddle this evening and I'd failed miserably.

"So, do you think he *could* have been talking to Mum?" asked Rowan, finally saying out loud what we'd all wondered.

I'd thought of nothing else for the entire evening, but to be honest, I couldn't see how it could be true. I couldn't believe that Dad would keep anything to do with Mum a secret from us (except for Tor – we *all* kept things secret from Tor, for his own sake). Especially not after four whole years...

So maybe it's a good time to tell you what happened with Mum. It's more complicated than you might think, mainly because there're are *two* versions: the short one and the long one (otherwise known as the white-lie version and the truth). I might as well tell you both, since the first one doesn't take up much room...

Tale of the Disappearing Mum (the short version): this is the one Tor believes. Mum loved all of us so much that she felt terrible about all the children in the world that have no one to care for them. That's why she decided to go away for a while – leaving us in Dad's safe care – and work for a charity that sends her to faraway places. There are lots of countries out there and lots of children to look after, and that's why she's been away so long. But she'll be home one day…

Tale of the Disappearing Mum (the truth): basically, Mum was only seventeen (and Dad was twenty-two) when the two of them started going out. Mum had just finished school and was working in the jeans shop in Camden, but was planning on hiring a craft stall in the market to sell all her paintings and pottery, then using the money she'd make from that to take off round the world for a year, before going on to art school. That was the plan. Then – oops! – she found out she was pregnant with Linnhe (think: Linny. Not that anyone calls her that. Except Rowan, that is).

Anyway, once they'd got over the shock, Mum and Dad were blissfully happy; and, by the time Mum was eighteen, she found herself in her own little flat, married to Dad and with a small bundle of baby to look after.

Fast-forward through ten very happy years (and they *were* happy – I remember lots of it, even though some of it's kind of hazy now), to the time when Mum had Tor. All of us knew that Mum had changed a little bit; she still laughed and had fun with us, but we'd sometimes catch her looking sad, even though she'd say she was all right ("Post-natal depression that just didn't get better," Grandma explained to us much, much later). Then, when Tor was three, Mum and Dad had this long chat with us girls one night (Linn was thirteen, Rowan was eleven and I was nine), and announced that Mum had decided to go travelling for three months, to see some of the places she'd meant to visit on that long ago year-round trip she'd had to cancel. It didn't sound too long to us; we were big girls and could cope, helping Dad around the house. It would be an adventure for us too.

Next thing, she'd been gone six months – always sending cheery letters and postcards home to us – and we three girls began to get suspicious. We *definitely* got suspicious when Dad started to get gloomy and Grandma sold her house and moved to a flat just along the road "so she could look after us better". I don't know when it was exactly that we all began to think she *wasn't* coming back, but eventually that's the way we all saw it, and the way we've expected it to be ever since…

(But you can see why we stick to the first version for Tor. You don't want a little kid to think he's the one to blame for his mother disappearing off into the sunset, for ever. It would be pretty tough to handle, figuring your Mum got ill 'cause she brought you into the world. The nice, fluffy, charity-work story is a lot better for him, if you see what I mean.)

So here we were now – the three eldest of the Love children – wondering if we'd got it wrong; if Mum really was closer at hand than we'd thought.

"Well, all that 'it's just like old times' and 'no I haven't told them yet' stuff Dad was saying on the phone," mused Linn. "It definitely *sounds* like he was talking to her."

"And he did go out on Wednesday night," Rowan chipped in, her face all taut and tense. "Remember? He said he was going for a drink with the guy from the plumber's next door to the shop."

"Oh, yeah…" I muttered, remembering Dad hastily scrambling out of the door, looking slightly overdressed just to go and sink a couple of pints in a local pub.

And we were bound to notice when Dad went out; he did it so rarely. After Mum left, I think he felt he had to over-compensate for the fact that we were one parent down, and he always tried to be around for us.

"And he'd done his hair that funny way – all greased back. Like it was in some of those old photos of him and Mum when they were young. We

231

were teasing him about it," Linn reminded us.

"Wow, do you think the pub story was just a cover?" asked Rowan, wide-eyed.

Frankie was trying to wriggle out from her heavy-handed stroking, I noticed.

"Maybe," shrugged Linn. "Maybe he got all dressed up to go and meet *Mum* somewhere…"

"But, hold on," I said, scrambling to my feet and going over to the big map of the world on my wall. "We got a letter from Mum last week, and she was *here*…"

I pointed to a blue pin stuck on a small island in the Pacific Ocean. Every time we get a letter from her, I check where it's from and mark it on my map.

"So?" said Rowan. "What difference does that make?"

I can be a prize-winning worrier, but Rowan *really* gets herself in a stressed-out mess. You know, forgets to engage her brain, she's so busy panicking. And right now it wasn't just the look on her face that was giving her away; it was the fact that she had Frankie in a vice-like grip in her arms. Poor Frankie – he'd only been looking for a warm lap to sit in and he'd found himself being used as a feline worry-bead.

"*Think* about it, Ro," I urged her. "Mum wrote that she was planning to stay where she was for a couple of weeks, so—"

"—so she *couldn't* be back yet," Linn finished off my train of thought.

"Probably not," I replied, not sure whether to be reassured or hideously disappointed by that realization.

"So, if it wasn't *Mum* that Dad was talking to on the phone," Rowan said slowly, "where does that leave us?"

"Back at square one," I sighed, flopping down so hard on the bed that Eddie – much to his surprise – found himself bouncing off the duvet and up into the air.

Chapter 4

SANDIE'S SMART THINKING

Q: What's white and red, and drips all over?
A: My mate Sandie.

Well, that would be the answer, this one particular Sunday afternoon.

Sandie's face had gone waxy white, but her rotten cold had left her with a scabby red nose and upper lip as a fashionable contrast. Add to that two nostrils that were running like taps, and you get the picture. (And it wasn't pretty...)

"How are you feeling?" I asked.

Stupid, really, since it was so obvious how she was feeling. And that was *lousy*.

I noticed that the carpet beside her bed was strewn with soggy, scrunched-up paper hankies, even though there was a wicker wastepaper basket strategically placed within chucking distance. But not placed strategically enough, by the looks of it.

"I feel absoludely derrible..." sniffed Sandie, punctuating her medical update with a parping blow into a man-sized tissue.

Her big Disney eyes were particularly pathetic –
all dewy-wet and sad. Or maybe she looked more
like one of the bunnies out of *Watership Down*.
Maybe the one with myxomatosis...

"You don't *seem* very well," I agreed, which was
an understatement.

I was perched on the end of her bed, well out of
the catchment range of tissue-chucking.

"Id's really sweed of you to come – bud you
shouldn'd have," she scolded me with a grateful
smile. "You mide cadge this cold!"

"Great! I get a legitimate excuse to stay off
school!" I joked.

I didn't mean it. It wasn't like I loved school to
pieces or anything, but I'd much rather have been
going to classes than looking as bad as Sandie did
right there and then.

I moved further back on the bed, and hoped I was
well out of the germ radius.

Maybe it would have been a better idea to just
phone rather than visit.

"So, I guess *you* won't be coming back to school
tomorrow..." I said, astutely. Not.

Sandie shook her head. She was like this
disembodied head (a white, red and dripping head)
above a sea of cutesy teddies. Cutesy teddy duvet
cover, cutesy teddy pillowcase, matching cutesy

teddy pyjamas. All bought by her mother, I hasten to add. No fellow thirteen-year-old friend of *mine* would willingly sleep amongst cutesy teddies if he or she had freedom of choice…

"Mum says I'll have to sday in bed a couple of days ad leased," she mumbled forlornly, through her bunged-up nose.

I couldn't blame her for sounding down. Sandie's mother was one of those suffocating, overprotective mums at the best of times. But if Sandie was ill, she'd be even worse – fluttering about, plumping up pillows and shovelling her daughter full of medicine every five seconds.

The thing is, much as they love her, Sandie's parents are the reason she comes round to my place so much. They're both about a hundred and ten (OK, so I exaggerate, but her folks *are* old), and treat Sandie (their only kid) like she's a cross between a china Dresden doll and a precious, delicate butterfly. Thank goodness they approve of me, or Sandie would have no fun at all. Mind you, they've never seen my house. They would probably never let her through the door ever again if they saw how ramshackle our place is (despite my Grandma's best efforts to civilize it). And if they knew how many animals there were, they'd be apoplectic about Sandie catching cat-flea allergies, or distemper from the dogs or something.

"Ally, can you do me a favour?" Sandie sniffed, pointing over to the candy-pink painted table by her bedroom door.

Honestly, you should see her room. Everything in it is pink; and not that mad, raspberry pink that Rowan's done her room in (which sears your eyeballs to the back of your brain, but is still somehow cool). No, everything in Sandie's room is in shades of candy or bubblegum pink. With frills. It's like being in Life-Sized Barbie's room, for God's sake.

And Sandie hates it.

I know, I know, it was her choice in the first place ... but that was when she was *eight*. She's been desperate to redecorate it for the last three or four years, but her parents won't let her. They think her room is "just adorable". If you ask me (and even if you *don't* ask me, I'm going to tell you), I think it's 'cause they want to keep their little girl *little*, if you see what I mean. Growing up, having periods, snogging boys; I think they've blocked all that out and are just pretending it's *never* going to happen.

(And, just for the record, Sandie *is* growing up – she's got bigger boobs than me, but then *every*one does; she *has* started her periods – aged twelve at my house and Linn sorted her out; and she *has* kissed boys – even though it was just during games of Spin the Bottle and that kind of stupid party stuff.)

"What is it? What are you after?" I asked, scanning the top of the table, and hoping Sandie didn't seriously want the white teddy sitting on it with the silk heart that had "We wuv you!" embroidered on it. (A Christmas present from her parents. *No*, not when she was at primary school; *this* year…)

"Can you pass me thad new box of dissues off the dable?" she asked.

I had to laugh.

"You sound just like Billy did yesterday," I smiled at my own joke.

"Whad – does he have a cold doo?" frowned Sandie, all concerned.

"No," I shrugged. "I was just torturing him by twisting his nose off."

"Why?" Sandie quizzed me, looking confused.

"He's a boy, he's annoying … what more is there to say?" I shrugged.

It's funny; Billy's my oldest mate and Sandie's my best mate, but they just don't really hit it off together. They like each other and everything, but they just don't seem to gel. We do all go out as a threesome sometimes – mostly to the movies, where they don't have to speak to each other too much – but usually I see them separately. Billy's told me he thinks Sandie's too quiet, and he doesn't know what to say to her. But to be fair to Sandie, he *does* tend to act more stupid and show-offy in front of her. Nerves, I suppose. And Sandie says she thinks he doesn't like her, which to me translates as Sandie feeling a bit insecure about me having another close friend, other than her.

It gets on my wick a bit, actually, but I like both of them so much that I don't let it bother me most of the time.

"So whad did you do lassed nide?" asked Sandie, using her nail to spear the new box of hankies I'd just given her.

It took me a second to translate what she'd said from virus-speak to English.

"Last night? Nothing…" I replied.

"Billy nod up for doing anything?" she asked, checking I wasn't getting too friendly with him behind her sickly back.

"No – he was seeing some guys from his school," I told her. "And I phoned Chloe and the others, but no one was up for doing anything."

Sandie looked quite pleased. I think she'd have felt like she was missing out if I'd ended up spending a brilliant Saturday night out with Billy, or Chloe or Salma or any of our other friends from school. And who could blame her – I'd probably be the same if it was the other way around.

"So whad did you do?" she asked.

"I just stayed in with Dad and Tor and watched telly," I explained. "But something weird *did* happen…"

Sandie's enormous eyes seemed to light up. But maybe that was just fever.

"Whad?" she demanded through her blocked nose. "Whad happened?"

You could tell how bored she was after two days of being incarcerated at home. The remotest *hint* of something gossip-worthy had got her going.

"My dad – me and the others overheard him having this phone call. He was saying all this stuff like 'I can't wait till next time' and everything…"

"Whad – like he's been on a *date*?" she practically squealed.

Sandie loves anything remotely romantic, she really does.

"Well, me and Linn and Rowan *almost* thought he might have been out with … with our mum."

Sandie's jaw dropped.

Like Billy, she knows the whole story to do with my mum and her disappearing trick. To everyone else at school, I just say my mum lives abroad. No one gives me a hard time about it – I guess one good thing about so many people my age coming from broken and re-modelled families means that having a mum living abroad doesn't raise anyone's eyebrows or interest too much.

"Do you really think id's your mum?" she gasped.

"Actually, no – I don't think it can be," I admitted. "It doesn't add up – she's still supposed to be out on the Cook Islands for a while. We had a letter; she *couldn't* be back…"

"Well, id's obvious, then," said Sandie, matter-of-factly.

"What is?" I frowned.

"Your dad," she continued, "is seeing someone new."

Sandie isn't what you'd normally call intuitive. When it comes to the two of us, she always shuts up and lets me do all the talking or deciding (which drives me crazy sometimes). And she was *well* off-course here; my dad seeing someone new? How ridiculous! It must be those cold germs short-circuiting her brain…

There was no *way* my dad was seeing someone new.

No *way*.

Or…

Or was there?

Chapter 5

RING, RING – WHO'S THERE?

I squinted at my plate, and tried to figure out what it was we were supposed to be eating.

It was Rowan's turn to make the Sunday tea again. How did her turn come around again so quickly? What had we done in a previous life to deserve it?

"This is—"

Dad stopped to cough.

"—lovely, Rowan. Er, what is it?"

Bless him, he always tries to pretend Rowan's efforts are edible. (I know I serve up fish fingers, spaghetti and beans with boring regularity when it's *my* turn to make meals, but at least people don't get *food* poisoning from it...)

Linn swirled her fork round in the pink sludge with a look of pure horror on her face. And she hadn't even tasted it yet.

"Is it pudding?" asked Tor.

"No," said Rowan, sitting down at her place round the kitchen table and looking slightly flustered. "Who ever heard of getting just *pudding* for tea?"

"Well, if it's not pudding, why's it pink?" Tor asked her straight out.

"It's *pink*," sighed Rowan, as if she was a world-class chef who was being questioned by a lowly punter, "because it's got *beetroot* in it."

"Beetroot's red," I pointed out.

And not unfairly, I don't think.

"I put it in the liquidizer, with natural yoghurt," Rowan explained. "To make a sauce..."

I gulped.

I had to ask the next question, if no one else would.

"To make a sauce for *what* exactly?" I asked, gingerly poking about in the lumpy pink goo with my fork.

"Roasted vegetables," she replied.

"Roasted vegetables?" said Dad, raising his eyebrows enthusiastically. "*They're* good for you!"

"And fruit," Rowan added.

"*Fruit?*" squealed Linn, spitting out her first, tentative mouthful. "What kind of *fruit*?!"

"Peaches," said Rowan defiantly. "I found a tin in the cupboard. I thought it would make it a sort of ... sweet-and-sour thing."

You know, sometimes I think Rowan stares at the fairy lights in her room too long...

Suddenly the phone shrilled out louder than Linn's

protests, and Dad went rushing out to the hall before any of us could get up off our seats to get it.

"Look – he's shut the door!" Linn hissed over the table, the terrible tea soon forgotten in the face of more secrecy on Dad's part.

"Yeah – he must be expecting this call, and doesn't want us to hear!" Rowan pointed out.

"Why not? Why doesn't he want us to hear?" Tor piped up, reminding us all that we should keep our mouths well and truly shut in his presence.

"Because it's just boring business stuff," I assured our little brother, wrinkling up my nose. "Hey – doesn't that sound like one of the cats yowling outside?"

It was smart thinking on my part – in a split-second, Tor had leapt out of his seat and tugged open the back door, heading out into the garden in search of any four-legged friend (or three-legged, in Colin's case) in need of his help.

"Listen," I whispered to my two sisters, while we had a moment to ourselves. "Sandie said something today…"

Linn rolled her eyes. At a time like this, she wasn't exactly scintillated by the notion of listening to whatever my best friend had to say – *that* was plain to see.

"What? What did Sandie say?" asked Rowan.

Bless Rowan – she's a weirdo, but at least she's a

weirdo who's prepared to listen.

"Sandie said that maybe…"

I lost my nerve for a second.

"…Um, that Dad maybe has a new girlfriend," I finished off. "Maybe."

Linn and Rowan's jaws dropped till they nearly hit the hideous pink creation on their plates. But they said nothing, so they were obviously considering the idea.

"I think…"

I stared at Linn, waiting to see what she made of it all. Normally, I was quite happy for my know-all big sister to keep her opinions where the sun don't shine, but tonight, for once, I actually wanted to hear what Linn thought.

"I think," she began again, "that Sandie could be right."

Rowan looked like she might cry. She hangs out with her cool, older friends and everything, but she's all marshmallow inside, really.

"So, what do we do?" I asked Linn, hoping she had a smart answer.

"We watch and listen," said Linn, staring from me to Rowan and back again.

"Spying, you mean?" Rowan gulped.

"If that's what it takes, yes."

Linn would make a great Bond girl, she really would…

Chapter 6

I'LL TELL YOU MINE, IF YOU TELL ME YOURS

There's this kind of broad, tree-lined avenue that leads into Alexandra Palace (one of about seventy thousand ways to get into the whole park area).

It's not really open to cars, except when there's some big, fancy exhibition going on at weekends. But during the week, it's shut off as a road by these big ornate gates, with just the odd cyclist using it as a scenic short-cut, away from the traffic, or people with pooches on their way to the grassy expanses of the park.

Course, there are times of the day when the avenue – and all the old wooden benches that line it – gets busier. Like after four o'clock on week-days; that's when it becomes the unofficial snogging (and smoking) venue for loads of people from our school.

I was there this one Monday, idly wondering if the greeny-coloured, damp mould that covered the bench I was sitting on was going to stain my trousers. I was also letting my finger run along the groove of a badly carved heart, with the initials "E.K. luvs S.W." inside. I wondered if they belonged to anyone I knew. I couldn't help feeling momentarily jealous; I hate vandalism of any sort (and hacking love-hearts on park benches with a pen-knife is vandalism, I suppose) but I couldn't help wondering if there'd ever be a time when someone scratched "X.X. luvs A.L." on a lump of wood for *me*.

Though, I think I'd prefer someone more literate. Like someone who could spell "love" properly, for a start...

Now before you get the wrong idea, no, I wasn't there snogging anyone. And no, I wasn't there smoking either (please, credit me with a *brain*). I was there because the avenue is also quite a good place to hang out and gossip (usually about the people who are snogging), if you're not in the mood to hurry home.

Today, since Sandie was still lying in her snotty sickbed, I found myself sitting on a bench chatting with Kyra. Or more like *not* chatting with Kyra.

I stopped picking at the carved initials and stared at her as she checked the messages on her mobile phone. The one she was listening to seemed to be going on for ever, and whatever was being said wasn't exactly lighting up her life.

"Sorry about that," she apologized, finally clicking

off her phone and slipping it back into her bag. "I was hoping for something a bit more exciting than my mum ranting on about the fifty million things I've got to pick up from the shops on the way home…"

I shrugged like I hadn't noticed how long she'd been. I wasn't really sure what to say either; the ins and outs of Kyra's relationship with her mum were still a mystery to me (all I knew was that it was bad, and that her mum had some kind of drinking problem). And since I didn't know Kyra well enough yet to go noseying into her life, I'd decided to keep schtum till she told me herself. *If* she ever wanted to.

"So, I see Teresa Smith's got zero taste in men!" said Kyra, brightening up.

I looked where *she* was looking and saw Teresa Smith – only the prettiest girl in the year above us – losing her street cred with amazing speed. There, in front of anyone who cared to watch, she was holding hands and staring slushily into the eyes of some non-entity in a Muswell School for Boys uniform. It wasn't the fact that he wasn't anything special that was ruining her reputation; it was the fact that with the hand she *wasn't* holding, he was slowly and unself-consciously scratching his bum. And not just a genteel one-finger scratch. Oh, no – this was a fullhanded gouge worthy of any of the baboons down at London Zoo.

"Hope she's not going to hold *that* hand now…" I muttered to Kyra.

"It's one of those times you wish you had a video camera, isn't it?" giggled Kyra. "We could send it into that TV show; make ourselves a bit of money!"

I knew she was only joking (wasn't she?), but it didn't seem like Kyra particularly needed any extra money. Apart from living in one of the poshest turnings in Crouch End, Kyra had a few trimmings that definitely spelt "dosh", and plenty of it. Like, her phone – it wasn't any old standard mobile. It was one of those snoot, tiny ones I'd seen advertised for more money than my dad pulled in at his shop in a slow week.

Not that my dad would buy stuff like mobile phones even if he *had* the money. Technology kind of passes him by. We clubbed together and bought an answering machine for the shop one Christmas, but Dad just ended up taking it back to Argos and swapping it for a new tool box because he couldn't figure out how to work the thing. And as far as computers go, he can't get his head around websites and the Internet at all, even though Tor's tried to explain it to him loads of times.

Plenty of my friends have got their own phones

and computers. It doesn't really bother me that I don't, and it doesn't bother me that the most gadgety thing in our house is a video we've had for a hundred years (that was second-hand in the first place), mainly because I know how tough it is for Dad to keep everything together for us on his one, unspectacular wage. It doesn't bother Tor or Rowan either, but I know it *really* bothers Linn. That's why she's been frantically looking for a Saturday job – so she can start keeping herself in the style to which she'd *like* to become accustomed.

"Hey, what's up?" Kyra suddenly burst into my thoughts. "You're not drooling over Scratchy Boy, are you?"

I realized I'd had my eyes fixed a little too firmly on the bum of Teresa Smith's repulsive boyfriend for the last few seconds while I daydreamed. No wonder Kyra had got the wrong idea.

"No! No way!" I grimaced. "Disgusting geeks aren't exactly my type!"

Scruffy, I don't mind. A boy with the manners of a pig, I don't *think* so.

"So what *is* your type?" asked Kyra, narrowing her eyes at me.

We were still at that getting-to-know-you-better stage, me and Kyra. And Sandie, of course. Ever since we'd had the bust-up and make-up over the

History project we'd done together, we three had all started to hang out a bit more. My other friends – Chloe, Jen, Salma and Kellie – thought me and Sandie were insane. They still reckoned that Kyra was a number-one show-off and a pain-in-the-doodah (and I understand why, since I used to see her in exactly the same way). But I'd come round to thinking that it was just a bad case of new-school nerves that made her try too hard and come over so bolshy and full-on.

"*I* don't know about what *type* of boy I go for!" I said, trying to laugh off her question.

Which was a downright lie, actually. Like most people, I can fancy all sorts of different boys for all sorts of different reasons, but I wouldn't need to do much thinking to come up with my *perfect* boy.

"Come on!" said Kyra, nudging me in the ribs with her elbow. "You tell me your type, and I'll tell you mine!"

The only person (apart from me, natch) that knew about my mega-crush on Alfie was Sandie, and I wanted it to stay that way. But what harm could this do? I could describe Alfie, without ever saying exactly who he was...

"Well," I mused, "I guess I like boys with short, messily spiky blond hair..."

"And?"

Kyra raised her eyebrows at me, egging me on.

"And light-grey eyes," I sighed. "You know – the sort that make you go a bit wobbly when you look into them, they're so spooky and pale."

"Go on!"

I didn't need much encouragement. Speaking about Alfie, even anonymously like this, was pretty much a pleasure.

"And I like guys who have great smiles. And maybe a little gold tooth somewhere at the side. That's cute. And I don't like jewellery on boys much, but you know those leather strappy bracelet things you get in Camden Market and places?"

Kyra nodded.

"Yeah, I like them," I continued, "on boys with skinny, muscular arms."

"So," said Kyra, staring at me intently now. "Who is this guy?"

"What guy?" I replied nervously. "You just told me to tell you what type I liked!"

"Come on, Ally!" she grinned. "That's not a type – that's a police photofit! You've obviously got one person in mind…"

I'm *so* transparent, I really am. I think I'm being clever and subtle and everything, but all the time I'm easier to read than a Year One ABC book.

"There's no one!" I blustered on, hoping against hope that she'd believe me. Kyra laughed out loud.

"You liar!" she giggled. "This guy sounds all right by your description, so what's the problem with him? Why can't you say who he is? What's the catch – is he only eleven or something?"

"He's four years *older* than me, actually!" I contradicted her bad-taste joke, and at the same time walked right into her trap.

"Aha! So we're getting somewhere!" shrieked Kyra, clapping her hands together as if prodding at my love life was the best game in the world. "Does he go to our school?"

"No. He goes to a sixth-form college over in Highgate…" I mumbled.

"Well? So tell!" she shrugged. "What's the point in keeping it from me?"

I couldn't think of *one* point, right at that moment, and although I thought I'd probably regret it, I ended up telling her who it was.

"His name's Alfie. He's best mates with my sister Linn," I explained, sheepishly.

"Does Linn know you fancy him?"

"God, no!" I squeaked.

The very idea made my blood run icy. Linn would *not* approve of one of her sisters fancying her best buddy – that would be far too juvenile for her. She'd never bring him around to the house ever again.

"Does he fancy you?"

"God, *no*!"

If only.

If only I could speak to him without turning into a gibbering, babbling fool, that would be a start.

"Why not? What's so weird about that?"

I was stumped. What a strange concept – Kyra honestly couldn't see why Alfie might not be interested in me. I'd spent the last few years stacking up all the reasons why someone like him could never be interested in someone like me, and now Kyra was putting a completely different spin on things.

Maybe it wasn't such a terrible idea talking to her about it after all...

"Oh – that's my phone! It could be him!"

Kyra jerked at the twittering tune jangling from her mobile, and dived into her bag to retrieve it.

I was feeling instantly deflated now that our Alfie conversation had been interrupted.

"Him who?" I asked distractedly, as I watched her practically turn her bag upside down to find her mobile.

"My new boyfriend!" Kyra grinned and whispered quickly, before she answered her phone.

Her new boyfriend?

Since when?

She hadn't even got round to telling me what *type* she went for yet, and now she had a *boyfriend*?!

Chapter 7

CUPID STRIKES AGAIN (NOWHERE NEAR ME...)

You know what was doing my head in? The fact that Kyra Davies had lived in Crouch End for about five minutes, and she'd got herself a boyfriend, just like that.

Me? I've lived here all my life, and all I've managed to chalk up is four (lousy) dates with Keith Brownlow when I was twelve and had no taste.

All the way home from the park, I couldn't help festering over how jealous I was. Not jealous of *Kyra* exactly (it wasn't like I wanted to get a voodoo doll of her and stick pins in it); just jealous of the whole idea of having a boyfriend. And that made me really mad with myself – it was so pathetic that I wanted one anyway. What was the point? My two friends who *had* had boyfriends (Salma and Jen) spent half the time they were supposed to be happily dating just moaning on about the boys, and how they never phoned when they said they would, drooled over other girls when they were out with them, and how generally useless they were. Their experience of boyfriends (as well as my *own* fleeting experience) should have put me off the whole idea.

But it didn't.

"Hello!" I shouted to no one in particular, as I barged grumpily through the front door.

I let my schoolbag drop with a clatter on to the floor and shoved my jacket on to the coat rack.

"Hello," I heard a small voice say, as I stomped past the staircase towards the kitchen, where Radio Two was blasting out some corny old song.

(Me and my sisters always retune to Radio One at breakfast, and Grandma switches it back to Radio Two when she gets in after picking up Tor from school.)

"What are you doing?" I asked, stopping to squint at my little brother.

Tor had his legs wrapped round a pole in the bannister, and was dangling backwards, his fingertips nearly touching the wooden hall floor.

"Being upside down," he stated, slightly breathlessly.

"Your face is bright red," I pointed out, turning my head around to get a better view of his beetroot-tinted features.

"Is it?" he replied, seeming quite pleased about it.

"Shout if you need a hand down," I told him, as I strolled off into the kitchen, where the smell of something good managed to lift my spirits.

Ah, the joy of Monday to Friday, when Grandma makes our tea. When everyone's guaranteed not to moan, or end up with violent indigestion.

"He's still upside down, is he?" muttered Grandma, leaning down and prodding at something in the oven.

"Yep," I said, flopping on to one of the wooden chairs around our big old table. "What's he up to?"

"They did something about bats in school today," she replied.

Well, that explained that. Tor loved animals so much that it wasn't a great surprise that he was trying to turn into one.

"What are you making, Grandma?" I asked, sniffing the air like I was one of the dogs. (Talk about *Tor* turning into an animal...)

"An aubergine and mascarpone bake."

"Huh?"

"Well, a vegetable and cheese bake, in plain English," Grandma explained, closing the oven door and straightening up. "Saw it on *Ready, Steady, Cook* the other day."

"Smells great," I nodded.

Grandma's always trying out new recipes off the TV on us. And I'd just like to take this opportunity to personally thank all the programme controllers for putting so many cookery shows on – if it wasn't for them, our weekday teas would be a lot less interesting.

"Well, you'll just have to tell me what this one's like – I can't stay and eat with you tonight," said Grandma, peering into the small mirror beside the back door and primping up her already immaculate blondey-grey hair.

"Why – what are you doing?" I asked, while marvelling at how neat Grandma was.

Not just in the way she looked and dressed, but the way the kitchen was so spotless and ordered, even though she'd been busy throwing food together for us five seconds before. I'm the total opposite – I even manage to make a mess at breakfast. There's always sticky bits on the table where I've poured (and dribbled) orange juice, and I always have to do a toast-crumbs-in-my-hair check in the hall mirror before I leave for school.

"I'm going out…" Grandma hesitated, looking uncharacteristically flustered for a second. "I'm going on what you girls would probably call a *date*."

Well, knock me down with a vegetable and cheese bake. One minute I'm in the park with Kyra, getting told she has a boyfriend (and being deserted two seconds after she gets off the phone, 'cause she's got to meet him, and promising she'll tell me more later). Next thing I'm home, and my Grandma is telling me more or less the same thing.

"Who is he?" I demanded, feeling even more rejected and loveless now that even my sixty-year-old grandmother had pulled.

"His name's Stanley, and I met him at my friends' wedding-anniversary party a couple of weeks ago," said Grandma, matter-of-factly.

"Is he nice?" I asked, a little more warmly.

It was silly to be so grumpy with her. It wasn't her fault that *I* wasn't going out with anyone, and it wasn't as if I was going to be too jealous of her new bloke.

"Very nice. He's a retired engineer."

Yep, I definitely didn't have the hots for Stanley the retired engineer.

"So, where are you two going?" I asked, wondering if I should push it and make a joke about her being sure to get home to her flat by eleven o'clock or she'd be grounded, but Grandma looked a little too self-conscious about the whole thing to take a joke.

"Just one of the restaurants near Crouch End Broadway. I forget which one he said," muttered Grandma, wafting her hand vaguely around in the air. "Anyhow, Rowan's outside taking in the washing. Why don't you give her a hand?"

I was dismissed. Grandma had had enough of gossiping about her love life with me, that was for sure. It's funny; her and Linn are so alike. If they're done talking to you, it's like the shutters come down and that's that.

Pulling open the squeaky back door, I saw Rowan wrestling for control of a pink, flowery pair of pants with Winslet.

"Let go! Leave! I said, *leave*!" she squeaked.

But Winslet didn't *want* to leave. She'd carefully selected the pants from the mound of newly dried clothes in the laundry basket lying on the grass, and was planning on adding them to the ever-changing collection of stolen items hidden under her doggy blanket. (She may be a short, hairy, grumpy dog now, but she *has* to have been a magpie in another life – it's the only explanation.)

"Need a hand?" I asked, bending down and grabbing Winslet by the scruff of her neck.

(It's a good trick that Tor taught me: get hold of a dog or cat by the scruff and they automatically open their jaws and drop whatever's in them – toys, mice, stolen pants...)

"Thanks. Yeuchhh! *These* are going straight back in the washing machine..." said Rowan, wrinkling up her nose and holding the knickers at arm's length.

"Those are Linn's, aren't they?" I asked, peering

at the floral pants.

"Oh, yeah, so they are!" said Rowan, brightening up. "Oh, well – I'm sure they'll be fine. I mean, what's a little dog saliva between friends…"

She dropped the knickers back in the pile of clean clothes and turned back to the washing line, a small, smug smile playing at her lips. Well, it's not often she manages to get one over on our bossy big sister.

"So," I began, holding out my cupped hands for Rowan to drop the pegs into. "What about Grandma having a date tonight, then?"

"Well, it's not really a big deal, is it?" Rowan shrugged. "Not compared to this stuff with Dad…"

Urgh – I'd managed to forget about that. Call me a coward (you're a coward, Ally Love), but I suddenly understood why ostriches bury their heads in the sand when trouble lurks. I'd put any thoughts about the business with Dad away in a small, dusty corner at the back of my mind, and now here was Rowan, reminding me about it all over again.

"I suppose so," I mumbled, as I half-heartedly shooed Winslet away from the laundry basket.

"Anyway, you know what Linn said about us keeping our eyes open?" Rowan whispered, peering over my shoulder at the open back door.

"You mean, about spying on him?" I said, more frankly.

"Yeah," Rowan nodded, making the halo of tiny, metallic butterfly clips holding her dark hair off her face glint in the late-afternoon sun. "Well, I found something!"

"Like what?" I asked, bending down and grabbing Winslet by the neck.

Automatically, the thief-dog dropped one of Tor's Pokémon socks and stared ruefully up at me.

"Like, I spotted the notepad beside the phone this morning," Rowan garbled, her eyes wide and shiny with her secret. "And on it, it said 'Wednesday', with these doodles of stars all round it!"

"OK, so he must have done that when he was on the phone last night – that call where he closed the door on us…"

"Exactly!" Rowan agreed with me. "So he must be going out with *her* again on Wednesday!"

Suddenly, I realized that I didn't care about Kyra having a new boyfriend. And Grandma seeing someone was just sweet. But what I did care about very, very much was the whole idea of Dad getting romantic with someone.

Someone who *wasn't* our mum…

Chapter 8

KYRA GOES TWINKLY

"Hi, Ally," said Kyra, hurrying along the school corridor towards me. "Listen, sorry I disappeared yesterday, but I *had* to meet Ricardo."

"Ricardo? Is he Italian, then?"

I hadn't even found out his name the day before, Kyra had been so desperate to sprint off and meet Wonderboy.

"Well, his family are, way back, I suppose," Kyra shrugged, leaning up against the radiator I was parked on. "Ricardo Esposito... Sounds really nice, doesn't it?"

Kyra was looking totally twinkly-eyed. The way she'd said it I had the feeling she'd already played that game of running your name together with his. "Kyra Esposito..." nah – I wouldn't run down to the registrar's to book the wedding straight away if *I* was her.

It was the start of breaktime on Tuesday morning, and I was idly mooching around, waiting to meet up with any of my friends who happened to amble by. (Not Sandie, though – she was still at home sinking under the weight of soggy tissues and being smothered by mother love.)

"So, come on – tell me about him," I grinned. "What's he like? When did you meet him?"

I'd decided I might as well be enthusiastic about this. If I didn't have a love life of my own, I might as well get a kick out of somebody else's.

"Well—" said Kyra, her light-brown skin flushing unexpectedly.

She comes across so loud and over-confident normally that it's always a surprise when you see little chinks of shyness like that (never mind the big chunks of insecurity I know are hidden away there too).

"—I went shopping in Wood Green with my dad on Saturday, and we ended up in one of those phone shops. Anyway, it looked like Dad was going to be in there for *ever*, so I said I'd wait for him in Burger King."

"And?"

I was intrigued. Girl Finds Love in Burger King. It didn't sound too promising...

"And Burger King was mobbed. So I spot this *really* cute lad sitting on his own at a table, and I asked if I could sit there for a while," Kyra gushed, her bushy, high ponytail bobbing as she talked. "*He* tells me he's keeping the table for his mates, but then he says of course I can sit down, if I want to!"

Amazing. If *I* saw a really cute lad sitting at an empty table, the last thing I'd do is ask to sit down. I'd never have the nerve. I'd just cower in a corner and stare longingly at him from a distance. But then maybe that's why Kyra had got herself a boyfriend and I hadn't.

"And then he asks my name, and I ask his, and we get talking… We must have been talking for about half an hour; then I look up, and see my dad coming in. So I say, 'Here's my dad – I better go', but he says, 'Quick – write down your phone number!' and shoves a serviette across the table at me. And I scribble down my number with this old eyeliner pencil I found at the bottom of my bag!"

"And he phoned you yesterday?" I asked.

"Yesterday? Huh! That was the *third* time he'd phoned me," Kyra beamed happily. "He already called on Saturday night, *and* Sunday afternoon!"

It was official: I was impressed. Compared to my one, pathetic attempt at going out with someone, this was like a Hollywood blockbuster.

"What's he like, then?" I quizzed her.

"Like I said, he's cute. He's got dark-brown hair, big brown eyes, a big cheeky smile. Looks a bit like he could be in a boy band. And he's dead chatty and funny."

So, definitely *not* like Keith Brownlow.

"When you saw him yesterday, what did you do?" I asked, raising my eyebrows at her, and getting a little cheeky myself.

"We just hung out. He jumped on a bus from his school—"

"Which school?"

Kyra frowned and glanced around like she was trying to figure out which way was north. She still hadn't been in this part of the world long enough to get the geography sorted out in her head.

"Um, can't remember the name. It's somewhere over that way, I think."

"Wood Green?" I guessed from the direction she was pointing, through a set of school walls. "I wonder which one it is…"

"Whatever," Kyra shrugged, not interested in boring details like schools. "So we just hung out for a while and talked."

"And … anything else?" I ventured.

She knew and *I* knew that we were talking snogging. It just seemed a bit tacky to come right out and say, "Did you snog, then?" even though it was the one thing I wanted to know.

"Maybe," grinned Kyra, shooting a sideways look at me. "But anyway, best of all, we're going out properly tomorrow night!"

"Where to?"

"Skating up at Alexandra Palace."

It's good up there. Good for boy-spotting that is, not for skating. Well, very good for skating if you *can* skate – which I can't. Tor has to hold my hand and literally *drag* me round the ice whenever we go there.

"That'll be fun," I mused.

Lots of hand-holding and giggling – skating has great touchy-feely potential. Good choice, Kyra.

"But you know what's stupid?" Kyra shrugged.

"What?"

"I don't know what to wear! I mean, on Saturday, he just saw me in my old combats and a T-shirt, and yesterday I was in school uniform. Tomorrow I'd really like to look different. Y'know – really nice!"

I knew the feeling. Whenever there's a party or something, it always takes me about a week to work out what to put on. All my mates are the same, and we have this thing where we try on outfits in front of each other just to road-test them. It's a real laugh, and we always end up swapping and borrowing stuff from each other. Maybe that's what Kyra needed – a bit of the dress-rehearsal treatment…

"Well, why don't I come back to yours after school today and help you choose something?" I offered.

OK, so I had an ulterior motive: I also wanted to check out her posh house in her posh street. And maybe get a glimpse of this mother she didn't get on with.

"Uh, nah – it's OK," she said, looking suddenly ruffled. "I'll probably just shove on a jumper and my padded vest top. We're going skating, after all, so I guess it'll just have to be warm stuff…"

Did I hit a raw nerve? I wondered to myself. *Doesn't she want to have anyone back to the house?*

"Um, anyway, I better go to the loo before the bell rings," she suddenly muttered.

Ooh, it did look like she wanted to change the subject.

"OK," I shrugged. "Shall I wait for you?"

"No, it's all right," she shook her head. "You go on without me!"

I got the hint.

Just as I turned to head towards my Maths classroom, as the end-of-break bell trilled, this horrible image popped into my head: Keith Brownlow. All this love stuff had brought it back to me – i.e. our rubbish attempt at dating – when I'd done a really good job of forgetting it for a long, long time.

You see, it started in that way that it often does in real life, and never, *ever* in movies. Keith Brownlow was this kind of cute-looking boy in a crowd of lads in the year above me. Then one day, out of the blue, one of his mates comes over and says, "My mate Keith fancies you. Do you want to go out with him?"

Now, I did a stupid thing: I was *so* flattered that someone cute-looking (and in the year above!) was interested in little old me, that I persuaded myself in two seconds flat that I was madly in love with him.

And so me and Keith Brownlow went out four times (twice, we just hung around the park; once, we went to Pizza Hut; and once, I watched him play football and hung out with him afterwards).

And it was all a horrible disaster. Partly, it was my fault, because I was spending all my time trying to persuade myself that I fancied him, when I didn't really. The rest was his fault – I mean, he may have looked cute, but he hardly ever *talked*. Every time I saw him, I ended up babbling like crazy, and all he'd do was grunt in reply. And I should never have let him kiss me. To be honest, I didn't even know he was going to *do* it. One minute he was hovering outside my gate, slugging on his Coke, after walking me home (in silence) from the football match. Next thing I know, he's lunged at me, suctioned his lips on to mine, and done that unforgettable burp, right in my mouth. Talk about a memorable first kiss.

I think he knew he'd blown it then. I scurried inside the house after he walked me home and hoped against hope that he'd never phone me or come near me again, and luckily he didn't. We'd both done this thing ever since, where we never looked at each other at school. Maybe it was juvenile, but it was a lot easier to pretend we'd never met than to remind ourselves what a huge, embarrassing mistake it was.

I shook the memory out of my head and tried to concentrate on where I was going. Right now, there were about a million people coming down the stairs that I was trying to go up, to get to my Maths class.

"Don't push!" I yelled, as this surge of Year Seven boys came towards me.

But of *course* they took no notice of me, and of *course* they kept on pushing. Next thing, I'm on the floor, with everything in my bag spilt everywhere.

I was just thanking my lucky stars that I'd decided to wear trousers and not a skirt that day (landing on your bum in full view of loads of people is bad enough – having your skirt over your head at the same time would be just *shameful*), when something made me look up.

Stepping over my scattered books right at this second was the one, the only, Keith Brownlow. He was doing our trick, I noticed, as I scrambled, red-faced, to my feet. He was staring down at the tiled floor and pretending he couldn't see me.

Phew.

And then I spotted what he was actually staring at.

The little blue box I kept in my bag had burst open, and my tampons were fanning out across the shiny red floor tiles...

Nice one, Ally! I told myself, wondering if I should just ram my empty bag over my head and make like an ostrich.

Chapter 9

SPEAKING IN DISGUISE

I was sitting at one end of the sofa, with my school books spread all around me, when Linn came bustling into the living room.

(Grandma had left ten minutes before, which is why I had my homework with me in the living room instead of upstairs at my desk. She's got this pet theory that you can't study properly in the same room as a TV; and to be honest, she's right. Instead of doing anything remotely swotty, I was gazing blankly at some holiday programme, while simultaneously reliving my humiliation in front of Keith Brownlow the previous day and stroking Colin the cat, who was gently snoring on top of my opened textbook.)

"I just saw Dad come out of the bathroom..." Linn hissed, scooting over and shifting some of my books so she could sit down.

At Linn's pronouncement, Rowan roused herself from flicking through her magazine. And Tor stopped playing his game of Spin the Bottle on the floor (which consisted of him hugging Rolf or Winslet, depending on where the empty plastic Coke bottle ended up pointing).

"…and he's done his hair all fancy!"

It was Wednesday night – the night we girls were primed to watch out for signs of Dad going out again. And you didn't get much more of a sign than Dad doing his hair.

"He's greased it back?" I asked, feeling my heart rate pick up.

For a long, long time we'd only ever seen it as short-ish, curly-ish and style-free. But years ago – and we had the photographic evidence in the albums in cupboard – he always wore it smoothed back, all slick and shiny like the teddy boys did in the fifties. That's what had first made our mum and dad fancy each other; they were both really into fashion – only fashion that was several *decades* out of date. Dad had this kind of rockabilly style, with his greased hair and checked shirts, worn with turned-up jeans and Doc Marten boots. Mum's style was straight out of the seventies, with her long wavy hair, velvet jackets and hippie dresses. They must have made a weird couple. But cool too, I think.

So Dad's retro hairdo *had* to mean something. He'd done it like that the previous week when he'd disappeared off for the pint or two with his "plumber mate" – but strangely enough, he hadn't said anything about going out tonight. Only the scribble on the phone pad had given that away.

"He's coming down the stairs!" whispered Rowan, hearing the thudding of footsteps a microsecond before the rest of us.

We must have looked like dress-shop dummies when Dad came into the room. Rowan, Tor, Linn and I were silently and stiffly glued to the TV, as if the story about scenic coach-trips for the over-sixties was just about the most fascinating thing we'd ever seen.

"Um, listen, I forgot to say…" said Dad, hovering in the doorway, awkwardly. "I'm just going out for a couple of hours. Just … popping out for a pint."

"With the plumber?" I asked, hoping I looked innocent.

"Um … yes, with the plumber. Jake, yeah…"

He didn't sound too convincing. And he didn't *look* too convincing either. He was wearing his best white shirt, and both it and his jeans were ironed, if I wasn't very much mistaken. What bloke would iron jeans (that were never normally anywhere within an eight-kilometre radius of an iron), just to go to the pub with a mate?

"Sorry, guys," he apologized. "I should have checked with you first. None of you are going out are you? Is someone OK to look after Tor?"

"Of course!"

"Yes!"

"Sure!"

The colliding voices of his three daughters must have caught Dad by surprise. I don't think he'd ever heard us sound so definite when it came to babysitting duties.

"Well, all right. Thanks, you lot," he said sheepishly, as he disappeared into the hall. "I won't be late!"

Linn darted over to the window as soon as we heard the front door shut.

"OK, he's gone," she said, ventriloquist-style through clenched teeth, as she smiled and waved Dad off.

She spun round, ready to talk over events with us, when something made her stop.

"What's happening?" asked Tor, narrowing his eyes at all three of us.

Tor – we'd forgotten about him in all the intrigue. He'd silently listened to us gossiping about the business of Dad's hair, and he'd played along with keeping quiet and watching the telly when Dad had walked in the room. But really, he hadn't a clue what we were all up to – and we wanted it to stay that way. After all, the night before, he got kind of worked up when Dad and us had been joking around about Grandma's hot date (we knew he was worked up because he didn't make his food into any shapes before he ate it, like he normally does). We finally got it out of him that he was scared Grandma wouldn't love him as much if she had a boyfriend. And if he was scared of *that*, then we sure didn't want him freaking out about Dad seeing someone else...

"We're just taking the mickey out of Dad, that's all," I tried to reassure him. "Just 'cause he's putting all that slimy gel in his hair!"

"It's wax, actually," he corrected me, earnestly.

You've got to watch it with kids sometimes; they're smarter than you think.

"Hey, do you suppose I should run after Dad?" asked Linn, trying to sound normal but staring meaningfully at me and Rowan. "You know – to check he's got his *keys*?"

It suddenly clicked – we were about to have a conversation in code. Me and my sisters sometimes do this when we want to keep stuff well over Tor's head. (And Grandma's, now and again. There *are* times when you don't want your gran to know *everything* that you're up to.) According to the code so far, Linn was letting me and Rowan know that she planned to follow Dad and see where he was going ... and who he was *really* meeting.

I glanced over at Rowan to make sure she'd sussed the code thing – sometimes she's too busy being an airhead to notice what's going on. But Rowan shot me a quick look back and I knew we were all on the same wavelength.

"That's a good idea!" I nodded at my eldest sister. "We might be in bed by the time Dad comes back, so he'll need his keys to get in!"

(Translation: "Go for it, Linn!")

"But he *took* his keys!" Tor piped up, before Linn could head for the door.

"Er, no he didn't!" said Rowan.

"He *did*! He was jingling them in his hand!"

Never underestimate the observational skills of a seven year old.

"Was he?" I smiled at Tor, "Well, that was clever of you to notice."

Annoying, more like.

Me, Rowan and Linn were silent for a second, stumped, now that our first attempts at proper spying had been stalled.

"Oh, I think I'll go to the shop!" Rowan burst out, scrambling out of the armchair. "I really fancy … some … Wine Gums!"

(Translation: "Now that Linn's plan is down the dumper, I've tried to come up with an alternative excuse to get out of the house and follow Dad.")

"*Grrandma* says Wine Gums stick in your teeth and rot them," Tor squinted at Rowan dubiously.

"Well … maybe I just fancy having rotten teeth, OK?" Rowan shrugged, searching the floor for her shoes.

(Translation: "Leave me alone, Tor – I know it's lame but it was the first stupid thing that came into my head!")

"You'd better hurry, Ro – the shop might close!" said Linn sternly.

(Translation: "Hurry up if you're going, or you'll never catch up with Dad!")

"But the shop stays open past my bedtime!" Tor chipped in.

I gritted my teeth together and knew my sisters would be doing the same. It was like living with a junior member of MI6.

"I think the shop is closing early tonight. I'm sure I saw a sign in the window saying that…" I tried to pacify him.

(Translation: "Tor, we love you but shut up and let us lie to you!")

"I can't find my other shoe!" whined Rowan, knowing that time was ticking away. "Winslet – have you taken it?"

(Translation: "I'll never catch up with Dad at

this rate, because that stupid dog's hidden my shoe under a bed somewhere!")

"Ro, listen: forget the Wine Gums," Linn sighed, shoving her hands on her hips. "You can get them another day."

(Translation: "Give up. Dad'll be *well* gone. We'll try another time when Inspector Tor isn't listening in.")

Tor glanced around and seemed to notice that all of us were deflated for some reason or other, and he didn't like it.

Since I was the only one still sitting, he fixed on me.

"Winslet would like a cuddle," said Tor, struggling to pick up and carry the reluctant, hairy sausage of a dog over to the sofa, and scrambling up next to me with her.

(Translation: "Tor would like a cuddle.")

And who was I to refuse those big brown eyes. (Tor's, I mean, not Winslet's...)

Chapter 10

LOVE AND CHIPS

I know I moan about Linn, but she was really cool when Billy phoned and begged me to come out and see a movie with him before his brain exploded with boredom.

OK, so it was obvious that it didn't need all of us to stay home and look after Tor while Dad was out with … well, *whoever*, but in the circumstances, I felt like I should be there, showing solidarity with my sisters.

But as soon as I came back in the living room and said how I'd told Billy I couldn't come out, she'd told me not to be so silly and to get back on the phone and tell him I'd meet him up at Muswell Hill Odeon at half past six.

And so here I was, sitting in the darkness next to Billy, nudging him to pass me the giant bucket of popcorn he was hogging.

The only problem was, the new sci-fi movie we were meant to be seeing (Billy's choice) was sold out. So we'd been forced to give up until another day, or opt for this romantic comedy thing that was starting around the same time. And since neither of us was in the mood to go home (me, because I'd just worry about what my dad was up to; Billy because, well, he was plain *bored*) we stuck it out.

"Ally, how come that girl keeps on crying?" Billy whispered loudly, pointing up at the screen as I wrestled the bucket of popcorn from his other hand.

"Because she loves that blond guy," I whispered back, "but she thinks she doesn't stand a chance with him."

Boys aren't too sharp at picking up emotional stuff, are they?

"Oh, OK..." Billy nodded, but sounded unconvinced. "But how come the bloke with the blond hair keeps being horrible to her?"

"Because he loves *her*, but he's trying to hide it."

Even in the semi-dark, I could see Billy frowning.

This film wasn't doing much for his understanding of the intricate ways of romance. And who could blame him for struggling with it? After all, the two characters we were watching would spend an hour and a half going through a whole pile of complicated misunderstandings, but just before the credits rolled – shazam! – they'd come to their senses, realize how in love they were and live happily ever after. And surprise, surprise, life's not like that. (If it was, after all these years of fumbling, blushing conversations and awkward silences, me and Alfie would be well on our way to announcing our engagement or something by now.)

"I don't get it – who's this other guy *here*?" asked Billy, forgetting to whisper now, which must have been just fantastic for the people sitting around us.

"He's her boss. He's in love with her too."

While I was trying to explain the film's ludicrous romantic entanglements to Billy, for a fleeting second, I thought not of Dad and his mystery date, but of the other hot date that was going on – Kyra and Ricardo, slip-sliding their way around Ally Pally ice rink.

I immediately shoved the thought to the back of my mind. The best *I* could do with my Wednesday night was explain storylines to my dense mate. And speaking of that, it suddenly struck me that I'd just learnt an important life lesson, which is: only attempt to watch romantic movies with a) girl mates, or b) boyfriends. Girl mates are always up for a good chick flick, and boyfriends will at least *pretend* to like them, for the sake of their girlfriends. But romantic movies and single boys don't mix – it brings out the worst, most cynical streak in them.

Basically, watching a romantic film with a boy

who *isn't* your boyfriend is just *asking* for trouble.

"*Burrrrrrrrrrrrrrrrrrrp!* Oooh, sorry!" sniggered Billy.

As the tutting started behind us, I slunk so low I practically slipped off my seat...

OK, another life lesson is *not* to tell Billy anything vaguely important and expect a useful answer.

"But you don't know for *definite*!" said Billy, through a mouthful of tomato-sauce- and (blee!) mayonnaise-drenched chips.

We were strolling along Muswell Hill Broadway, heading towards my bus stop. I had been a bit dubious about telling Billy what was going on with Dad, but for some strange reason (I think the film was so bad in the end that it turned my brain to mush) I told him everything that was rattling around in my muddled head.

The reason that I *hadn't* planned on telling him was the fact that he's not too brilliant with "sensitive" stuff. (Put it this way: he isn't Sandie, who's so sensitive that she can cry at *car ads* on the telly, if they're slushy enough.) Here's an example: there was this one time, years ago, when I got a bit upset at how long Mum had been gone, and all Billy did was go very quiet, then tell me I could borrow his DS Lite for an unlimited period if I wanted. I mean, OK, so it was really sweet, bless him, but a girl buddy would give you a hug, wouldn't they?

(Actually … you know something? There I am moaning on, but I've suddenly just remembered that I was quite chuffed at the time. I'd never had a go at a DS Lite before and within one minute of playing on it, I'd got totally addicted and managed to forget about Mum for a bit. Maybe Billy isn't so useless after all. And maybe I'm just a bit of an ungrateful moo…)

But anyway, as we queued at the fish and chip shop opposite the Odeon, common sense was telling me that I should stick to talking about how much he'd hated the movie (loads); how much his school was bugging him (loads); if he still had a crush on the eighteen-year-old girl who'd moved in next door to him (most definitely); the usual stuff. But instead, I blurted. Well, Billy and I have known each other since we were little kids, so it's hard *not* to tell him what's going on. Even if he generally doesn't have anything remotely helpful to say about it.

"What do you mean, I 'don't know for definite'?" I asked, wondering how he had room in his skinny body for the mound of chips he was stuffing his face with. He'd already hoovered up *triple* his fair share of popcorn in the cinema.

"Well, you don't know for *certain* that your dad is

out on a date with a woman," Billy shrugged.

"What are you saying – that he's out on a date with a *man*?"

I know I was deliberately misunderstanding him, but I was a bit irked at Billy's unwillingness just to go with what I was telling him.

"No! I don't mean that. It's just that I think maybe you've got it wrong!"

"Look, Billy," I said, regretting that I'd ever opened my mouth, "I think I know my own father pretty well, and I know when something weird is going on!"

"Yeah, but I still think you're overreacting!" he mumbled, as he rammed more chips in his mouth. "I mean, my mum and dad go out all the time, and *I* don't know what they're up to. They're just out – like tonight – *doing* stuff."

"Billy – you can't compare me and my dad to you and your parents!"

"Why not?" he blinked at me, looking slightly hurt.

I couldn't feel sorry for him, though. Not while he had this disgusting dribble of tomato sauce oozing down his chin.

"It's totally different!" I tried to explain. "Dad is really close to all of us – we all know what's going on in our family!"

Well, that wasn't quite true. None of us knew what Dad was up to this particular evening; *that* was the problem.

"So, what are you saying – that I'm not close to my mum and dad?" asked Billy, coming to a halt beside my bus stop.

"Well, you're not, are you?"

It wasn't like Billy and his folks didn't get on – it was just that they all drifted about in their biggish house, all doing their own thing. Whenever I went round there, Billy's mum was always popping out to her coffee mornings and the garden centre and her evening classes. And his dad was always the same – saying a cheery hello to me and then burying his head in the paper for the rest of the time.

"We *are* close!" Billy protested.

"Billy – you don't even know what your dad does for a *living*!"

"I – I do! He works for … an insurance company!"

"Doing *what* exactly, Billy?" I tested him, my hands on my hips.

Boys are rubbish at knowing important details. They really are.

"Uh…"

Billy was saved by the fact that my bus drew up just then, opening its doors with a swish of hydraulics.

"See you up the park on Sunday, if I don't talk to you before!" he yelled, as the doors swooshed closed behind me.

I felt a bit mean going on like that at Billy, and tried to make it up by hurtling up to the top deck and waving at him like mad before the bus whizzed round the roundabout and dipped down the steep hill towards Crouch End.

As Billy waved his greasy fingers back at me, the bus driver did the usual kamikaze trick of hurtling down the forty-five-degree incline at an alarming rate, hurtling me bum-first down on to the seat. Normally, I hate this part of the journey (I tend to play out a whole morbid scenario in my mind: the screech of brakes, the bus tilting over, the local-paper headline, "Bus Careers Out Of Control On Perilous Hill – All Passengers Horribly Squashed"), but tonight I quite enjoyed the sensation. With the top of the bus to myself and the carpet of lights of London spread out down below, it was kind of like being on a Disneyland ride.

I was almost disappointed when the bus finally squealed to a halt by the junction at the bottom of the hill. But just as I stuck my feet up on the back of the seat in front and relaxed, something caught my eye.

The couple huddling in the bus shelter on the other side of the road were doing some seriously steamy snogging. It was better than anything in the film I'd just watched, that was for sure. I squinted for a better look; the way they were going, it was like a cross between mouth-to-mouth resuscitation and a WWF wrestling competition.

It was at that second that a passing car illuminated the couple in the glare of its headlights. Although I couldn't see her face, I recognized the girl's high, bushy ponytail instantly.

Oh. My. God. What was Kyra Davies *like*?!

Chapter 11

DAD SLIPS UP

"He's whistling!" whispered Rowan, as if Dad whistling first thing in the morning was the wildest thing to happen in our house all year.

Rowan was attacking some bread on the worktop, waving the long breadknife at me ominously as she made her point.

"So?" I whispered back, as I grabbed myself a glass out of the cupboard.

Speaking of wild things, Rowan's hair would've scored a definite nine out of ten on any wild scale this morning. She had it done up in two short plaits (nothing wrong with that), but the bottom of her plaits were tied with whole streamers of different coloured ribbons that trailed down over her white school shirt. If she stood still for too long, she was in danger of having small kids use her as a maypole.

"*So*, if he's whistling like that, maybe it means he's happy. You know, maybe he had a good time last night!"

I heard what Rowan was saying, but I glanced

over my shoulder to check that Tor hadn't. Luckily, we had the radio up loud and Tor was pretty much absorbed in carving his toast into something specific.

"Ro, whistling doesn't mean anything. We need more to go on than that..."

Rowan looked a little huffy with me. She grabbed the mound of bread she'd just cut (all squint), turned and plonked it down on the table.

"Hi, guys!" Dad's voice suddenly boomed above the radio.

"Hi, Dad!" said Rowan, Tor and I, simultaneously.

"Ah," exclaimed Dad, settling into his usual chair at the table, and rubbing his stomach. "Pass me some of that bread, Ally Pally – I'm starving!"

At that point, Linn breezed into the kitchen, looking as immaculate and ironed as she always does.

By contrast, an uncomfortable damp sensation made me look down at the cuff of my own white school shirt, which was currently soaking up a pool of orange juice right by my plate. I yanked my arm up and sucked at the cloth, and wished – for a split-second – that I was just slightly *less* of a clumsy geek and slightly *more* like Linn. (And you don't hear me say that too often...)

"What's this about being starving?" smiled Linn, bending over to peck a kiss on Dad's forehead before she sat down. "What have you been up to that's made you so hungry, Dad? Bit of a night last night, was it?"

Good one, Linn! I thought proudly, as my big sister launched today's offensive before she'd even had any cornflakes.

"No, no," Dad shook his head, concentrating intently on buttering his wonky slice of bread. "Quiet night, really. Few drinks, and a bit of chat. That's all."

"What pub did you go to, Dad?" asked Rowan, getting in on the act.

"Um, it was just that one off the Broadway," he muttered, vaguely.

I watched Rowan open her mouth and then close it again. She was obviously just about to question him about which of the many pubs off the Broadway that he meant exactly, when she realized she might incriminate herself. (I guessed Rowan didn't *really* want Dad knowing what me and Linn already knew – that she'd been in most of those pubs at one time or another, thanks to hanging out with her two best mates, who were both eighteen.)

My turn.

"So how's Jake?" I asked, studying Dad to see if he'd give himself away.

"Jake?"

A hint of a puzzled frown crossed Dad's face.

Aha! Got him... I thought, desperate to glance over at my sisters and check that they'd spotted that too.

"Oh, Jake! Yes, fine," Dad attempted a recovery. "Yes, Jake's ... OK."

Yeah, *right*. And just how long have you had this imaginary friend, Mr Love?

"And what did you two talk about, then?" I continued, practically giddy now that I was sure we'd caught Dad out in his lie.

"Um, just ... sport. That kind of thing," he said casually.

To add weight to his casual act, Dad picked up the marmalade jar and pretended to be fascinated by the wording on the label. Who was he kidding? And what was with the "sport" conversation? Dad watched cycling stuff like the Tour de France on telly, but beyond that he knew as much about sport as he did about the nutritional value of marmalade.

"Don't we have any *normal* stuff?" Tor suddenly interrupted, while trying to ram a piece of bread that lurched from being ten centimetres thick at one side to a sliver at the other into the toaster.

"Sliced? No we've run out. We've only got that," said Rowan slightly tersely, feeling her culinary skills were being criticized once again, even if it was only bread in question.

"But I can't finish what I'm making with this!" Tor whined, flopping the bread in the air.

"What *are* you making, Tor?" I asked, squinting at the carved piece of toast already on his plate.

Tor trotted back to his place at the table and put the toast up to his face.

"Cool!" mumbled Rowan, nodding at the sight of the chunky (toast) specs our brother was balancing on the bridge of his nose.

"I needed more toast for the arms!" Tor explained, looking at us all through the holes he'd so expertly cut out, while pointing at the space between his home-made glasses and his ears.

The technical specifications of his work of art were certainly making our normally monosyllabic little brother very chatty this morning. I was just about to quiz him on how he'd planned to *fix* the arms to the rest of the edible specs when a screech from Dad's chair alerted me to the fact that he was on the move.

"Where are you going?" asked Linn, seeing our prey slip away.

"Um, I just remembered there's an early delivery

due at the shop this morning," said Dad, heading out of the kitchen armed with his bread and marmalade. "Better get round there now…"

"Damn!" muttered Linn, under her breath.

"I *heard* that…" muttered Tor, disapprovingly.

So, we got nothing out of Dad. But luckily, *someone* was willing to talk – and tell all. Even if it was on a totally different subject.

"…and then he was skating *straight* towards me, and I was screaming and everything, but he *deliberately* crashes straight into me, grabbing me and cuddling me." Kyra giggled at the memory. "And we were laughing like mad, and then he says, 'I'm freezing – do you fancy warming me up?' And *I* said, 'Sure – you want me to buy you a coffee from the machine?' Geddit?"

I got it. So much for Kyra giving a cool backhander to his saucy line; it sure looked like they were doing a good job of warming each other up when *I* saw them the night before – and that was what I was *really* interested in hearing about. I still hadn't quite got over the shock of seeing Kyra and Ricardo re-enacting a scene out of some steamy movie, specially since the setting was a bus shelter on the W7 bus route.

To be honest, I wasn't exactly blown away by

the sound of Ricardo's unsubtle charms, but I was having quite a good time listening to Kyra's tales, or at least as much as she could squeeze into the short journey along the corridor between English and Maths classes.

"And he definitely wants to see me again!" gushed Kyra, her upturned nose crinkling as she grinned, so that her sprinkling of freckles disappeared. "He's asked me to go to his mate's party in Muswell Hill with him on Saturday!"

"Yeah?" I said dolefully, a sinking feeling suddenly washing over me, so that I totally forgot to tease her about the bus-stop snog-fest.

"What's wrong?" asked Kyra, scanning my face.

"Nah, it's nothing," I tried to laugh, thankful that the door of the Maths class was looming up and I'd be spared any further explanation of my Party Complex.

So I didn't want to tell Kyra about it there and then ('cause I didn't want to sound like the pathetic, sorry-for-myself geek I know I can be), but basically, *this* is my Party Complex: hearing about a party that you *know* you're going to get an invite to is exciting. Hearing about a party that you're *not* going to get an invite to is just sheer torture.

I mean, parties can be rubbish, can't they? But there's always that potential; the potential to have a brilliant laugh with your mates, to meet new people, to meet new boys… (Uh-oh, I'm off on the boy thing again.)

But that's the problem with hearing about parties and knowing you're not invited – all that potential is going on and you're stuck at home playing Junior Scrabble with your little brother while your kleptomaniac dog keeps running off with random vowels.

OK, I'm speaking about myself here, but you get my drift.

"Anyway, I'll keep you posted!" Kyra grinned at me conspiratorially, before she darted off to her own class.

"Yeah, keep me posted on what fantastic things are happening next in your charmed life, Kyra," I mumbled grumpily.

Chapter 12

STUNNED? ONLY A HUGE BIT...

"Yeeeeooooowww!"

Grandma, who was busy pulverizing some potatoes into submission with a masher, shot me this look that said, "I told you so!"

And she was right. When you've got an old coffee jar (painted bright blue with paper stars stuck on it – one of Rowan's early artistic efforts) that's stuffed with kitchen utensils, it's really dumb to try to turn the fishcakes you're frying just with your fingers.

I was just about to run my stinging hand under the cold-water tap, when I heard the phone ring in the hall.

"I'll get it!" I yelled, hurrying through to grab the receiver.

I presumed it would be Sandie; she was going to phone me back once she'd had a think about what film I should bring round with me on Saturday night. I'd called her as soon as I'd got in from school to see how she was getting on with her pet virus. Her horrible cold had turned into some even more horrible gastric thing, and she'd been confined to her little pink bedroom for the entire week by both her doctor and her mother. She was now going completely round the bend after days' and days' worth of mollycoddling (her mother was asking for regular updates on the state of her "bowel movements" for goodness' sake), and was desperate for me to come and inject some normality in to her life. ("Do you want me to bring anything?" I'd asked her. "Just a DVD. Oh, and maybe you could get me something from the hardware shop too." "What?" I asked, wondering if the virus had affected her brain. "One of those big industrial padlocks," she sighed. "So I can lock my stupid mother out of my room…")

"Hello?" I said down the phone, suddenly aware that I could smell something fishy at close quarters…

"Can I speak to Ally, please?" said a voice that wasn't Sandie's, but that *was* vaguely familiar.

"Yeah, it's me," I replied, sniffing at the hand that was holding the phone and sussing out that it was the one I'd been flipping the fishcakes with. Poo.

I cradled the receiver awkwardly, between my head and neck, and – using my non-burnt, non-smelly hand – lifted a corner of my shirt and wiped away the grease from the plastic handle.

"Oh, hi! I thought it was maybe one of your

sisters," I heard the girl's voice say, as I transferred the phone to my other ear with my clean hand.

"Kyra?" I said, clicking who it was.

"Yeah, it's me! What are you up to?"

"Not much..." I shrugged, holding my greasy, fishy-fingered hand well away from me.

What could I tell her? That after I heard that she was going to a party on Saturday night with her new boyfriend, I spent the whole of Maths feeling particularly hacked off? And then I'd walked home from school (feeling particularly hacked off); tried to do my homework but couldn't concentrate (because I was too hacked off); phoned Sandie on her sickbed to see if I could come round and see her on Saturday night (so I wouldn't be the only one hacked off at not going to a party); and finally that I'd nearly deep-fried my hand because I was too hacked off to pay attention when my grandmother told me to use a spatula instead of risking third-degree burns?

"Hey, listen, Ally," said Kyra. "I've got a bit of a proposition for you..."

I was intrigued...

"Like what?"

"Do you remember what I told you at school today? About Ricardo's mate having a party on Saturday?"

Did I remember? The fact was only *seared* into

my brain...

"Yes, the party. I remember something about that..." I mumbled, trying to sound like I couldn't care less.

"Well, do you fancy coming?"

A wave of happiness steamrollered over me. I wanted to scream "YES, PLEASE!!", but I decided very quickly that that would not rate too highly on a cool scale.

"Uh, yes – sure, I'd like to come!" I squeaked, instead.

(While a small voice in my head was also shouting, "And what about Sandie?" and I was doing a wonderful job of ignoring it...)

"Great!" said Kyra. "Only there *is* a catch..."

Isn't there always?

"What is it?" I frowned, becoming aware of a rasping sensation on my fingers.

I glanced up and saw Colin the cat, perched on a stair at shoulder-level to me, stretching his neck through the bannisters and enthusiastically licking my fishcake-scented fingers.

"It's like this," Kyra began. "I was just talking to Ricardo on the phone, and he was saying that he wants to bring this mate of his along to the party too, so I said, 'Well, can I bring *my* mate as well?' "

Me. *I* was her mate. And if I wasn't very much

mistaken, I was just about to have my very first blind date.

"—and Ricardo says, 'Hey, it'll be like *Blind Date!*'"

Kyra didn't look much like Cilla Black, but I can't say I cared. And I know blind dates can sometimes be a disaster, but on the boy front, it was the best offer I'd had all year. And in a week where I'd not only made a fool of myself in front of Alfie, but also in front of the only boy I'd ever been out with too, I kind of thought I deserved a change of luck.

"No problem. It could be a laugh," I giggled, trying to keep the wobble of hysteria in my voice under control.

Wait till I tell Chloe and the others at school tomorrow! I thought frantically. *Wait till I tell Sandie! Er, on second thoughts…*

I was debating whether to phone Billy and boast about it, or leave it till I saw him on Sunday to blurt my news out, when Kyra wrapped up the call pretty suddenly.

"Oh, gawd … my mum's just come in. I've got to go. Speak to you at school tomorrow!"

And with a clatter from her end she was gone.

Slowly, I put the receiver down and walked back into the kitchen in a daze, only narrowly avoiding falling over Colin, who was weaving (make that *hopping*) his way around my legs, in the vain hope that I was carrying any spare fish in one of my pockets.

"All right, Ally?" asked Grandma, giving me one of her X-ray looks.

She must have thought I was ill, the way I was wandering about like a zombie. Probably thought I'd contracted Sandie's Horrible Thing.

"Grandma – I've got a date on Saturday!" I blurted out.

"Have you, dear? Well that makes two of us!" she smiled brightly, clattering plates on the table.

"Stanley again?" I asked, remembering her dinner date earlier in the week.

"Of course it's Stanley. What do you think I am, some wanton woman going out with two men in the same week?" she said, brusquely. "And who are you going out with?"

I didn't take offence at the brusque business – it's just the way Grandma talks. Mum isn't like that, though; she's more ditzy, like Rowan (well, from what I remember). It's funny how it kind of skipped a generation, with Linn ending up like a mini-clone of Grandma.

"That's the thing," I said, responding to Grandma's question. "I don't know his name. Well, not yet."

"Blind date, is it?" Grandma frowned. "You're not meeting him on your own, are you?"

"No, I'm going out with my friend Kyra and her boyfriend. And some boy *he's* mates with."

I felt myself blushing as I explained it to her. I was probably going to spend the next two days blushing about it. I'd be luminous *red* by the time I finally got introduced to this boy. He'd probably think I had some strange tropical disease and insist on a note from my doctor before he'd go anywhere near me.

"Hello, girls! What are you two gossiping about?" said Dad, coming into the kitchen and scooping Colin up into his arms and away from my legs.

"Nothing much," shrugged Grandma.

She's great that way. She knows when there's things that we might not want to tell Dad about. I mean, I *would* tell Dad before I went out on Saturday, but only once I'd stopped being a gibbering, girlie wreck about it.

"Well, it didn't sound like that to me!" Dad grinned, standing in the middle of the kitchen in his bare feet, oldest faded jeans, scruffiest black T-shirt and with the purriest cat in his arms.

And with his hair normal and curling, he didn't look anything like he had done the night before, when he'd seemed so smartened up (for *him*, I mean; my dad's not exactly the kind of guy you'd ever see in a suit...).

"Just girls' talk, Martin," said my Grandma, in that tone of hers that means "that's it – you're not getting any more explanation than that!".

"Oh, that's right!" he teased us. "Just you two keep your little secrets from me!"

"Ah, now, speaking of keeping things from you – I nearly forgot," said Grandma, glancing up at him from fixing the table. "Someone rang earlier, when you and Tor were out feeding the rabbits in the garden. I was going to come and get you, but she told me not to bother."

She?

At the mention of that one word – that one *pronoun*, if we're going to get pernickety – I came out of my date-induced walking coma.

"Er, who – who was that, then?" asked Dad, looking suspiciously sheepish.

"Sorry, can't remember her name. I should have written it down," said Grandma, clattering the forks and knives into place. "All I remember is the message."

"And that was...?" asked Dad, his voice sounding ever so slightly strangled.

"If you're still up for Sunday, then give her a call. Does that make sense?"

Grandma looked up at Dad with her steely grey eyes.

"Uh ... yep. Yes – that makes sense. Oooh, smells like tea's nearly ready. I better give everyone a shout!"

Dad – and Colin – were out of the kitchen door at the speed of light.

I looked at Grandma.

She looked back at me.

I saw her fractionally raise one eyebrow and, in that unspoken second, *I* knew that *she* knew that *I* knew that *she* knew *something* was going on.

If you see what I mean...

Chapter 13

SMALL, BUT SMART

We were just heading out of the doorway of the pet shop when Tor tugged at my sleeve.

"The parrot!" he whispered to me, his eyes wide and earnest.

I glanced back at the shop's resident grey parrot, whose cage stood above the cash desk.

"What *about* the parrot?" I asked, ducking to one side to let another customer in.

"He said my name!" gasped Tor.

Tor does this thing, where – after we've chosen what we need to keep our menagerie going – *I* do the dull stuff like queuing up to pay, while *he* talks Tor-talk to the mice and hamsters in their cages. He also tries to bond with the resident parrot by giving it long, meaningful stares.

I thought about it for a second as I hustled Tor out of everyone's way and pointed him in the general direction of the café a couple of doors along. Call me cynical, but to me, the sound the bird made was your basic "squawwwk!" type parrot noise. But

I guess it *could* sound a bit like "Torrrrr!".

If you stuck your fingers in your ears and hummed a bit, that is.

Still, who was I to burst Tor's bubble?

"Wow! He said your name? That's cool!" I nodded down at Tor, putting my hand firmly on his back and steering him into Shufda's.

As we waited for our two hot chocolates – a regular treat after our Saturday-morning pet-shop expedition – Tor took out the new goldfish scoop-net we'd just bought from the plastic bag and proceeded to capture the salt cellar with it.

"Watch you don't knock it over, Tor," I whispered.

Tor's a good kid – you can take him most places and never be embarrassed by him, unlike a lot of other children. Even when he was really little he was kind of laid-back. Other two year olds would be having screaming hissy fits on the bus because they weren't being allowed to eat the bus ticket or something, and Tor would just stare at them with his big, brown eyes, like he was trying to figure out what their problem was.

"I'm being careful!" he assured me, as the waiter came over with two steaming mugs.

"OK. So how've things been at school this week? Are you friends with Freddie again?"

I liked these chats we had on our own. I mean, I always did most of the chatting (no surprise), but it was still pretty nice, just the two of us.

"Uh-huh," nodded Tor, licking chocolatey froth off his spoon.

"What was it you two were fighting about, anyway?"

"Stuff," Tor shrugged.

Tor maybe didn't say much – especially at school – but he was still a popular guy. There was always a procession of small chums from his class trampling around our house being introduced to all the pets. Maybe different things make you popular when you're older, but when you're seven, having the equivalent of a petting zoo at home works pretty well.

"What kind of stuff?" I pushed him.

Today in particular I was quite up for losing myself in Tor's world. It distracted me from what was looming in front of me ... i.e. my blind date. I was planning on keeping myself really busy until it was time to get ready, just so I wouldn't go round the twist thinking about it.

"Stuff," shrugged Tor again, taking a slurp of his drink. "I did a picture of a snail and Freddie said it looked like a big poo."

I know ('cause I remember) that when you're

Tor's age, things like that matter – a *lot*. But still, if that was all he had to worry about, then I was pleased. He had plenty of time to grow up and worry about life, the universe, exams and everything.

"You and Linn and Rowan..." said Tor suddenly, fixing me with a serious stare.

I was tempted to lean over and wipe away the frothy chocolate moustache on his upper lip, but I thought he might get grumpy about me babying him.

"What? What about us?" I asked, sneaking a look at my watch. (Nine hours to go before I had to meet up with Kyra...)

"You all think Dad's got a girlfriend."

I choked so much on a mouthful of hot chocolate that it nearly sprayed out of my nose (mmm!). Frantically, I tried to think of something to say – some reassuring denial – but my mind let me down. Several pathetic explanations popped into my brain, and were so pathetic that they popped right out again.

Tor kept staring at me as his nose disappeared back into his mug.

He may be a weird kid, but he's so smart. Smarter than his three sisters put together, that was for sure. We thought we were so clever, hiding everything from him, and he saw through it all.

"He's going out with her on Sunday," said Tor

matter-of-factly, wiping his mouth with the back of his hand.

It was just as well I hadn't taken another slurp of hot chocolate, or it really would have been spraying out of my nose in surprise at *that* little pronouncement. It seemed that Tor not only knew what *we* knew, he knew *more*…

"He's going out on Sunday? How do you know?" I quizzed him, giving up any pretence at denying anything. Why bother?

"I asked Dad if we could go to the City Farm on Sunday," Tor explained. "He said he couldn't, he had to do a *thing*. And he went bright red."

Look at that – my brother was even smarter than our *dad*, seeing through his excuse straight away. (Still, saying he was doing a "thing" was a pretty *pitiful* excuse on Dad's part and not *that* hard to see through, I guess.)

"Are you going to follow him this time?" Tor asked straight out.

I was slap-bang stunned. Again.

"Did you know that's what Linn and Rowan were trying to do on Wednesday night?" I asked him, remembering how his questioning had put a stop to my sisters' attempts at spying.

"Uh-huh," nodded Tor, playing around with the fish-scoop again.

"Why didn't you tell us you knew what was going on?"

"You were leaving me out," said Tor simply.

I guess he had a point.

"Listen, we'll talk to Rowan and Linn when we get home," I told him. "And we won't leave you out again, OK?"

Tor nodded happily. I guess we thought we were protecting him, but all the time we were making him feel lonely and pushed out with our sisterly secrets.

Still, it looked like Love Child No. 4 was just about to join the family firm of private investigators.

Dad didn't stand a chance.

Chapter 14

THIS WAY FOR A SPEEDY EXIT...

Time was dragging. It had been a busy (and draining) day, but this last couple of hours before I was due to go and meet Kyra were stretching out like the world's biggest elastic band...

My day had gone like this: after my brother's little bombshell in the café, the two of us had traipsed home, rounded up Rowan (Linn was out), and filled her in on Inspector Tor's powers of deduction. What Tor had said about Sunday tied in with the suspect message Gran had given Dad the other evening, but until we could get hold of Linn, there was no point working out what to do about it.

After that, I went round to see Sandie. I was in serious grovelling mode; she'd said on the phone that she didn't mind if I blew her out for the party (and the date), but I knew she was gutted really. She'd asked me all these questions: "What's this boy like?" (I didn't know); "Where's the party?" (I didn't know); and "What are you going to wear?" (Yep, I didn't know – since none of my other friends were going, the dress-rehearsal ritual hadn't happened). And all the time, Sandie kept looking at me with her big Disney eyes all soulful and sad.

I finally escaped (from the guilt) when her mother came up to take her temperature and check she hadn't developed the *plague* or something. On the way home, it suddenly struck me that Sandie was probably worried that me and Kyra had got too buddy-buddy while she was stuck at home with her gastric-flu thing. It wasn't really like that, but I could see why she thought it might be.

But as they say, that was then and this is now. And right about now, I was standing under the shower, feeling very, very sick.

(Mind you, it's not hard to feel ill in our bathroom. Mum painted the walls deep ruby red, 'cause she wanted to put lots of plants in here, and thought the greenery would look great against it. Only it practically gives you a *migraine* if you stay in the room more than ten minutes.)

His name was Bobby, this guy I was feeling sick about. Kyra had told me that much, and that was *all* she'd told me, apart from the fact that him and Ricardo went to the same school. I guess that was as much I could expect from Kyra, considering she'd only been going out with Ricardo for a week, and probably didn't know that much about him either (apart from an intimate knowledge of his snogging technique).

So, with two hours to go, I was standing in the shower, letting the torrent of water batter over my head, and – get this – trying to think of things I could talk about with Ricardo's mate.

How pathetic was that? But you know, that was (actually, it still *is*) something I worry about a lot. A *lot*. I mean, what are you meant to speak to each other about on dates? Once you've run through all the stuff about *likes* and *dislikes*, and who your mates are and everything, I worry that you just dry up. At least, it was like that when I went out with Keith Brownlow (urgh, don't remind me...), and even though we're about a million light years away from *ever* dating, it's like that with Alfie too – my mind just goes blanker than blank when I get the chance to talk to him.

Now Billy, that's different – 'cause he's just a mate, same as Sandie, or Chloe or the others (well, with a couple of genetic differences...). I can talk to Billy for *hours* about *anything* (mostly rubbish, if you want to know, but it's always pretty entertaining rubbish).

So what happens to your brain when you fancy someone, or you're out on a date? Why does it seem like having a normal conversation is about as alien as nipping to Saturn for your summer holidays?

My eyes suddenly started stinging with shampoo, so I rammed my face under the flow of the water, and tried to distract myself from the pain by coming up with things I could talk about.

And this was all I managed…

1) Ask him what subjects he's doing at school. (Nah – it would make me sound like a total swot…)

2) Ask him what football team he's into. (What's the point? I don't know anything about football, so it would be a really *short* conversation. Him: "And what football team do you support?" Me: "Uh, none." Him: "Oh." See? Not exactly scintillating…)

3) Tell him the stories behind my brother and sisters' names. (Nope – he'll think we're all weirdos. Which isn't far off the case when it comes to Rowan…)

4) Ask him what he wants to do when he leaves school. (Sounds too heavy. He'll expect me to ask how many children he wants and if he's got a pension plan next…)

5) Tell him that I share a house with two dogs, five cats, three hamsters, too many white mice to count, a one-eyed iguana, four rabbits, a couple of tanks of fish, a pile of stick insects, a recuperating pigeon and whatever else Tor's brought home lately.

(*Definitely* not – I want him to think I'm this cool, intriguing girl, not Dr Dolittle…)

It was no use.

I gave up, turned the shower off and stepped out of the bath, dripping. The water pipes to the shower shuddered to a halt, like there was a tiny man behind the wall, hammering like crazy. (Maybe there is – who knows? Or a poltergeist of an irate Victorian plumber?)

Wiping away the steam on the old, chipped, wood-framed mirror above the sink (a junk-shop treasure my mum once came home with), I checked out my reflection – and saw a big pink prawn staring back at me. I'd obviously stayed in the shower just a *little* bit too long. In fact, I was *so* pink, I clashed horribly with the red walls. I had to get out of there – get up to my room, open the windows wide, and cool down. How could I go and meet the mysterious Bobby if I looked like I'd fallen asleep under a sun-lamp?

Rifling through the towels in the cupboard, the only one I could find that was big enough to cover my bits was one of those emergency towels – an ancient, threadbare, ratty one that you keep in case the others are all in the wash, and hope you never need to drag out. But it would have to do; today was laundry day and all the half-decent towels were

outside twirli...
clothes.

"Mmm – very ...
dripping, pink, ratt...

The old bolt on t...
as ever, and I had t...
open.

Does nothing in this st... I
moaned to myself, realizin...
starting to sound worryingly ...had her
choice, Linn's dream house ... some ultra-
modern, ultra-sleek, ultra-minimalist effort like you
see in those interiors magazines – not a pipe-rattling,
door-sticking, madly-painted wreck like our place.

In my general stress-induced state of grumpiness,
I hadn't noticed the creak on the stairs coming up
from the hallway. Suddenly, I saw Alfie's scruffy
blond hair coming into view, just when I was about
as far away as I could be from the escape route of
the stairs to the attic (which were at the other end
of the landing).

Emergency! If there was one thing I was sure
of, it was that I did *not* look like a moist-skinned,
semi-nude goddess. I looked like I'd been *stewed*,
for God's sake, and I could feel an ominous draft
whistling round my bum, from what must have
been a large hole in this disgrace of a towel.

...sely zero chance of ever
... If he saw me like this, my
...ip down to minus a *million*.

...ly, Alfie's face was turned and looking
...own at Linn, who I could hear chatting behind
...im. This gave me a split-second's grace to vanish,
before I embarrassed myself more than I'd ever
been embarrassed in my life (and there were plenty
of times *that* had happened, I can assure you...).

The closest door to me led into Dad's room and,
quick as a pink flash, I slipped in there, shutting the
door silently behind me. Sighing, I leant my whole
weight against the door. (What for? In case Alfie
had caught a glimpse of me and tried to barge his
way in after me, unable to control his passion at the
sight me in my peek-a-boo towel? I don't *think* so.)

As my heart rate began to slow down (from frantic
to only marginally *less* frantic), my eyes drifted across
the room. It was flooded with a cosy orange glow,
partly from the early evening sunlight streaming in
through the window, and partly because the walls
themselves were orange (a kind of ginger-cat colour
– Colin was completely camouflaged whenever he
came in here for a snooze).

Outside on the landing, I could make out the
mumble of conversation and the squeaky tread of
stairs, as Linn and Alfie headed up to her room. I

could relax... Or at least give myself a chance to cool down, and nick a pair of jogging bottoms and a T-shirt from Dad's wardrobe so that I could get back up to my room with a little more decorum.

I walked over to the wardrobe and pulled the door open. It was packed – but not all with Dad's stuff. There were loads of Mum's dresses and everything in there. All beautiful, patterned fine cottons and Indian silks, a couple of velvet jackets, and some cheesecloth tops. I knew without looking that all her favourite chunky old jumpers would be where they always were, folded up in the big bottom drawer of the chest by the bed. Dad's kept all her stuff just as she left it – perfume bottles, make-up (not that she ever wore much) and an old hairbrush all sit on the dressing table, in case she just happened to stroll through the door and want to pick up where she left off...

There are reminders of Mum all over the house – not just in the way she decorated it, but her paintings and pottery and everything are on every wall and on practically every spare surface. But this room in particular is like a mini-shrine to her, and it's nice to come in here now and again, just on those weird occasions when I feel like I'm starting to forget little things about her, and smell her perfume or pull out her favourite clothes.

And of course, there's her self-portrait right above the bed. Not that you might recognize it as a self-portrait, since it's just all a mass of swirly oranges and yellows. In case you were wondering, it represents her aura. (An aura is some spooky electric current that we all have around us, according to … well, people who read auras. Normal people can't see them, but aura readers can; and one of them told Mum that hers symbolized "awakening". I think I go through so many feelings and moods in a day that *my* aura would be brown – like when you get all those brilliant Plasticine colours that turn to sludge when you mix them.) Anyhow, my mum came back home after getting her aura reading done at a Mind, Body and Spirit Festival at Alexandra Palace, and immediately started working on this painting. She left home on her travels about two weeks after that, so I reckon that aura reader's got a lot to answer for, if you ask me…

But back to that afternoon, when all I had on was that awful scabby towel. Suddenly, I found myself sitting on the edge of Mum and Dad's big old squeaky wooden bed, staring at her painting and remembering the Sunday mornings when we all used to pile in – even Linn. Nowadays, Tor still dive-bombs Dad occasionally (along with Winslet and Rolf), and it's funny to see, but it's not the same as those long-ago times when all us girls and Mum were part of the fun.

I shook myself, aware that I was starting to get too sad about everything. Quickly – before the tears had a chance to get hold of me – I got to my feet and began hunting through the wardrobe, yanking an old denim shirt off a hanger and hauling it on. Some more searching, and I'd found a pair of Dad's jogging bottoms that were far too big for me but at least made me look more human and less like pond-life.

I went over to the dressing table to check out my general redness levels, when I spotted something lying open by the side of the bed.

It was a photo album – one of the ones that normally lived in the cupboard in the living room. What had Dad taken it up here for?

I flopped down on the floor and pulled it round to face me. It was open at a page of photos of Mum: Mum holding her long skirt up and paddling in the sea; Mum laughing at some unknown joke; Mum in the long, wispy lavender dress she got married in; Mum grinning by a muddy stream, wearing wellies, dungarees and stroking her round, pregnant tummy.

What had made Dad dig these out?

I glanced up again at the large framed painting hanging over the bedhead.

"Oh, Mum," I mumbled, wishing I was looking at her face for real, instead of a bunch of stupid orange and yellow swirls. "What do you think's going on? Do you think Dad's feeling guilty about something...?"

Chapter 15

BLIND DATES AND FRAYED NERVES

It was the first time I'd ever seen Kyra without her hair scraped back into her bunched-up ponytail. With her curls waxed, her mid-brown hair looked darker and glossier, pinned back from her face with coloured butterfly clips.

It suited her. You know how she's got those sort of sticky-out ears? Well you couldn't even tell they were sticky-out at all with her hair like that. Not one bit.

"I know I've said it already, but you look really nice," I told her, in a squeakier-than-normal voice.

It was a tough job keeping my frayed nerves under control. I couldn't do much about my voice, but at least I could stick my hands (which were suffering from a bad case of tremble), deep down in my trouser pockets.

"Thanks! You look pretty OK too!" she smirked, raising her eyebrows at me.

We'd just got off the bus and were heading for Ricardo's house, with Kyra holding a scruffy bit of paper with directions on it. We were now on the north side of Alexandra Palace, not a million miles away from Billy's house (I hoped we wouldn't bump into him – he'd have killed himself laughing if he'd seen how dressed up I was). Now that we were here, I realized that if I'd known how close Ricardo's house was, I'd have suggested that we just walk over the park.

But then I took a look at the black, satiny wedge sandals that Kyra had on her feet, and knew that grass, earth and those shoes would definitely *not* go…

I was just wearing a pair of trainers (but my best pair, of course). I can't wear anything with heels – they make me walk like a duck. And unlike Kyra, who was wearing a little chiffon, flowered skirt, my legs were well covered up, in my cut-off khaki trousers. Kyra had dared to bare with her top (a little black halterneck thing), but again I played safe, sticking to my favourite T-shirt: the khaki one with the red star on the chest.

It wasn't so much my clothes that would have made Billy laugh – it was my make-up. Or more like *Kyra's* make-up. When we'd met at the bus stop, she'd frowned at me, then rummaged in her bag and pulled out a little pot. Next thing, she's holding up a mirror and showing me the twinkles of glitter she's daubed on my cheeks and eyelids.

"That looks so cool on you!" Kyra had announced, and I didn't have the guts to contradict her.

A couple of lads in a car honked their horn at us as we trotted along the road, still searching for Ricardo's street. I didn't know whether it was the sight of Kyra's long brown legs that had driven the boys to hammering on their horn, or if the glitter on my face was blinding them and they were trying to let me know I was a traffic hazard.

"Is it far now?" I asked, trying to sneak a peek at the squiggles on the piece of paper Kyra was holding.

"No – this is the road here!" she announced, swinging a left into a street full of small terraced houses.

"Thanks again for inviting me," I muttered, even though at that point I felt so nervous I was pretty tempted to turn and run – very fast – all the way home.

"No problem," said Kyra, brightly. "I kind of felt sorry for you after what you were saying earlier in the week…"

Great. She hadn't fixed me up on this double date because I was smart, or funny, or interesting or pretty – she'd invited me because she felt *sorry* for me. How useless did that make me feel?

"After I was saying what exactly?" I quizzed her.

I tell you one thing: getting defensive is a good way to stop feeling nervous.

"Oh, it was when you were talking about fancying that friend of your sister's. The one you said you don't stand a chance with," said Kyra, bluntly. "So, I just thought it might cheer you up to snog Ricardo's mate."

An avalanche of nerves descended upon me again.

Oh my God. Did this guy *assume* I was going to snog him? If Kyra was sure it was going to happen, then her boyfriend must be sure too, and – naturally – his mate as well. I mean, I had no objection to the idea of kissing someone if I really liked them, but the thought that everyone expected it to be a done deal was only completely petrifying...

I didn't have any more time to think about it (or invent a sudden illness that had struck me out of the blue so I could get away *fast*) – Kyra was sashaying up to a navy-blue front door and ringing a bell.

I gulped, and just knew I'd gone pink again.

"Hi!" said a dark-haired lad, pulling the door open.

He glanced my way for a nano-second, then grinned slowly as he eyed Kyra up and down. Joey out of *Friends* had nothing on this guy.

"Hi, Ricardo!" Kyra smiled coquettishly, twirling

and swaying on the doorstep. "This is Ally…"

"Yeah? I couldn't remember what you said she was called," said Ricardo, with minimum tact and charm.

Mmm, it might be a bit of a struggle to like this guy, I decided.

"Anyway, this is my mate," he continued, pointing his thumb back over his shoulder in the general direction of the hallway, where a tall, shadowy figure ambled towards the doorway.

"Hi, Bobby!" said Kyra, wafting her fingers in a wave towards Ricardo's buddy.

I took one look at Bobby and froze.

He took one look at me, and seemed like he was going to laugh or hurl – one of the two.

"His name's not Bobby," Ricardo snorted. "It's Billy!"

"Bobby … Billy," Kyra shrugged off her mistake with a cheeky air of casualness. "What's the difference?"

It's the difference, I felt like telling her, between having a proper blind date, and being set up with your own best *mate*…

Chapter 16

THAT'S SOME PARTY TRICK...

I glanced around the room. Yep, it was just like I suspected when we first walked in: everyone at this party seemed a *lot* older than us – fifteen or sixteen at least. I hoped I didn't look as young as I suddenly felt.

Just as I was nervously checking everyone out, I became aware of a pair of eyes staring at me, from only a few centimetres away.

"What *is* that stuff on your cheeks?" asked Billy, wrinkling his nose up as he inspected my face.

"Pure gold dust. What did you think?" I replied, sarcastically.

Some party this was shaping up to be. The whole of the flat we were in was crowded with people (i.e. boys) I'd never met, and I'd never get a *chance* to get to know any of them – not with Billy in tow. Even if a cool sixteen year old was interested in going out with someone who was only thirteen. (Like, fat chance...)

It's at times like these you suddenly appreciate

the differences between female and male friends. If I was with Sandie or Salma or someone, people would assume I was single. But standing with this lanky dork of a boy – especially when he was pawing at my face the way he was – anyone was bound to suppose we were an item.

"Gerroff!" I moaned, pushing his finger away from my eyeball.

"I just wanted to see what that stuff was!" he whined. "Is it like little bits of metal, or what?"

"It's a gel, with glitter in it," I sighed, knowing I'd better give him an answer or he'd just keep annoying me. "Kyra's got a little pot of it. Why don't you go and ask her if you can try some?"

I stared over at Kyra and Ricardo, who were busy getting to know each other better on the sofa (i.e. recreating their snogathon at the bus stop when I saw them the other night).

"Nah, I won't bother," grinned Billy. "Just looking at you, I can see that it's crap."

"Thanks!" I said, rolling my eyes.

I still hadn't quite got over the shock of finding out that Billy was my date for the night. Billy, of course, thought it was the funniest thing in the world. It turned out that Ricardo had only told him he was set up on a blind date about half an hour before me and Kyra arrived (like I said before, boys are useless when it comes to important details).

"He told me your name was Emma, or Wendy or something," Billy had told me, as we'd headed off to the party after our bizarre "introduction" on the doorstep – *and* once Kyra and Ricardo had stopped wetting themselves laughing.

"But didn't you even recognize Kyra's name when he was talking about her?" I'd asked him.

Kyra was pretty unusual (the name *and* the girl), and he'd heard me moan about her enough when she'd first started at school and got right up my nose.

"I didn't know what she was called. I just knew Richie had a new girlfriend, that's all," he'd shrugged. (See what I mean about being useless?)

And there was the other twist of the night. Ricardo wasn't an unknown quantity to me at all – Billy had mentioned him loads of times in the passing, but as Richie, not Ricardo. He wasn't a close friend of Billy's or anything, it was just that they played on the same football team. The one nugget I'd remembered hearing about "Richie" was that he was a real success with the girls. Billy was slightly in awe of his success rate in actual fact: Richie seemed to be going out with a different girl practically every week.

Which didn't exactly bode well for Kyra...

"Come on – let's dance!" said Billy, trying to drag me into the centre of the room as a hip-hop track burst on to the sound system.

"No, I'm not in the mood," I shrugged.

"Aw, Ally!" he pleaded, tugging at the bottom of my T-shirt and doing this goofy little dance in front of me, rolling his shoulders and jumping around on the spot.

"No!" I giggled, shaking free of him.

He's such an idiot, you can't help laughing at him sometimes. And the thing is, he just *looks* funny as well – like he grew too quickly and bits of him haven't caught up yet. It's like his whole body's skinny-boyish, but he's got this big, man-sized nose and these huge hands and feet.

God, I'm not selling him too well, am I? I mean, despite all that, he *is* kind of cute-looking. To be honest (and I'd never tell him this), I don't really get why he hasn't got a girlfriend yet…

"*Course* you want to dance!" Billy grinned at me, grabbing me round the waist and lifting me into the centre of the room, and into the throng of dancers.

"Billy – put me down!" I squealed, battering on his shoulders with my fists. See what I mean about goofy?

As he let me slither to the ground, I noticed something behind him. Over by the far wall, a couple of guys were watching us. They looked like they might be about sixteen, and one of them – dressed in baggy skate gear and with spiky short dark hair – was grinning this cute grin. At *me*.

I checked again, just to make sure he wasn't looking at some gorgeous model-type girl lurking behind me. He wasn't – there was that grin again.

I decided to stop protesting and dance. I'm a pretty good dancer. I know that sounds big-headed, but there are plenty of things I'm *not* good at (and I'll be the first to say so), so when there *is* something I can do quite well, I don't think it's too awful to admit to it.

Anyhow, I figured that I might just impress Skate Boy, if he was still watching me. I'm rotten at flirting (see? *There's* a thing I can't do!), so dancing well was my best shot at getting his attention. Maybe.

Three tracks later, and I'd worked up enough courage to sneak a peek in the direction of the wall.

No Skate Boy, or his mate.

Well, that was a waste of time, I grumbled to myself.

But I can't say I wasn't surprised. And anyway, I felt kind of nervous about the whole idea, if you want to know the truth. It's like, if I didn't know what to speak to Keith Brownlow about, I sure didn't know what I'd find to speak to a really cool sixteen-year-old boy about, if he'd decided to come over and talk. Which he hadn't.

"Billy – I'm going to the loo," I yelled in his ear, above the music.

"OK!" Billy yelled back, still dancing.

I'd kind of needed to go to the loo for ages, but because I'd been on my mission to impress, I'd put it off. I wished I hadn't, though – there were already three people queuing outside the bathroom door.

To take my mind off my expanding bladder, I started to daydream about the Skate Boy. What if I caught him looking at me again? What if he asked me to dance? What if we got talking? What if he asked for my phone number? What if tonight I ended up with a date after all? But I was rushing way, way, *way* ahead of myself.

I took a long, slow, deep breath… Once I'd been to the loo, I decided, I'd trawl through the flat, and see if I could locate him in the crush of people. I might not have the courage to go right up and talk to him (like, duh!), but at least if I hung out in the same room as him it would up my chances of getting to know him. And I'd just have to worry about what to say to him when (if!) it happened…

"Ally! Oh, brilliant – you're next!"

Kyra appeared at my side, irritating everyone

who'd started to queue behind me. While I'd been daydreaming, I hadn't even been aware of the fact that the three people in front of me had been and nearly gone.

"I'm absolutely desperate, Ally – can I nip in before you?" Kyra pleaded. "I'll be quick!"

"Well…" I said, dubiously, knowing I was about to get steamrollered.

"Aw, thanks!" Kyra smiled, crossing her arms across her chest and doing tiny hopping movements from side to side.

At that moment, the bathroom door opened, and practically before the poor girl had come out, Kyra was barging past, dragging me in tow.

It seemed we were to have our first girls-gossiping-in-the-loos moment.

"So how are things going with what's-his-name?" giggled Kyra mischievously, as she plonked herself down on the loo.

"Don't!" I moaned. "And it's all *your* fault. If you'd remembered which school Ricardo went to, and got Billy's name right in the first place, I *might* have sussed it out…"

"Whatever," yawned Kyra, in that irritating way she's got.

But that's what Kyra's like – really good fun and also kind of infuriating. But as I was getting to know her, I was slowly learning *not* to get too wound up by the infuriating side of her character.

"So?" I asked, sensing that she was probably more interested in talking about her own situation than mine. "Are you having a good time?"

In the harsh bathroom light I couldn't help noticing the vivid red rash below her bottom lip and on her chin. A telltale sign of her snogging marathon…

"Well, yeah. It's OK…" Kyra replied, scrunching up her face slightly.

"*That* doesn't sound too enthusiastic!" I frowned.

I'd expected her to be raving on about how fantastic Richie/Ricardo was. What was going on? Had something happened? Maybe Richie/Ricardo was up to his old tricks; maybe Kyra had spotted him eyeing up next week's potential girlfriend.

"Well, I've decided I'll probably chuck him," said Kyra matter-of-factly, as she stood up, smoothed her skirt back down and turned on the sink tap to wash her hands.

I knew it was my turn to go, but I was too surprised to do anything about it.

"You want to *chuck* him?" I gasped. "How come?"

"I'm kind of bored with him. He's really into football and stuff that's just dull, dull, dull…"

Kyra was gazing into the mirror above the sink,

inspecting her reflection and running her finger under her eyes where her mascara had started to run.

"Are you going to chuck him *tonight*?" I asked.

I felt almost sorry for Richie/Ricardo, even if he hadn't done or said anything to make me like him. It looked like the heartbreaker was in for a bit of a shock.

"Nah. He's a good kisser. I won't chuck him till tomorrow."

Maybe I'm really dumb, but I always thought you needed to *like* someone if you were going to kiss them. But then, Kyra was pretty good at baffling me.

"I thought you needed to go?" said Kyra unemotionally, glancing over towards the loo.

"Yeah, yeah," I muttered, distractedly unbuttoning my trousers and taking my turn.

If I *was about to chuck a boy*, I thought to myself, *I think I'd be a wobbly pile of jelly*.

Kyra was being so cool it took my breath away. I wondered what had happened at her other schools. Had she been out with lots of boys? Was she always this hard-nosed about them?

"And what about you, Ally? Seen anyone you like here?" asked Kyra, fluffing her curls up with her fingers and readjusting some of her butterfly clips.

"Um, well, I saw this cute boy when I was dancing earlier…" I said, slightly shyly.

"Yeah? What's he like?" she asked, her eyes lit up at the prospect of gossip.

Before I could tell her, there was a hammering at the door.

"Hurry up! Get out of there! NOW!" came a muffled male voice, along with other mumbles from a variety of voices.

I glanced at Kyra, both of us a bit shaken at being yelled at like that, even if there was a large chunk of wood between us and the shouty lad.

Quickly, I got myself together, flushed the loo and opened the door – only to be pushed aside by two lurching boys falling into the room.

"Jeez! Too late!" growled a guy I recognized as Skate Boy's mate, just as Skate Boy hurled projectile vomit all over the bathroom floor.

And Kyra's satin wedge sandals…

Chapter 17

IT'S ALL DOWNHILL FROM HERE...

It wasn't particularly late (we'd left the party early, because it had turned out to be so rubbish), but on the road that circled round the walls of Alexandra Palace, there wasn't a car to be seen.

"Look – see that flashing red light away in the distance?" I pointed out to Kyra. "That's Canary Wharf, down in the Docklands. And that light over there? That's the Telecom Tower, in the West End."

"Wow!" said Kyra, pulling her little black cardie tighter around her body in the chilly evening air. "I'll have to bring my dad up here – he'll love it!"

"You get a better view in the day, though," Billy chipped in. "You can make out the Dome then too."

"Why didn't you point out this stuff when we came up here to the skating the other night?" Kyra chastised Richie/Ricardo.

Richie/Ricardo just shrugged.

I felt like pointing out to her that they were

probably too busy snogging when they weren't actually skating at the rink. And when you've got your eyes closed and someone else's face in your way, it's hard to appreciate a view.

"And since we're sightseeing," said Billy. "You see that bench down there?"

"No," replied Kyra, peering down into the unlit, grassy expanse of the park below.

"No, neither can I," Billy, the big joker, agreed with her. "But anyway, there *is* a bench down there, and that's where me and Ally meet up every Sunday, with our dogs. Isn't it, Al?"

"Yep," I nodded, as I turned off the pavement and started walking down the steps into the darkness.

"Where are you going?" asked Kyra, sounding a little concerned.

"We're going down the hill," I told her.

The boys had offered to walk us to the other side of Ally Pally, where – back in the glare of the street lights – me and Kyra could make our separate ways home.

"What – straight down the hill?!" frowned Kyra dubiously. "But I thought we'd just follow the road around!"

"But going down the hill's much quicker," I explained.

(I was trying to convince myself as well as Kyra

339

at that point – I knew my dad would flip out if he knew we were cutting across the park at night; he thinks that's way too dodgy. OK, so I wouldn't do it on my own, or – like that night – if it was just me and Kyra, but since the boys were going to keep us company, and it wasn't exactly *late* late, I figured it would be fine, just this once. And I planned on sticking the money Dad had given me for a taxi back into his jeans pocket, since it's not like he's got gallons of money to chuck about.)

"And going down the hill's more fun!" grinned Billy. "Come on – run!"

And with that he grabbed my hand and pulled me after him, running headlong into the darkness, where only the tallest branches of the trees stretching up into the starry sky showed any shape.

Half-laughing, half-shrieking, I tumbled after him.

"*I'm* not running down there – it's dark! I could step in dog poo and not realize it! Why can't we just— No, Ricardo! Ricardo! *Waaaaaaahhhhhhh!*"

From the thudding of running footsteps and shrieking giggles coming from Kyra, it didn't sound like Richie/Ricardo had given her a choice. They were right behind me and Billy as we crashed through the rustling, tall grass, halfway down the hill.

Mind you, I didn't know why Kyra was so bothered about the risk of getting dog poo on her precious shoes – not when they'd already been barfed on that night. Even though we'd done a good job of cleaning them up at the kitchen sink, they were still pretty much ruined…

Actually, I think it's safe to say that after the barfing incident, me and Kyra both had a change of heart about our boys. Once we'd cleaned off her shoes and made our way back to the living room (Kyra leaving a trail of wet footprints where she walked), it suddenly became blindingly obvious that practically every lad at the party – not just Skate Boy and his mate – was horribly, obnoxiously drunk. By comparison, Richie/Ricardo and Billy were reassuringly sober, and it was a relief to be back in their company.

"Where have you been?" Billy had asked me when I finally found him, now slouched on the sofa beside Richie/Ricardo. "I thought you were off trying some of that lethal cocktail stuff. I thought I was going to have to roll you home!"

The cocktail stuff that Billy had heard about was the reason so many of the lads (and loads of the girls) at the party were trashed. Billy had heard that someone had found a big bowl and was pouring *everything* alcoholic into it – whatever bottles people had brought had been chucked in there, as well as stuff that had been raided from the house.

I felt kind of sorry for the boy whose party it was – his parents were going to kill him when they saw how trashed their house was and how much of their own booze supply had been raided. But Billy told me not to waste my time: the guy whose party it was the one who was making the "cocktails"...

"Yeah, suckers – we're beating you!" Ricardo called out, streaking past us with a yelping Kyra, the two of them just hazy blurs in the darkness.

"You want a race? You've *got* a race!" Billy yelled after them. "C'mon, Al!"

I gasped breathlessly as we hurtled headlong down the hill, Billy still holding my hand tight. It was funny; I'd been building up the party in my head since I'd heard I was going, and yet this – acting like a ten year old, with my best mate – was much more fun than anything else had been the whole night. (Although, in a *weird* way, I'd quite enjoyed Skate Boy's little party trick – it was just the novelty of a boy making a fool of himself in front of *me*, instead of the other way round...)

Finally, the hill slipped away into the flat, grassy expanse at the bottom, and the occasional window light from the flats that backed on to Ally Pally lit our faces with a watery light.

"We won!" Billy panted, holding my hand aloft in the air.

Richie/Ricardo and Kyra didn't say anything – they just grinned and tried to get their breath back. But I noticed the way they were standing with their arms round each other. It looked like Kyra might have changed her mind about chucking him quite yet...

"Hey," said Richie/Ricardo, once he could speak. "You said you lived over in Palace Heights Road, didn't you?"

He was talking to me (and I suspected he still didn't remember my name).

"Yes," I nodded.

"Well," he panted, "that entrance over there is closest to you. But the entrance over there is closer to Kyra's. So we're going *that* way..."

Even in the faintly lit gloom, I could see the way that Kyra was gazing mushily into his eyes. Looked like the two of them were telling us in no uncertain terms that they were off for a romantic stroll – and we were not invited.

As we waved the two of them off, I turned to Billy.

"You don't have to come any further," I told him. "You'll just have to go all the way back up over the hill."

"Nah, it's all right," he shrugged, starting to walk down towards the alleyway. "I'm thirsty after all that running. I'll walk you down to that twenty-four-hour shop on the main road and get a Coke or something, and then maybe get the bus home."

OK, so I was doing a total turnaround. Suddenly, I remembered one of the advantages of male friends compared to female friends – they can act like your protector the way a girl can't.

We had just come out of the alleyway into a sleepy little street, when Billy came out with something that nearly squeezed what little air I had left right out of my lungs.

"Hey, I meant to say," he shrugged, his hands shoved in his jeans pockets. "What was my mum phoning your dad about the other night?"

"Huh?" I blinked at him.

Sure, my dad knew Billy's mum, but only vaguely. My own mum had been quite pally with her – they'd met when Billy and I were in playgroup together. But Dad didn't know her or Billy's dad particularly well at all. I mean, if they bumped into each other round Crouch End, then they'd stop and say hello and stuff, but calling each other up?

"What, didn't he say she'd phoned?" asked Billy.

I shook my head, silently.

"Well, maybe I got it wrong. It was just that I heard her call whoever it was 'Martin', and I just thought of your dad. It was probably some other guy

344

she knows. She knows loads of people. She's got a better social life than *me*."

I tried to tell my befuddled head that that was the answer. She was talking to someone else, not my dad. No way.

"You know, it must have been someone else, 'cause she was arranging to meet them on Sunday. Tomorrow, I mean," Billy shrugged.

There were shivers zipping up and down my back. I didn't know what to think, what to say, what to do.

"Billy," I suddenly found myself choking out, "thanks for walking me over the hill, but I've got to run, I'm really late..."

I didn't even give Billy a chance to say bye as I pounded the pavement at top speed. I didn't even think about the fact that he must be wondering what I was on about (late? How could I be late when we'd ducked out of the party early?). All that was in my head was the memory of Gran passing that message on to Dad on Thursday.

"If you're still up for Sunday, then give her a call," I muttered, repeating the message as I ran, my heart pounding.

Call "her".

Billy's mum.

I just couldn't believe it...

Chapter 18

IT CAN ONLY GET WORSE...

I stared at the map on the wall, faintly lit by the light from the street lamp outside my window, since I'd left my curtains open.

I felt restless and hot under the covers, and kicked my duvet off me.

An indignant "Prrrp!" from the bottom of the bed made me realize that a small, furry entity had been adding to the temperature of my overheating bed.

"Sorry," I whispered, to a cat that wasn't Colin, as I sat upright and hauled the duvet off it.

Before I could identify which cat it was, it thumped off the bed in a grump, heading off to another part of the room where its sleep wouldn't be so rudely disturbed.

Now that I was sitting, I let my hand stretch up the wall and touch the jutting-out coloured pins that mark all the places Mum has sent letters home from. Sometimes the pattern of the pins confuses me; they seem so random, like she's doubling back on herself a lot of the time. One time, she'll be in

Thailand, then a couple of months later we'll get a letter from America, then it'll be back to Indonesia again. "How can she afford it?" I asked Linn once, when I was old enough to work out that travel wasn't free. "All the long-term backpackers know how to live on next to no money," she'd told me, like she knew the answer to everything (which she usually does). "They all tell each other where the cheapest places are to stay, or where they can go and work for a while. And look what Mum's said when she's written – she's painting T-shirts and selling them, or waitressing sometimes too. That's how she pays for travelling."

What was most annoying was that she was on the move so much, she never had an address long enough for us to write back to her. That was hard, only having this one-way contact with her. There'd been plenty of times when I really, really felt that I needed to talk to her. Like now...

But what could I possibly write? "Dear Mum – remember your friend Sharon? Billy's mum? Well, it looks like she's having an affair with Dad..."

I shuddered at the thought and felt suddenly cold. Gathering up the duvet, I bundled myself up against the headboard, and – with only my nose sticking out – I stared off out of my window at the faraway outline of Alexandra Palace.

I mean, Billy's mum, of all people! She's *so* not like my mum. She's this neat-freak with a house full of stuff that's so new it's practically still got the price tags on. She runs some clothes section in a department store in Wood Green. The kind of clothes she sells, they're all sort of *womanly* and *middle-aged*, if you see what I mean. You know – jackets with gold buttons and knee-length skirts, worn with smart, high-heeled shoes. I know she's got to dress like that at work, but she dresses like that at home too. I think if I ever went round to Billy's and saw her in a pair of jeans and without her hair blow-dried, I'd faint.

I know I might sound like I'm judging by appearances (guilty!), but there's another thing about Billy's mum – she orders people about in that patronizing management way in the store, and does *that* at home too. "Billy," she'll say, lifting his feet off the coffee table, "we have standards!"

I don't know how Billy's dad stands it. (Not that I know Billy's dad too well even after all these years; he's one of those people who looks at children and teenagers like they're an unknown species, as if he's never been one himself and has no idea how to communicate with them.) Billy says his dad just agrees with everything his mum says and keeps his head down in his newspaper or whatever.

*Well, he might not have to do that much longer …
not if his wife's running off with my dad!* I thought
gloomily, feeling a sorry-for-myself pool of tears
forming in my eyes.

A thump on the bed heralded the return of a cat
that wasn't Colin. Tor always says that animals can
sense your emotions (I don't know if that goes for
stick insects too), and that they'll come to you when
you need comfort. I reached my hand out from my
duvet cocoon, and stroked the purry furball – and
when I felt the short stump of tail, I knew it was
Fluffy.

"Hey, puss – what's going to happen, eh?" I
whispered.

Fluffy rubbed her face against my nose in
response.

"What if she tries to move in here?" I muttered.
"She'll want to paint everything – she'll want to
throw all our furniture in a skip. She'll want to get
rid of loads of our animals, just so she doesn't get
pet hairs on her precious business suits!"

I jolted as soon as I'd said it.

Precious.

She'd want to take her horrible, yappy, manicured
poodle to live with us, while Rolf and Winslet would
be relegated to a hut in the garden, or worse.

Then another thought struck me.

Billy – Billy would be my step-brother!

I flopped back in the bed and flung the duvet over my face.

It was all too weird and it was making my head go positively twisty…

Chapter 19

ACTION STATIONS!

If it was twisty before, my head was totally muzzy when I woke up.

There was too much noise and barking and voices and sounds blaring from the TV and the radio for this early in the morning. I forced one eye open and looked at my alarm clock – and got a shock when I saw it was half-eleven already.

I felt a dead weight on my legs and peered down the bed, to see that Fluffy had transformed into Colin at some point. He snuffled in his sleep, as I pulled my feet out from under him and swung them off the bed.

Dad and everyone must have thought I wanted a long lie-in this morning, since I was partying last night, I decided, as I pulled an old cardie over my PJs and headed for the door.

Dad had been snoring in an armchair in the living room when I got in the night before – the house was still and quiet apart from the tappity-tap of Rolf and Winslet sleepily padding over the wooden floors to investigate who'd just got in. But it wasn't the party that had tired me out and let the morning slip by – it was the fact that my brain was working overtime and hadn't shut down till who knows what time in the early hours of the morning.

"Morning, Ally – or should I say afternoon?"

I blinked down the stairs and saw Grandma gazing up at me from the hall. She was helping Tor into his jacket. Tor, meanwhile, was swapping a packet of Wotsits from one hand to the other, while trying to keep them out of Winslet's reach. So *that* was what all the barking was about.

"Hi, Grandma," I replied, rubbing my eyes and stepping down the stairs. "What are you doing here?"

"Me and Tor are going to the City Farm, aren't we?" she said, turning back to my little brother.

"'Cause Dad can't take him..." I muttered, remembering what Tor had told me over our hot chocolate the day before.

"That's right – he's busy today," said Grandma, giving me what looked like a hint of a meaningful stare.

"Busy," said Tor, giving me a *big* meaningful stare.

I suddenly felt wide awake. I had to talk to my sisters – Linn in particular – to find what our plan of action was.

"Is Dad still here?" I asked Grandma, at the same

time nicking a Wotsit out of Tor's upheld bag, now that I was standing beside him.

"Yes. He's in the shower, I think. Right then, Tor – are we ready?"

"Uh-huh," nodded Tor, heading for the door.

"Have fun. Bye!" I called out, as I padded off towards the kitchen.

"Ally…!"

I turned and saw Tor at the opened front door, holding his thumb up to me.

That was "good luck" in code, if I wasn't very much mistaken. I nodded and put my thumb up in return.

"At last!" said Linn, looking up from the Sunday supplement she had open on the kitchen table in front of her. "Even Rowan's beaten you to it this morning."

That was amazing. Rowan was always the last to emerge from her bed at weekends. But there she was, sitting in her tartan, flannelette pyjamas, looking only three-quarters still asleep.

"Sit down, Al," Linn practically ordered me. "We haven't a lot of time. Dad's going out in half an hour. Says he's going to help 'Jake' fix his bike this afternoon!"

Linn's voice dripped with disbelief at Dad's lame excuse.

Before I did sit down, I stepped back to the kitchen door and pushed it closed. Then I walked over to the radio and turned it up louder – there was no way I wanted Dad earwigging on *this* conversation.

"Has Rowan told you what Tor heard?" I asked Linn, who was fully dressed in a black top, black jeans and trainers. Me and Rowan must have looked like bag ladies beside her...

"Yeah, she told me last night. I just wish you hadn't slept in when we needed to talk about this!" said Linn, a little snappily.

The longer I hadn't come down, the more uptight she'd been getting, by the looks of it.

"Listen," I began, ignoring her snippy tone. "You're not going to believe what Billy said to me last night!"

"What?" asked Rowan, pushing her unruly hair back off her face.

"He said..." I paused, checking in my head that I hadn't dreamt the whole horrible thing, "that his mum had been on the phone to Dad – arranging to meet up with him today!"

Linn and Rowan stared at me with similar open-mouthed expressions. For once, they actually looked alike.

"Your mate *Billy*? His *mum* and our *dad*?" Linn repeated, incredulously.

Both of them knew who she was. At least, they knew her to say hello to, if nothing much more than that.

"Billy's mum?" squeaked Rowan, her brown eyes the size of saucers. "But isn't she married? To Billy's dad, I mean?"

"Well, *yes*," I said, rolling my eyes at her.

"What's Billy saying about it? Was he freaking out?" asked Linn, almost managing to slip back into her organized and in-control self after the shock.

Still, her skin looked paler than pale against her almost-blonde hair.

"No! He didn't get the significance – and I didn't really want to spell it out for him," I told her.

"What did he say exactly?" asked Rowan.

"Just what I said. Literally, just that he overheard her talking to 'Martin', saying she'd meet him on Sunday."

"Ally – quick, before Dad gets downstairs," said Linn urgently. "Phone Billy; ask him if he heard where they were supposed to be going!"

"If he heard it, he won't remember!" I protested. "He's a boy! Boys don't remember details!"

"Ally, you've got to try!" Linn flashed her eyes icily at me. "It's going to be really hard trying to follow Dad if we don't know where he's going, but if Billy *has* overheard something, it'll make it much easier!"

I sighed – there was no saying no to Linn.

"I'll try," I promised, pushing my chair back and heading for the hall. "But don't get your hopes up. It *is* Billy we're talking about after all…"

"Just do it," said Linn firmly.

Peering up the stairs, I could hear Dad still singing in the bathroom, while the taps in the sink rushed and the pipes gurgled and rattled.

Quickly, I dialled Billy's number.

"Hello?" came his familiar voice, after a couple of rings.

"Billy? It's me," I told him.

"Oh, hi, Al! I was just heading off for the park. Aren't you coming?"

"Uh, I hadn't thought about it," I replied, slightly flummoxed.

My brain was too fried to deal with ordinary, run-of-the-mill habits. But he'd pricked my conscience – I gazed around me in the hall, and saw two expectant doggy faces gazing back up. Rolf even had his Frisbee in his mouth.

"What are you phoning for, then?" asked Billy. "Are you OK? Did you get home all right last night? You ran off pretty fast. I thought—"

"Billy," I interrupted him, lowering my voice to a whisper, even though the singing and pipe-rattling showed that Dad wasn't about to walk out of the bathroom on me. "I need to ask you a question."

"Fire away," he said, sounding intrigued. "But why are you whispering?"

"It doesn't matter – just listen," I snapped at him, Linn-style. "Is your mum still there?"

"Uh … no. She's just gone out. About five minutes ago."

And Dad was leaving soon too. Urgh, the whole mess *had* to be true…

"Billy, this is going to sound weird, OK, but when you heard your mum on the phone the other day – you know, when she was speaking to my dad or whichever Martin she was talking to – did you hear her say *where* she was meeting him on Sunday? Today, I mean?"

"Uh … I don't remember."

Wow, what a surprise.

"Are you sure?" I pushed him.

"Hold on!" he said, brightly. "Dad's just through in the living room. He might know. Wait and I'll ask—"

"No!" I yelped down the phone.

It was complicated enough trying to work out what was going on with Dad and Billy's mum – we didn't need to alert Billy's dad to the fact that his wife might be cheating on him. Well, not *quite* yet…

"Why not? What's up?"

Any other day, I might have been able to come up with a sharp excuse (i.e. white lie) to cover my tracks, but since my brain was as scrambled as the eggs going cold and rubbery on Tor's plate through in the kitchen, I failed miserably.

"Billy, can you come round here? Now?"

"Why?"

"Just come, will you?"

"Um, OK. I'll be there in about half an hour. I'll take Precious with me…"

"No!" I yelped again.

My wide-awake nightmares came flooding back; I didn't want Precious coming here, trying to get his horrid little paws under the table.

"Why not?" asked Billy, sounding confused.

"Just come, will you? And quick – come on your bike?"

"Why?"

The singing suddenly stopped, and the pipes were gurgling to a halt. Dad was going to pull that door open at any second.

"See you in ten minutes!" I hissed down the phone, before slamming it back on the receiver.

Rolf nuzzled his damp nose under my hand and whined.

"I feel like that myself today," I muttered, ruffling the spiky fur on his head.

Chapter 20

I SPY WITH MY LITTLE EYE…

I don't know if Dad thought it was weird or anything, the fact that the four of us were all hovering about down at the end of the garden, but there wasn't much else we could do. The trouble was, he was wandering up and down the house too much, getting ready to go out, and the garden was just about the only place we could talk without risking him overhearing.

"*My* mum and *your* dad!" Billy exclaimed for the fortieth time since I'd told him what we suspected.

He'd taken it better than I thought he would, but to tell you the truth, I don't think it had sunk in. He had this stunned-yet-dumb expression on his face, like he'd just heard that Lara Croft had come to life and moved into the house across the road from him.

Me, I was feeling marginally calmer after my middle-of-the-night flip-out, but only marginally. I mean, I still felt really down about it all, but not so *frantic*. I know it's the sort of thing Grandma comes out with, but that stuff about "things always look better in the morning" is true, kind of. I maybe still felt totally weird about my dad being up to something with Billy's mum, but at least I'd got over that *ridiculous* idea of Billy being my step-brother. I mean, *as if*!

(Oh, please, please, *please*, God, don't let it come true!)

"Billy, are you *sure* you didn't hear where your mum was supposed to be going today?" Linn tried him again.

She was perched on the old swing, while the rest of us (and both the dogs) were hunkered down on the grass. Even at a time like this, it was pretty funny to see that Linn was still making sure her clothes stayed clean and free of grass blades.

"Nope, that's all I heard her say on the phone." He shook his head.

"Damn!" hissed Linn. "I suppose I'm just going to have to follow him when he leaves, and hope I don't lose him…"

"I'm sorry," shrugged Billy, petting Winslet, who'd moseyed up beside him and flopped her head in his lap.

"Hold on, Linnhe – how come you're saying '*I'm* going to follow him'?" Rowan demanded, peering at our sister through the pink, hexagonal sunglasses she'd shoved on to come outside. "Why should *you* go? Why don't we *all* go?"

Rowan had a point. But I had a better one.

"If anyone goes, it should be me and Billy – since *his* mum's involved in all this…"

"Rowan," said Linn flatly, completely ignoring the fact that I'd spoken. "For a start, you couldn't spy on anyone – they'd spot you a mile off."

Rowan opened her mouth to protest, then shut it again, with a slight wobble of her lip.

Linn was right, of course, and even Rowan could see that. Our in-between sister didn't know the meaning of dressing down, and no matter how well she hid, it would be practically impossible for Dad not to see a *glint* of something to do with Rowan, out of the corner of his eye.

"And *you* two," Linn continued, turning to me and Billy. "Well, OK, I see your point, but I'm coming as well."

Aha! She *had* heard me after all. And now She Who Must Be Obeyed had spoken, so it looked like the three of us had better get our spy-heads on…

"Winslet! Leave Billy alone!" I said, suddenly noticing that our small, hairy monster was showing her terrier side and trying to bury her way into Billy's jacket pocket.

"It's OK," Billy grinned, trying to gently remove her frantically snuffling nose from the inside of his jacket. But it didn't do any good. "I must have a couple of doggy biscuits left over in there from walking Precious."

There was nothing for it but forcible removal. I grabbed Winslet round the tummy and lifted her off her feet and out of Billy's pocket.

"Ewwwww! What's she eating?" cringed Rowan.

I turned her round to face me and heard the crunch of doggy treats. The trouble was, Winslet hadn't been very selective about what exactly was in Billy's pocket and also seemed to be chewing on an old snotty hankie and a piece of green notepaper.

Time for Tor's trick: I plopped her down on the grass and grabbed her by the scruff of the neck. And *voila*, her jaws flipped open and out tumbled the remains of her snack.

Winslet let out a long, low growl of irritation.

"Sorry, Billy," I apologized, picking up the piece of scrawled-on green paper by the least-chewed side. "Is this important?"

"Nah, I can't even remember what it is," he replied, flipping it round from one side to the other. "Oh, yes I can – it was just the name of this new Xbox game Richie phoned me up to tell me about. That's all. It's noth … oh."

"Oh?" I repeated, watching as Billy squinted at the writing on the other side of the note.

"'The Chesterton Hotel, W1. Sun. 1 p.m.,'" Billy read out in a monotoned mumble. "Hey, this is my mum's handwriting!"

"Bingo!" I cried out, feeling my heart leap at our unexpected breakthrough.

"Really?" said Linn, out of the blue, her eyes ridiculously wide. "Hey, sounds like a good party!"

Me, Billy and Rowan stared at her. Had the sun gone to her head?

Then it clicked – we were talking in code. Dad must be in the area.

I turned around, shielding my eyes with my hand.

"Hi Dad!" I chirped, hoping I sounded cheerful (and innocent).

"Hi guys!" said Dad, wandering over in his normal weekend jeans, T-shirt and old denim jacket.

If he hadn't have slicked his hair back with gel or whatever, he wouldn't have looked at all suspicious.

"So what are you lot up to?" he asked, gazing around at all four of us.

"Oh, just hanging out. Talking about the party Ally and Billy were at last night," said Linn, very convincingly. (Give the girl an Oscar!)

"Good, was it?" he smiled down at me and Billy in particular.

"Hu-unghh…" Billy croaked, obviously too fazed by the situation to communicate in English.

"Yes!" I answered brightly, to make up for him.

"Great stuff!" nodded Dad. "Well, I better be going. Um, see you later, guys…"

"Have fun fixing Jake's bike!" Linn couldn't resist calling after him, as he strolled back to the kitchen door.

"Linn!" I hissed, once Dad was safely inside. "That sounded really sarcastic!"

"No, it didn't – you're just paranoid," said Linn, pushing herself off the swing. "Right, as soon as Dad's gone, I'm going to have to make a quick call to Alfie and blow him out – I was supposed to meet him this afternoon. Rowan, like I said, you can't come. But make yourself useful and look up the address of that hotel in the Yellow Pages. OK?"

"Uh-huh," nodded Rowan, looking none too excited by her role in the action.

"Come on, Billy," I said, standing up and hauling my brain-numbed friend to his feet. "Operation Parent-catcher starts here."

Billy blinked at me for a second, then turned the collar of his jacket up and the brim of his baseball cap down.

"Ready for action!" he saluted me.

"Billy," I sighed, "you look more like a failed member of a boy band than a spy."

I yanked the brim of his hat down till it covered his whole face…

Chapter 21

THE FOUR MUSKETEERS...

"How much longer do you think we'll have to wait?" Billy whinged.

"For as long as it takes till they both come out," Linn said, her voice tinged with irritation.

Billy was drumming one knee up and down so fast under the table that our nearly empty cups and saucers were rattling gently on the formica table. I knew that was going to drive Linn insane (it was bugging me too, but Linn's levels of irritation are *infinitely* more finely tuned than mine...).

I stuck my hand across and grabbed Billy's knee – then pushed down hard.

"What?" asked Billy, his eyebrows knitted in confusion.

"Quit it," I told him, eyeballing him hard and trying to communicate to him through my stare that he was testing Linn's patience.

Billy scrunched up his face into an expression that said "Huh?"

Subtlety goes right over boys' heads, doesn't it?

"You're drumming your leg. It's annoying. Stop it," I spelt out for him more graphically.

Billy flopped his elbows on the table and rested his chin on his hands in real hangdog mode, but I didn't have the energy to talk him round. My nerves were ... well, all the things nerves *are* rolled into one. You name it and they were doing it: straining, fraying and jangling. And the pathetic thing was, it wasn't just the tense waiting game that was causing it, it was all because we had an extra spy in tow...

When Linn had phoned Alfie and told him she couldn't hang out with him that afternoon and why, he'd only gone and decided to invite himself along. It was a bit of a cheek really – as if he was joining us on some excellent adventure, instead of trying to find out something that could have pretty far-reaching implications on both our families and futures.

Well, that's what I'd have thought of any *other* person muscling in our spying mission, but we *were* talking Alfie, here. And I know I've got the invisible version of Rowan's rose-tinted sun-specs on when it comes to him, but what can a girl do? When your heart goes ping! your heart goes ping...

"What time is it anyway?" I asked, glancing round the café for any sign of a clock.

My heart skipped a beat or three as I spotted Alfie's messy blond hair over by the counter, where he'd gone to buy us more refills.

"Coming up for three o'clock," Linn muttered, staring down at the watch on her wrist.

We'd been sitting in the café, which (lucky or what?) was right across from the entrance to the Chesterton Hotel. By the time we'd got into town (the Tube seems to run in slow motion on Sundays), it was just after one o'clock. We weren't too bothered about missing seeing either Dad or Billy's mum heading into the hotel: as long as we knew they were there, we were happy to wait. (OK – bad choice of words: we were *willing* to wait…)

There was one little problem, though – a small niggle that kept pulsating through my mind. I wanted to say it out loud, but I was a bit scared. Scared of Linn *growling* at me over it.

Still, time was ticking away. For one thing, I had to say it out loud now, before Alfie came back to the table and I turned back into the burbling birdbrain I always was in front of him. (Luckily, both the bus and the Tube we'd taken into town were crowded, and Billy and I had had to sit at a safe distance away from Alfie and Linn. Safe, because I was far enough away not to open my mouth and say something stupid in Alfie's hearing, but not so far away that I couldn't ogle him from time to time…)

The second reason I had to make my point was

that Dad and Billy's mum could come out of the hotel at *any* moment. Therefore…

"Um, Linn…?"

"What?" said Linn, staring intently over at the entrance to the hotel.

"Linn – if, I mean *when* Dad and Billy's mum come out," I began, sheepishly, "what are we … well, what are we going to do?"

"Film them and send it in to *You've Been Framed*?" Billy jumped in, before Linn could say anything.

(I blamed mild hysteria for his bad joke. But then *all* Billy's jokes are pretty bad…)

Linn was frowning. I wasn't sure whether it was Billy being frivolous that had irked her, or me daring to question her authority (i.e. ask awkward questions). But I had a feeling I was about to find out.

But before Linn opened her mouth, someone else spoke.

"I just think you guys should play it cool…" Alfie's voice drifted down, as he hovered by my side with the tray of drinks.

I couldn't look up at him – I was frozen to the spot. I'd never, ever been this close to him before. My heart did a backflip as he leant right across me – the heat of his breath brushing my face – passing a coffee over to Linn.

"How do we play it cool?" asked Billy. "Do we say 'Hi, there! So you two are having an affair? Hey – no problem!' "

Linn flashed her eyes at Billy for daring to take the mickey out of whatever Alfie had said.

"No – I just mean, don't go out there yelling or something," Alfie drawled in his lazy, laid-back voice.

I went cross-eyed staring at his lightly tanned arm as it passed dangerously close to my nose. As he dumped a can of Lilt in front of Billy, I turned into Winslet and sniffed the air manically, trying to breathe a bit of Alfie in.

"Like, if I was you, I'd just walk along the opposite side of the pavement, saying nothing, till they saw me. Then let *them* do the talking..." Alfie continued, putting a steamy cup down in front of me. "Hot chocolate, wasn't it, Ally?"

I had to respond. I would look like a total twerp if I didn't – I'd already sat for two hours at this table letting everyone else do the talking so I didn't have to make a fool of myself.

"Cue!" I squawked.

(Translation: "Thank you!")

I turned and focussed my eyes on his face, only centimetres from my own. Those bony, high cheek-bones, that long, thin nose, those pale, pale grey eyes ("same colour as a collie dog's!" Tor had so kindly pointed out once), those lips…

Er, rewind to the pale grey eyes. Where exactly were they staring right at this minute?

Only at my hand, the one that was still clutching Billy's knee next to me.

And – once again – I'd managed to make the one boy I'd *always* fancied think I was going out with the one boy I'd *never* fancy…

Chapter 22

WATCHING AND WAITING. AND WAITING SOME MORE...

"What time is it now?" I asked Linn.

"Nearly four," she mumbled, without dragging her gaze away from the entrance to the Chesterton.

She'd got into the habit of checking her watch every few minutes like a reflex action, and was probably counting every second in time with her heartbeat.

"*Yeahhhh!*" came a loud roar from the back of the café.

Linn narrowed her eyes and shot a dark look at the two boys playing on the fruit machine.

It had seemed really considerate of Alfie to suggest a turn on the machine to Billy, when Billy had begun to look a bit maudlin earlier and started mumbling stuff about his "poor dad". But half an hour later, and it looked like they were enjoying their game just that little bit *too* much; like they'd somehow managed to forget the whole purpose of our "jaunt" today...

"Boys…" tutted Linn, folding her arms across her chest. "They've got the attention span of a *newt*."

"Yep," I agreed with her.

Although, to be honest, I was kind of glad they'd moved away. I hadn't been able to look at, never mind *talk* in front of Alfie since he'd clocked me clutching Billy's knee.

"You don't think Dad and Billy's mum have left already, do you?" I asked my all-knowing sister, while systematically tearing apart the plastic cup I'd just drunk my Coke out of. (The café owners must have been toying with giving us *shares* in the place, the amount of time and money we'd spent in there.)

"Left? How could they have left?" said Linn, sounding a little short with me. "We've been sitting here watching that entrance for nearly three solid hours. Well, at least *you* and *me* have…"

"I know," I tried to agree with her. "But maybe they snuck out the back entrance or something. You know, just in case they were spotted!"

"For one thing," sighed Linn, "they aren't *expecting* to be followed, so there's no *point* in them sneaking out the back. For another, they wouldn't *go* sneaking out the back because they're not *film stars*, for God's sake. It's only *famous* people who sneak out through the kitchens – or hadn't you noticed?"

Forgive me for having such a lowly brain compared to yours, Miss Smart Alec! I felt like saying.

Except I didn't.

"Hey, I was thinking," I said instead, while eyeing up the phone box on the other side of the road, just along from the entrance to the Chesterton. "Rowan'll be at home going crazy – we should let her know what's going on."

Or *not* going on. Watching a Sunday afternoon's worth of traffic zip by was about as interesting as it had got.

"Yeah, good idea," nodded Linn.

The tension was starting to show on her, I noticed. It wasn't just her excessive snappiness (a couple of degrees up on her *normal* snappiness), it was also the fact that a couple of tendrils of hair had escaped from her scraped-back ponytail, and she *hadn't bothered fixing them*.

I rest my case.

"I've got some change. I'll go and call her from over there," I pointed to the phone box opposite.

"OK," said Linn, sounding weary.

It was all getting to her, it really was. Linn does such a good job of hiding all her emotions away (apart from the grumpy ones) that I think the very *effort* of doing that tires her out more than the rest of us.

I glanced back into the café as I made my way out of the door, and saw Billy staring intently at the display on the fruit machine while he hammered away on the buttons. At the same time, Alfie was cheering him on, grinning his wide grin and showing off that twinkling, gold back tooth.

I felt my knees buckle...

But my knees had to behave themselves once I got out in the fresh air (or traffic-polluted air, since we were in the West End of London). I had to make it across the road and into the phone box quickly, just in case Dad appeared at the front door of the hotel at that moment. I didn't really fancy getting stuck in the middle of the road and confronting him with "What exactly do you think you're doing, Dad?" while a stream of black cabs thundered in front of me, drowning me out.

Once I was safely (and breathlessly) in the phone box, I dialled our home number, then turned to stare back at the now-nearby hotel entrance while I waited for Rowan to pick up.

"Hello?" I heard her say.

"Ro?" I panted. "It's me. Listen—"

"No, hold on, Ally – I'm so glad you phoned! I've got some news..." she interrupted me.

As she began to tell me her news, I stopped staring off into the distance. Instead, I just saw my own reflection in the glass panels on the phone-box door. And all over my face was written "Oh. My. God."

The pips sounded – my twenty pence had run out. But it didn't matter; I'd heard all I needed to hear.

I replaced the handset and pushed the door open. But instead of crossing the road straight away, I made my way along the pavement to the entrance of the hotel. Right before I walked up the few marble steps that would take me into the foyer, I glanced across at the café, and saw Linn sitting where I'd left her, in the window seat, frowning over at me and mouthing "What are you doing?"

"Hold on!" I mouthed back, holding up my hand to her.

I didn't need to go all the way in to see what I needed to see. From out here on the top step, I could peer through the glass double doors at the noticeboard standing just inside. The noticeboard that had all the details of what was going on the hotel's various function suites.

"So it's true!" I heard myself say out (very) loud, as my eyes fixed on what Rowan had told me to look for…

Chapter 23

DAD'S DARK SECRET (AHEM)

"Wow. I mean, *wow*!"

It was all Sandie had been able to say since we'd filled her in on the whole sordid story. (Not, thankfully, that there was anything too sordid about it in the end...)

Sandie was sitting on the swing next to Kyra's, wrapped up (by her mother) in a padded black coat that looked a bit like a duvet. She must have been sweltering – it was a warmish Sunday evening and the rest of us weren't even wearing jackets.

"So you and Billy spent three hours sitting in some café this afternoon for *nothing*?" said Kyra, a hint of a teasing smile on her face.

I was mildly tempted to run over and shove her off the swing that she was twirling on, but I couldn't be bothered untangling my crossed legs and getting up off the ground. Also, it seemed a bit mean, since I was feeling practically giddy with relief right now.

"Well, it wasn't exactly for *nothing*, was it?" said Billy, perched on the saddle of his mountain bike and leaning on the handlebars. "I mean, we had to try and find out what was going on, or *if* anything was going on!"

"But like you say, there *wasn't* anything going on – well, not what *you* two thought, anyway!" Kyra laughed, leaning her head languidly against one of the swing chains.

During the last couple of weeks of the Dad Drama, I hadn't breathed a word about it to Kyra. In fact, I hadn't told any of my friends except Sandie (because she's good at being super-sympathetic) and Billy (because I *had* to), and that's the way I thought it would stay. But as soon as we'd arrived at the park this evening, Billy had blabbed it all to Kyra – by accident.

What had happened was that me and Billy had arranged to meet up with Sandie in Priory Park at seven o'clock. (Billy had stayed at mine for his tea – well, after dragging him into a drama that was, after all, *not* a drama, asking him to stay for tea was the least I could do. And Rowan wasn't cooking, so it was safe.)

I was desperate to tell Sandie what we'd found out that afternoon, and Sandie was desperate to get out of the house and away from her pink cell, so the kids' playground – mercifully free of small, shrill children at that time in the evening –

was where we'd decided on to meet up and catch up.

What we *hadn't* expected when we got there was to find Kyra dangling on a swing, waiting to meet Richie/Ricardo (who obviously wasn't quite dumped yet). And what *I* personally hadn't expected was for Billy to suddenly launch into a blow-by-blow account of everything that had happened that day, which was supposed to be for Sandie's ears only. I guess with the business of the party and everything, he'd just figured (wrongly) that me and Kyra were a couple of stages further along the friendship trail than we actually were. But you could tell he was regretting it now; he wasn't as used to Kyra's cheekily sarky ways as me and Sandie.

"Where's your boyfriend? Isn't he late?" I said to Kyra, changing the subject. "Maybe you got it wrong – maybe he meant for you to meet him at the kids' playground up at Ally Pally instead. That would be closer to his house..."

"Nice try, but you're not getting rid of me that easily!" grinned Kyra, seeing through my feeble attempt to distract her. "I'm enjoying hearing all this stuff far too much!"

Actually, I didn't particularly mind her teasing. After the stresses of the last little while, it was kind of nice to have a laugh about it.

"Awww!" sighed Sandie, out of the blue, a soppy little smile on her face.

"Awww, what?" I frowned at her, wondering what planet she was currently residing on.

"I was just thinking about Tor – it's so sweet that he sorted out this whole mystery!"

You know how I said she can turn on the waterworks really easily? Well, right then, it looked like she was in danger of going all gushy over my little brother. Her eyes were looking suspiciously dewy. (But then she *had* been ill with gastric flu all week. Maybe she was just suffering from a case of conjunctivitus.)

"Fnar!" snorted Kyra. "That's the funniest thing about all this, Ally! While you and your sisters all managed to convince yourselves that your dad was up to no good, a *seven* year old is busy sussing out what's *really* going on!"

"Thanks, Kyra. Rub it in, why don't you!" I grinned back at her.

But she was right. It did seem ridiculous when you looked at it that way. After all, while me, Billy, Linn and Alfie had spent our Sunday afternoon acting like the cast of *Scooby Doo* (er, minus Scooby Doo) on the trail of skullduggery, Tor had got to the bottom of the mystery in one easy step: by asking the right person a straightforward question.

"Dad's acting weird," Tor had begun, as he and Grandma sat on the bus on the way to the City Farm. "Do you know why?"

And, as I should have expected, she did. Not much gets past our gran, whether it's something to do with us kids, or her grown-up son-in-law.

"So did your grandma know all along?" asked Sandie, so entranced with the whole story that Kyra's sarcasm was shooting over the top of her head.

"No," I replied, stretching my legs out in front of me. They were going to sleep the way I was sitting. "Like I said, she'd had her suspicions that something was going on, but it was only after she took that message for him – the one from Billy's mum – that she asked him what was up."

And here's what *was* up.

Billy's mum had no intention of getting her perfectly manicured claws into my dad (phew). Instead, it turned out she was trying to do the Girl Guide thing and do a good deed: she'd bumped into my dad on the Broadway one day a couple of weeks back, and started giving him a hard time about never getting out and having no social life (ever since Mum had gone, natch). Dad had wittered on about being happy to stay at home with us lot (bless him), but Billy's mum kept on at him. Finally, she persuaded (i.e. bullied) him to come along to the regular Wednesday evening class she and Billy's dad did.

What could Dad do? He's so easy-going, he'd never be able to say no to someone as determined and persistent as Billy's mum. And so, he found himself – wait for it...

Line dancing.

I know. Shocking, isn't it?

"No wonder your dad didn't want to tell you what he was doing!" sniggered Kyra. "I mean, *line* dancing, for God's sake! How corny is that?"

Exactly. That is *exactly* why he hadn't told us what he was up to. He said as much when we spoke to him about it this afternoon, when he'd arrived back home and seen from all our expressions that We Knew.

(Me, Linn and the boys had beaten him back to the house. After Rowan told me over the phone what was going on – Grandma and Tor had filled *her* in after they got back from their day out – I'd double-checked by reading the board in the hotel lobby. As soon as I saw "Ambassador Ballroom: Line dancing workshop, 1–5 p.m.", I'd run across the road, spilt my news, and we'd all beaten a hasty retreat back to Crouch End.)

"So you know, then?" Dad had said sheepishly, confronted by us all in the kitchen.

(By the way, we just let him believe we'd heard about his heel-toe-tapping adventures from Grandma. Admitting that we'd been trailing him halfway across London was just too sad and pathetic, and was one of those times that a white lie comes in very useful.)

"But, Dad, *line* dancing?!" I'd squeaked, incredulously.

"I know, I *know*. I don't even like country and western music!" Dad had laughed, his cheeks pink. "That's why I didn't tell you all. It was too embarrassing. And I kind of thought I'd go just the once to pacify Sharon – oh, no offence to your mum, Billy!"

"No problem!" Billy had said brightly, glad that his mother didn't have an illicit lover after all – only a stupid hobby.

"But then…" Dad shrugged and paused.

"Then what?" Linn had pushed him impatiently.

"I realized – and don't hate me for this – I *quite* enjoyed it."

None of us had a go at him for such a shameful confession. (Although it was on the tip of my tongue to beg him *never* to buy a cowboy hat, if he truly loved us.)

"So, my parents do line dancing?" Billy smirked. "My dad too?"

Scary, isn't it? That a boy can live in the same house as his folks and not have a clue what they do with their lives. Scary, but typical, if you ask me.

"Well, yes – didn't you know?" Dad had replied.

Billy shook his head.

"But your father couldn't come to this workshop at the hotel today," Dad had continued, "because of his bad back."

Billy looked confused.

"From hurting it at work?" Dad prompted him.

Billy had looked just as confused.

Not a clue about important details. Not one, tiny clue...

And Billy didn't have much of a clue about learning to shut up, either, as I realized now, sitting in the kids' playground this Sunday evening.

"Still, Ally, if your mum ever comes home, at least she won't find out that your dad's shacked up with someone new!" he said, tactlessly.

Sandie took a sharp intake of breath, knowing that wasn't an entirely sensitive thing to say. But that's Billy for you.

I saw Kyra pause on her swing and narrow her eyes at me, knowing that there was more of a story to my family than I'd ever let on. But she didn't push me this once, mainly because she's got more of a story too.

And I did find out her story, eventually … only I won't tell you now. I can't concentrate any more on my writing, 'cause Dad's playing some dreadful country and western track really loud downstairs and Rolf and Winslet are howling along like out-of-tune walruses.

Before I go downstairs and tell Dad that I'm going to report him to the social services for extreme mental cruelty to his children (there's no other way to describe that music), what I *will* say is that Billy was kind of right: I am glad that if Mum happened to wander through the door, all smiles and suntan and outstretched arms, the only romance she'd be hearing about is Grandma and Stanley's (going very well, apparently).

And I'd also like to say that while I love Billy like a brother, I'm so, *so* glad that he isn't going to be one to me.

That would have been *very* weird indeed…

So, until next time, I'll leave you with my top tips for avoiding embarrassing situations:

1) ALWAYS keep spare tampons safely stored in a zipped-up purse – they have a life of their own and tend to escape from bags when you least expect them to;

2) AVOID any home-made "cocktails" at parties,

unless you enjoy being violently sick; and

   3) Never EVER tell anyone that your dad does line dancing…

Want to know more. . .?

Meet the sparkly-gorgeous Karen McCombie!

★ **Describe yourself in five words. . .**
Scottish, confident, shy, calm, ditzy.

★ **How did you become an author-girl?**
When I was eight, my teacher Miss Thomson told me I should write a book one day. I forgot about that for (lots of) years, then when I was working on teen mags, I scribbled a few short stories for them and suddenly thought, "Hmmm, I'd love to try and write a book . . . can I?"

★ **Where do you write your books?**
In the loft room at the top of our house. I work v. hard 'cause I only have a little bit of book-writing time – the rest of the day I'm making Playdough dinosaurs or pretend "cafés" with my little daughter, Milly.

★ **What else do you get up to when you're not writing?**
Reading, watching DVDs, eating crisps, patting cats and belly dancing!

Look out for...

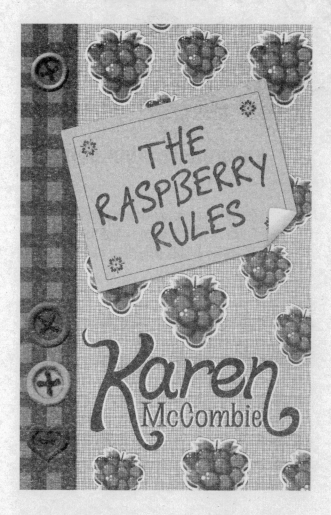

Dip into Rowan Love's secret diary, and discover her sparkly, silly and seriously addictive world!

Check out Karen's super-cool website!

karenmccombie.com

For behind-the-scenes gossip on Karen's very own blog,
fab competitions and photo-galleries,
join her website of loveliness now!